'Cushie Butterfield'

By

Gill Burnett

Other Books by Gill Burnett

Take Note
Note Taken
Last Note

Mack Book
Show Me A Sign!
Who Said That?

By Gill Burnett & Freddie Jones

Eddie the Elf

Copyright © Gill Burnett 2023
This book is sold subject to the condition that it shall not, by way of trade or otherwise, be lent, resold, hired out, or otherwise circulated without the publisher's prior consent in any form of binding or cover other than that in which it is published and without similar condition including this condition being imposed on the subsequent publisher.
The moral right of Gill Burnett has been asserted.

1) The Ten of Cups

The lights off the Christmas tree twinkled.

It was early. The house was quiet. But then it was always quiet, but sometimes it felt quieter than others, even if there was only her there.

It was Boxing Day. The gifts under the tree were opened, but as was her usual custom, she would leave them there until she found a home for them, in her wardrobe or on her wrist on in her ever-growing vinyl record collection.

It has been a good Christmas. Maggie liked family time. It was more precious than any of the gifts either given or received. Though she hadn't always felt like that. But life was better now. Easier. More settled.

It had been a long, long road to get to where she was. To being able to sit on her sofa at dawn on Boxing Day morning and have the feeling that all was well in her world.

A road that had twisted and turned. A road that had been thwart with potholes, bumps and many dead ends.

Christmas had a way of making you remember even if you didn't want to. There was always something that would trigger a memory.

Coffee in hand, sat on her sofa and let the twinkly fairy lights mesmerize her, memory lane beckoned......

2) *The Queen of Wands*

Margaret known as Maggie Hunter was born in Gateshead in 1969. She was the youngest of Doreen and Leslie Hunter's three children, their only girl.

Stephen was her eldest brother and Shaun the other. Because of the way their birthdays fell, Maggie and Shaun had always been in the same school year. It always fascinated Maggie how her mam had got herself pregnant so soon after having Shaun, more so when Maggie had children of her own, she could think of nothing worse than getting up close and personal with a bloke five minutes after giving birth. But then she hadn't had a relationship like her mam and dad's, Maggie's were much more complicated.

There were no dramas in Maggie's childhood. Her mam and dad were affectionate not just to their kids, but to each other too. Maggie had good relationships with both of her brothers, in fact, she still did, even if they had always thought her a bit odd, they had loved her for her oddness.

Both her mam and dad worked hard. Doreen had first worked as a dinner nanny at their senior school, which progressed into school secretary, much to her children's despair, it was difficult to be naughty when your mam was the school secretary and knew everything that they got up to. And Leslie Hunter worked on a digger at a quarry and in later years selling the stone in the quarry's saleroom, a place Maggie herself would begin her working life. A bittersweet experience.

It had been a happy childhood though.

Mostly it would just be the five of them. Doreen Hunter worked at a school so there was never an issue about having the children looked after while they worked. But Doreen would often help out with her own sister's childcare and their cousin Tom would come and stay with them for weeks on end.

Maggie loved her cousin Tom. Age wise he was in the middle of Maggie and Shaun, but unlike her football loving brother, Tom was sensitive and liked nothing better than sitting with a pencil and paper drawing. Maggie thought maybe Tom got bullied at school, but because they didn't live close to each other, Maggie couldn't be sure.

She just sensed it.

Like so many other things, Maggie just got a feeling about stuff. She knew what people were going to say before they said it and she lost count of the places she had been where she had the feeling that she had been before, even though it was impossible for her to have.

And this is what made Maggie odd!!

Doreen Hunter could often be heard saying to her husband 'Leslie our Maggie is just like your mother!'

Maggie was never sure if this was a good thing or not. As far as she could see her Granny Hunter was lovely. Maggie always loved any time spent with her Granny Hunter. She was much more fun than her other Granny, Granny M.

Granny M was always so miserable. There seemed to be little joy in her heart.

Both of Maggie's Granddads had died before she was even born, both miners, one in an accident and the other with some sort of bronchial complication. Granny M acted like it had only just happened and spent all of her days in mourning with barely a smile passing her lips. Granny Hunter on the other hand lived life to the full. She loved spending time with her family and friends and truly lived each day as if it was her last.

Doreen Hunter seemed to like neither her own mother or her husbands and it was a rare occurrence that either of her Grannies paid them a visit, welcome or unwelcome.

But Maggie and her brothers were frequent visitors to Granny Hunter's and if their cousin Tom was with them, they would visit Granny Hunter too.

Granny Hunter always made a fuss. She always made them lovely cakes and biscuits and always kept a bottle of dandelion and burdock pop in especially for them visiting, something they were never allowed to have it home, their mam said that it made them all silly. But Granny Hunter was silly and wouldn't mind her grandchildren tearing around her house at a million miles an hour. She would join in.

And Granny Hunter has a special soft spot for her granddaughter Maggie, maybe from the day that she had picked up Granny Hunter's funny looking pack of cards, shuffled them and picked a few out. She them told her Granny Hunter all about what the cards were saying to her. Maggie had no idea if her little story was right or wrong, but her Granny Hunter was delighted and from then on in, they would always get the strange deck out and pick a few cards and then Maggie would tell her Granny Hunter what each card meant and then what they meant collectively.

Granny Hunter told Maggie she had second sight just like she did. But Maggie had no idea what she meant by that. Maggie just thought she was odd because everybody told her she was!

When Maggie became the butt of jokes in junior school because she would take a book out or do a drawing before her class teacher had even asked her to; Maggie decided that whatever her head was telling her to do, she would ignore. So, before she even got into her teens, her second sight was dampened.

Unfortunately, her oddness remained though. Because she no longer listened to anything her head was telling her, she tended to just say and do things without thinking about it. It got her into trouble. Then because she got into trouble, she would not do anything and then appear to be aloof and a little bit out of it! It was a no-win situation.

Granny Hunter tried to explain what it was all about. They had ancestors who seemed to be magical people, Granny Hunter herself had used her 'second sight' over the years to forecast the future; she had been known to make a penny or two for her trouble too. Even the death of her husband in a freak mining accident had not come as a surprise to her, she had been expecting it allegedly. Perhaps Granny Hunter should have warned Granny M that her husband was going to die young and then maybe she would not be so miserable all of the time, Maggie often thought to herself.

But all Granny Hunter's knowledge did was confuse Maggie. She was the odd girl in class and there she would probably remain. All she could do was accept it and hope that the feelings she sensed and the little voice that sometimes told her what to do would disappear when she grew up. Until then she would just do her best to not let others see!

Granny M and Granny Hunter died unexpectedly within weeks of each other, just like their husbands had. It was a very sad house for a while, both of Maggie's parents lost their mother's. There were lots of arrangements to be made with regards to funerals and there were houses to be cleared. All of a sudden, their own home seemed to be filled with artefacts that neither Doreen nor Leslie seemed to want to part with. Sentimental value Maggie's mam said, but Maggie just found all the strange bits odd scattered around their home, trying their best to nestle in with the modern 80's look of their home. But they had arrived and for many years, there they remained.

Granny Hunter had left a gift for her only Granddaughter. Wrapped in brown paper packaging and tied up with string, Maggie had taken the gift and sat with it on her bed. She didn't need to open it to know what it was. It was the funny pack of cards that Maggie and Granny Hunter used to play with before Maggie's oddness got out of hand.

Maggie placed the package in the bottom of the jewellery box that she had received the previous Christmas.

And there they remained for years and years.

There they remained until Maggie had no choice but to open it.

Years and years until Maggie opened the package and read the note that Granny Hunter had left wrapped around the Tarot Cards.

Maybe if Maggie had untied the string and unwrapped the brown paper packaging and read the note Granny Hunter had left her, then she might have embraced her oddness.

Maybe then her life would have been different.

3) The Eight of Swords

By the time Maggie was 15 she became a bit of a handful.

Having two older brothers was a bit of a setback especially when one of your brothers was in your own social circle and a massive hit with all of your friends. But nevertheless, Maggie still managed to get into mischief. Those teenage years she spent most of her time being 'kept in' by her mam and dad and her bedroom became her world.

Blonde haired and big boobed, she was as tall as her brother Shaun and always stood out in a crowd.

If she was popular with boys, then her brothers certainly put any boyfriends off. Worse still her mam, Doreen was her school's secretary and absolutely nothing got past her.

So, Maggie became the joker in the pack. Always up for a laugh and game for anything. She would try to keep under the radar as much as possible. But schoolwork bored her, and she was prone to distract her classmates and end up being sent out of class, and of course her mam would always know within minutes and Maggie knew without any shadow of doubt that any plans she would have made for after school for the following days would need to be cancelled and she instead would spend the time in her bedroom.

It was a pattern that she would repeat over and over again in her final years at school. Maggie had made herself a chart and literally crossed off every day until she could leave school and gain some sort of freedom.

it certainly didn't help that Shaun liked school. He played football for not only for the school team, but for county and was hoping to get picked up by a football scout for a major club sometime before he left school. So, he went to school no bother, stayed, worked hard and was the complete opposite of his baby sister, or so everyone liked to tell Maggie.

She wished she had got a £1 for every time someone said it to her. 'Why can't you be more like your brother?' 'You would never guess that you and Shaun were twins, he is a pleasure to teach!!'

Maggie used to have to bite her tongue. 'He is only my brother not my fucking twin!!!' she wanted to scream. But she didn't, she would just put up and shut up before she got herself into more trouble.

The voices were still in her head and the sensing things was as strong as ever, she knew instinctively what teachers thought of her, which of her friends actually liked her and if anything, she did was going to get her into trouble. She ignored them.

Maggie was unsure what she wanted to do when she left school. Stephen got an apprenticeship at an engineering firm when he had left school. Shaun was going to go to college to do something sporty, but Maggie had no idea.

She saw her career advisor, who was no help. She attended open days at college, but nothing tickled her fancy. The only thing Maggie had ever really been good at was hairdressing. Her friends would often arrive in her bedroom to have their hair cut, or coloured or styled, or all of the above. She liked doing hair and making people look different, it played into her creative side.

Maggie's cousin Tom had his heart set on university and art. It was a long shot; university was for posh people and Tom certainly didn't have a posh family. Auntie Joan and Uncle Ken both worked in factories and even though Tom was their only child, the Grey's certainly weren't in a position to send their son to university. But Tom would not give up on his dream. There was scholarship or something and Tom was trying his best to secure one for when he finished 6th form. Maggie had to admit he was good, he made things with some sort of clay and then painted on them. She had a whole collection of them in her bedroom that she had received off Tom over the years for birthdays and Christmases; she kept her hairdressing things in them.

So basically, it had to be hairdressing. She called into local shops to see if she could get a Saturday job and was delighted when she got to about the 10th one, she had seen that Saturday morning and they said that if she had dyed her own hair, then she could have a job. She did and she got the job. Maggie was over the moon. The shop looked trendy, and it had lots of young stylists working there. Freedom. No mam or brothers keeping an eye on her working in a place like that.

But then everything went West. There was to be no Saturday job in a hairdressers for Maggie. No career in hairdressing at all. Leslie Hunter had secured Maggie a job at the paving slab showroom he worked at, as a junior typist or something. A job for life her dad said. The quarry had been in the same family for almost 200 years, he himself had been there all his working life and it hadn't done him any harm…

Maggie was gutted. She didn't want to be a typist and she certainly didn't want to be a typist for life. Her dad might have worked at Quarry's End all of his working life, but he had paid the price, he had the worst bad back and his knees were goosed. Even working in the showroom wasn't a cushy job for him, he still barrowed paving stones day in day out.

The money would be good for Maggie, probably more than being an apprentice hairdresser, but she really couldn't see herself sitting at the same desk with the same people day after day. She struggled enough at school and that was a shorter day and there was always a holiday on the horizon.

Now she would be working 8am to 5pm Monday to Friday with half an hour lunch. Same as her dad. And there would be nowhere that she could go to for lunch because you needed a car to get there in the first place and she could barely ride a bike never mind drive a car. But worse that, she would be working with her dad every day. And as much as she loved her dad, she had just had her whole school life not only with her 'twin' brother who wasn't her twin and her mam at her secondary school, now she was switching personnel to her dad. The freedom that she craved had been within touching distance to her.

But it had gone. Maggie would turn 16 in August and start at Quarry's End the following Monday.

As it turned out the Maggie's Christmas as a 16-year-old was very different to any Christmas they had ever had before. Maybe if she hadn't got used to dampening down the voices in her head and the senses, she felt things may have been different.

If only Doreen and Leslie Hunter had given Maggie her freedom and allowed her to go to the trendy hairdressers and not insisted that she went to Quarry's End and have a typist's job for life, they may have had a normal Christmas in 1985.

4) The Star - REVERSED

Maggie was allowed to have a party for her 16th birthday. Just in the house with some classmates, her cousin Tom Grey and of course her brothers would have to be there as well her mam and dad, who promised faithfully to stay upstairs in their bedroom unless they were needed.

Doreen Hunter had laid on a buffet that would feed the street, Maggie sat in her bedroom terrified that no one would turn up. She almost let her 'second sight' loose to see if her fears were founded but was saved by the arrival of her best friends Linda and Jude who had come extra early to have their hair done.

By the time all of their hair had been backed combed lacquered and tied in various Madonna style headscarves, the doorbell was ringing, and Tom Grey was ushering everyone into the dining room where the buffet was laid, balloons had been inflated and where the newly fitted patio doors would lead them into the garden.

Stephen was playing DJ and as the sun began to set, the group of former school friends were making their best moves to Tina Turner, Billy Idol and Dire Straits. He had been under strict instructions that there was to be no slow dances and to be honest, there was no one that Maggie wanted to slow dance with.

A lot of her friends had already 'done it' with boys from school. Linda and Jude had both 'done it' a lot, but for Maggie there had been no one. All Maggie had managed was a kiss with tongues and the last boy she had kissed had groped her mammoth chest. It had done nothing for her, she hadn't had the urge to let him do more. It certainly didn't help with Shaun being friends with the majority of the boys at school. And if they weren't friends with Shaun then they knew about him, and it sort of put Maggie on a 'no no' list.

It didn't bother Maggie. The boys that had kissed her been some of the bad lads of school, the ones that were cock sure of themselves and thought that they could handle Shaun Hunter if he came looking for them if he found out that they had been with his sister. The boys had been arrogant and usually had been drinking so it had never been a pleasant experience. So, when Linda and Jude talked of how good 'doing it' was, Maggie didn't get it.

So, the lack of slow songs wasn't a problem and when Stephen played DeBarge Rhythm of the Night as the last song; the whole house was jumping.

As Maggie said her farewells, she knew that there would be many of them she would more than likely never see again. They had all written in each other's jotter; they would love each other forever, good luck blah blah blah. But Maggie knew that her own jotter would not travel her life with her. It would be left at her mam and dad's house and long after she would move out, her mam would throw it in the bin, she might have valued her own sentimental relics, but a scrappy jotter wouldn't fall into the same category.

When everyone had left, Linda and Jude helped Maggie and Doreen clear away the mess. The girls were sleeping so rushed about making the house right again and then all rushed upstairs so they could get into their nighties and talk about the night's events.

Linda had been courting Paul for a few months, 6 months 3 weeks and 2 days to be precise. A long time for any school time relationship. Maggie was in no doubt that they would marry and have 2.4 children. They were already like an old married couple; they had even started collecting things for their bottom drawer.

Whereas Maggie would make for a record shop and Jude would go for clothes, Linda would drag them to Woolworths when they went on their little shopping trips into town. Linda was already working in an old people home, just in the kitchen where her mam worked, and Paul had an apprenticeship in a garage. Between them they were saving as much money as they could. They wanted to get married within two years. It baffled Maggie, it was lovely that they were in love so much, they were sickly sweet together, but neither of them had lived, not really lived and there they were, already booking Churches and Venues and picking best men and bridesmaids, obviously Maggie and Jude were to be bridesmaids. If either of the bride or grooms' parents had a problem with the youngsters marrying so young, they didn't seem to be voicing their concerns. It was even being arranged for them to live with Paul's family after they were married, after all there was more room at his house. And they would stay there until they had a home of their own.

Jude was less grounded. She just liked boys. Jude liked to be the centre of attention and because she was small and pretty and really a very nice girl, she was very popular and was never short of male admirers. She would get her eye on one boy, and he would be the total focus of her attention. Until she had him and then she would cast her eye around for her next conquest. To Maggie it seemed to be a game she played. She had split couples up with her twinkly eye, only to cast him aside once she had him. Her mam said there was a name for girls like Jude. Again, another peril of your mam working at your school. Not only did Doreen Hunter know the ins and outs of her own children's school life, she knew that of all their friends too. Jude was notorious, of course her mam would know all about her. But it always made Maggie feel uncomfortable, on edge when she had Jude over, she was never sure if her mam would say something to her!

In the privacy of Maggie's bedroom, the girls chatted away in hushed voices. They each brushed their hair within an inch of its life and a pot of Astra Cream and pack of cotton wool balls was passed around to remove their make-up.

Maggie was chuffed. The party seemed to have been a hit. Linda was always happy when she did anything and Paul there, you could literally stand them in an empty field in the rain and they would be happy. They just wanted to be together!

Jude was cooing. She was playing a game of Eye Spy with her friends. Teasing them about who she had her sights set on. All great fun until it became apparent that it was Maggie's brother. The letter S led them to Shaun, but Jude had been there and bought the t-shirt, something Maggie had always wondered about, no this time it was Stephen, the record spinning DJ of the night.

Maggie wasn't sure if Stephen would succumb to Jude's charms. He was older and up until a couple of months earlier had been seeing a girl. Maggie didn't want to know, what her brothers did was their business, they might have always poked their noses into her life, but she had no intention of playing cupid with theirs. She told Jude as much. This seemed to urge Jude on even more.

The chatter went on way into the night. But eventually Maggie's friends fell asleep, and she was left to stare at the ceiling, her mind whirling. In a couple of days, she would be starting work at Quarry's End. The thought of it filled her with dread. It had been bad enough having to pop into the trendy hairdressers and tell them that she no longer needed a job. Even when her dad had given her the money to get herself a nice haircut while she was there didn't take the sting away. She didn't book an appointment, she left the hairdressers and made her way to Boots the Chemists where she bought herself a new hair dye, a brush and a bottle of body mist. It would have been too depressing sitting having her hair done and imagining what her life could have been like if she had been given the opportunity to take the Saturday job.

Quarry's End was a dirty dusty place. Nothing glamourous about it even working in the office. Her dad had taken her up to meet the people she would be working with. Maggie had put a smile on her face and feigned an excitement she didn't feel. If anything, it made her feel worse. How would she ever keep her blonde hair clean and shiny with all the dust?

But it was done, and she would be starting her new life as a Junior Typist at Quarry's End on Monday. With her Dad. Freedom seemed like a very long way away!

5) *The Knight of Swords*

Maggie barely slept a wink the night before her first day at Quarry's End. It was difficult not to dig a little deeper into her thoughts and see if she could gleam what the days ahead would look like. But she had spent such a long time suppressing her heritage, apart from times when things were on-top of her before she realised, she didn't hear much. It was there, there would be that odd feeling she got when she went to somewhere new or met someone that she had never met before, and she had the overwhelming feeling she had been there before or that she already knew the person. But mainly any oddness she was seen to have these days, was just for being herself.

So, Maggie tried not to think and instead tossed and turned and rolled over and over until she had her blankets so twisted, she had to get back up, put on the light and remake her bed. Her digital clock illuminated 2.53am!!

Back in bed, Maggie closed her eyes again. Doing her best not to think of anything else, she started singing softly 'Swaying Room as the Music Starts ….. Strangers making the Most of the Dark… Two by Two their Bodies Become One ……I See You Through the Smokey Air ………' Maggie didn't even make it to the chorus and the next thing she knew was her mam shouting for her to get up for work.

Leslie Hunter seemed to be very excited that his daughter was going to work with him. He chatted about the people she would be working with and the things she would be selling. All the names were familiar to Maggie, she had been hearing about them for years, but had only met a handful of them and then she hadn't really taken much notice.

Maggie knew that it was still very much a family business. There was grandfather, father and son as well as some extended family. But for the life of her she had no idea who did what and where her dad even fit into the establishment. She maybe should have shown more attention!

And then they were there, and Leslie Hunter was ushering her into the building and to the little office at the back of the showroom which would be her place of work for the foreseeable or the rest of her life, who knew. Maggie's legs felt like lead, there was nothing glamourous about the showroom, it was full of paving slabs in various sizes, shapes and colours. Nothing like the trendy hairdressers she could have been working in. Maggie's heart felt as heavy as her legs.

Mrs West who was in charge of the little office, greeted Maggie like she was a puppy. She gushed over her welcoming her to the little team and told Leslie Hunter what a beauty his daughter was and what a credit she was to him. Then he was gone, promising to pop in and see Maggie on his dinner break and they could share the bait that Doreen Hunter had made for them. Despite her fear of having no freedom, Maggie didn't like the sight of her dad's back leaving through the door and leaving her in a room with strangers.

Maggie was ushered to a little desk by Mrs West. She had no typing experience at all, and Mrs West thought that it would be a good idea that for the first few days, she practiced. So, there she sat while Mrs West showed her how to put paper into typewriter and use all of the levers and buttons. There were pages and pages of script for Maggie to copy and Mrs West assured her that she would be back to check on her regularly!

Surprisingly the morning passed quickly. Maggie found she quite liked typing; it was a newish electric typewriter that made a sort of swishing sound when she hit the keys. Over and over, she typed 'THE QUICK

BROWN FOX JUMPED OVER THE LAZY DOG' and she soon found that she had a feel for where the keys were. By lunchtime she wasn't making as many mistakes and Mrs West shrilled that she was thrilled with her progress. Maggie beamed. Perhaps Quarry's End wasn't going to be so bad after all.

Mrs West seemed nice. She was hard to pinpoint an age on, maybe mid-forties, but for working in such a dusty environment, she was dressed really smart. Her two-piece skirt suit was smart and modern and hugged her tiny frame. Her hair was dyed red in a long bob, and she wore a damson-coloured lipstick which was either really expensive or she reapplied it every hour because it never budged.

By the time Leslie Hunter came to share his dinner with her, Maggie was feeling quite settled. There was just one other girl in the office beside Mrs West, Ann who Maggie thought probably wasn't that much older than her. Whereas Mrs West was petit, Ann was tall and thin, but had a ready smile on her face and shouted out encouragement to Maggie as she mastered her skills on the typewriter.

Leslie Hunter seemed satisfied that Maggie was doing ok and left to say that he had a delivery somewhere or other but would be back in time to drive her home. Again, Maggie thought that it was probably going to be ok working there. The office was busy with lots of people coming and going, though Maggie was concentrating far too hard on the typewriter to take much notice and there seemed to be a telephone constantly ringing. Before she knew it Mrs West was leaning over her should and telling her how pleased she was with her progress, and she could pack up for the day and get herself ready for her dad coming to collect her.

Maggie was just putting her arm into her coat when the door opened and in walked the most beautiful human being Maggie had ever set eyes on.

Just the thought of her thinking how beautiful he was made Maggie blush and she fumbled around putting things in her bag hoping that he wouldn't notice her.

But Mrs West, the ever professional scuppered any thoughts that Maggie would fade into the background. 'Tony, this is Maggie, she is our new junior and has only just joined us today. And can I just say she has done very well. She is Leslie Hunter's daughter!' 'Maggie this is Tony, Tony Sharp as in youngest member of the Sharp family, you know who own Quarry's End!'

A little more composed. Maggie lifted her head and stared into the darkest brown eyes she had ever seen. Tony held her gaze, eyes twinkling with amusement. To Maggie he seemed to have movie star looks; his hair was long, he looked like…. She couldn't find the name just the face. Her legs felt as if they wouldn't hold her as she smiled her most dazzling smile. Morten Harket. Tony Sharp looked like the lead singer of A Ha!

Leslie Hunter bundling through the door distracted her gaze from the Adonis in front of her. All of a sudden working at Quarry's End had appeal. Tony Sharp had appeal, every sense within her was awake. The alarm bells going off in her head were deafening, but she knew without a shadow of a doubt that she would ignore every single one of them. It was mumbo jumbo, no one knew what was in front of them, no one had the ability to look at someone and know that they were trouble. At that moment she refused to be the 'odd' girl at Quarry's End. Her Granny Hunter and all her grannies before her might have thought they had something magical about them. But the only magic Tony Sharp would see was in how absolutely magical it could be loving Maggie Hunter.

Smiling at her dad, she made for the door. Tony Sharp can take on me any day of the week she thought to herself as she slid into the passenger seat next to Leslie Hunter. The bells ringing in her head were more of a siren now. Nothing a couple of headache tablets wouldn't fix when she got home, Maggie thought to herself. 'Tell me about everyone that works their dad! I've really enjoyed today!!!'

6) The Emperor

Tony Sharp was heir apparent to Quarry's End, not quite a billion-pound conglomerate, but it had provided the Sharps with a wealthy lifestyle for generations. At 21 Tony had worked at the quarry since leaving school, starting at the bottom just as his dad and his granddad had done before him. Tony hadn't minded, he liked working with his hands and he liked the banter of the blokes that worked in the quarry. He was still working in the quarry much to his dad's disgust, Anthony Sharp wanted his eldest son on the road selling. But so far Tony had managed to duck out of the collar and tie, leaving the selling in the capable hands of his dad.

Tony's younger brother and sister had managed to avoid the quarry completely. Neil who was the next down was working as some sort of lineman for British Telecommunications and Angela, the youngest of the brood was learning to be a baker or a chef or something, Tony wasn't sure what it exactly what it was she did, he wasn't that interested in either of his siblings.

He could be thought of as spoilt or full of himself, but in his eyes, he was the one that had been stuck in the quarry so he would reap the benefits. And he certainly did that. Tony drove a Porsche 944 in red that he kept garaged at home. For work he drove a truck, the paintwork on the Porsche was far too precious to be covered in the dust that lay on everything within a 2 mile radius of the quarry.

Tony was smart and handsome and because he carried heavy loads around in the quarry, his body was strong and muscular. From being quite young he had always been a hit with the women, but no one at Quarry's End had ever tickled his fancy. Until Maggie Hunter, with her bouncing blonde hair and killer smile.

Leslie Hunter had talked about his kids a lot over the years, more so Maggie when he had secured her the job as a junior typist in the office. Tony Sharp made sure that he was about when Leslie Hunter arrived at work with his miserable faced daughter that Monday morning. But miserable face or not, she was a knockout and Tony knew that he would make it his business to be introduced to his new employee before the day was out.

Later in the day, up close, Maggie Hunter hadn't disappointed. Tony knew she had just left school so was no more than 16, but she was tall, almost as tall as him and there was something about her he couldn't put his finger on. All Tony knew was he had his eye on the prize and maybe going to work at the quarry might be a bit more interesting than it had been in the 5 years or so he had been working there!

Maggie May!!!

7) *The Two of Wands*

Maggie Hunter found herself looking forward to going to work. She would chit chat with her dad on the way there and then because she had picked up the skill of using a typewriter so quickly, she was already typing out quotes and orders. But the main thing that dragged her out of her bed, made her back comb her hair and gloss up her lips was Tony Sharp.

The second day she was there he had made his way into the office on his break and perched himself on the end of her desk, much to Mrs West's disgust. The office was Mrs West's domain but telling Tony West to leave the new junior alone was way above her pay grade, so she put up and shut up and grimaced through her damson coloured lipstick at the flourishing friendship between her little boss and her junior.

Maggie and Tony were totally enthralled with each other. He was quite immature for his 21 years and Maggie was an old 16 year old, they seemed to be somewhere in the middle together. Each breaktime Tony would be there. They were open about their friendship and had never left the office together, their conversations were about music and films, nothing too deep. But from the moment he plopped his bum onto her desk, their eyes never left each other's. Mrs West could smell trouble coming and poor Ann was much put out, she had been crushing on Tony Sharp since she had arrived at Quarry's End, he never even glanced her way.

Tony Sharp was sly and cunning though. He knew Leslie Hunter would spend his dinner break with his daughter, so there would be no sign of him between the hours of 12 and 2pm, he would only see Maggie on his morning and afternoon breaks.

But of course word got back to Leslie Hunter. Before her first week was even out her dad had mentioned Tony Sharp on their drive home. How that one day the business would be Tony's and that from what he could make out Tony Sharp was a bugger for the ladies. It was a shot across Maggie's bow. He hadn't needed to. The persistent shrilling in her head was testament enough to the dangers of Tony Sharp. Even the endless supply of pain killers that she took morning noon and night didn't dampen down the warnings. Maggie was choosing to put up with the pain and ignore them.

Maggie Hunter was smitten and when Tony Sharp asked if she fancied a ride out in his car one night, she had no hesitation.

They arranged to meet around the corner from her house, she could think of nothing worse than him turning up on her doorstep and her dad having some sort of seizure. No, it was only a drive out in his truck to the coast or something, pointless making a scene with her mam and dad. It may well be the one and only time she would see him.

Maggie hadn't even said anything to Linda or Jude. There was nothing to tell them, apart from having a crush, nothing had happened.

Sitting nervously on a wall waiting for his arrival, Maggie felt nervous. She had spent ages getting ready, making loads of effort so it looked like she had made none, she knew she was looking good. But as 10 minutes turned to 15 and there was still no sign of him, she began to feel stupid. Had it just been a joke!

Thinking that she would just go home and at least save some face, you just never knew who was watching. She couldn't just sit in the hope that he would turn up!! Deciding that she would walk forward and not in the direction she had come from, just in case someone was watching, she stood up to set off. Maggie heard him before she saw him, the steady roar of an engine. If she had been trying to meet Tony discreetly then turning up in his Porsche wasn't the way to do it. Tony pulled up the Porsche up to the kerb Maggie couldn't get into the passenger seat quick enough. The arrival of the Porsche had not gone unnoticed, glancing around Maggie could see curtains twitching and a flush crept up her neck.

In the safety of the Porsche, Tony smiled at her and before she chance to say anything, the Porsche roared off. Maggie had never been in a car like it, she felt that she was almost sitting on the floor. Tony drove it expertly and to Maggie looked the boss that he ultimately was. The smell of his aftershave filled the car. It was something like Shaun wore on special occasions only nicer and Maggie knew that for the rest of her life, the smell would always remind her of that night.

Dire Straits pounded out of the CD Player, it was loud, and it made talking impossible. Maggie sat back in her seat and enjoyed the ride. The speed, the smell, the sounds and being this close to Tony Sharp and them being completely on their own.

They drove for some time. Maggie wasn't even sure where they were. As a family they often travelled to the coast, but Maggie was always in the back with her brothers and usually in the middle, she seldom took notice of how they got to places. So, it was a pleasant surprise when Tony pulled into a car park and she realised that he had driven them to Whitley Bay.

They walked along the front, Tony bought them dab and chips and a bottle of dandelion and burdock pop, thoughts of Granny Hunter popped into Maggie's head, a warning? She swallowed it down and concentrated on Tony. He was good company, the conversation was light and then was no pressure. Even when he dropped her off in the Porsche later he only pecked her cheek. Maggie didn't know if she was disappointed or not. When he suggested that they do it again a few days later she could cope with the fact that he hadn't wanted to snog her face off.

And that was Maggie and Tony for the next few weeks, drives out in the car. The speed, the smell and the sound. They would drive somewhere, Tony would buy them food, they would walk and they would talk and then he would drive Maggie home, peck her on the cheek and roar off into the sunset. She was like a wired beast.

At work they continued as they had started out. Tony would show up on his breaktime, Mrs West would be grimacing, Ann sulky and Tony would perk his pert bot onto the edge of her desk, and they would chat. It really was all very innocent.

Maggie found that she was really enjoying working at Quarry's End. The money helped too, beyond the bits of money she received for her birthday or Christmas, she had never had any money of her own.

Now when she made her way into town with Linda and Jude, the record shop was forgotten and she would follow Jude into various clothes shops, buying nice tops and jeans before heading into Boots the Chemists for hair dye and perfume and magic creams that made your skin glisten. She still hadn't told her friends about Tony. He was her secret and hers alone, she wasn't ready to share, especially with Jude who would no doubt cast her beady eye on him and go in for the kill.

Or would she?? With Maggie being so focused on her 'new job' she hadn't realised what had been going on right under her nose. It seems that Maggie's oldest brother Stephen had been taking Jude out. They had been to the pictures and he had taken her to a party, Jude had even been to their house for supper, how had Maggie missed that? Jude for once seemed to be a one man woman, hard to believe when it was Stephen and Maggie always thought he was a bit on the boring side. But horses for courses and he may be the life and soul of the party away from their house. Jude seemed happy!

8) The Lovers

It was 3 weeks and 5 driving dates before Maggie and Tony kissed.

It had been worth waiting the 3 weeks and 5 driving dates for.

This was the kiss that Maggie Hunter had been waiting for. The kiss that made her want to push her body into a boys. Urge him to hold her and touch her. This was the type of kissing that would lead her to 'do it' just like her friends had.

Once they started kissing in the front seat of his Porsche in some car park beside the sea somewhere, they couldn't stop. It was dusk. The car park was deserted but even so. When he pulled her out of the car and down onto the beach she didn't resist.

There was no one on the beach. They found a spot, sunk into the sand and started with the delicious kissing all over again. She pushed her body as hard as she could against him and he answered doing the same. And then it got frantic, and Maggie entered some trance like state. Her body was melting against Tony whispered something in her ear, she thought he mentioned pills and said yes, she had taken some. This seemed to spur him on and despite the discomfort and his amazement that she obviously had never 'done it' before, it was the most magical time of her life.

Later lying in her bed, she mused at how quickly it had all been over. Maggie knew she was in some sort of shock about the whole experience, but from start to finish it couldn't have lasted for more than 5 minute. It had been good. She loved the feeling of being so wanted, but that had been before really, the kissing part. The actual act had been a little under whelming. There had been no explosions or fireworks. Surely with all the baloo about 'doing it' it had to be better than that. First time or not, it truly hadn't been what she had expected.

Still, Maggie went to sleep with a smile on her face. Maggie Hunter and Tony Sharp were girlfriend and boyfriend. Maggie Hunter and Tony Sharp were lovers.

They remained lovers the following months. Little drives to the seaside or deep into the countryside always resulted in lots of lovely kissing and then a frantic fumble. For Maggie things didn't really improve. She was always in a trance like state, delirium really. But when it got to the actual act, it was disappointing, over before she had chance to catch her stride and before she knew it, she would be back in the Porsche with the speed and the smell and the sounds and being dropped off around the corner from her house.

For 16 year old Maggie is was all a little confusing. Tony Sharp continued to spend his breaks perched on the edge of her desk. Mrs West still grimaced but Ann no longer sulked. She had met a boy and was distracted by him. Maggie and Tony were of little interest to her. Maggie was becoming quite a proficient typist and was now given extra duties to carry out, Mrs West was very pleased with her, she told Maggie so on a daily basis. And Leslie Hunter obviously knew that Maggie and Tony were girlfriend and boyfriend because the journey in the car to and from Quarry's End was silent and frosty. Maggie didn't even try to fill the silences, there was nothing she could say.

As November headed into December, Tony broke the news that he was going away on holiday with the family over the Christmas and New Year period, three whole weeks at some house in France where they went every year. The skiing was amazing he stated. Maggie wasn't bothered. No one knew they were even boyfriend and girlfriend so she could hardly have been expecting an invite. And for the life of her and as hard as she tried, she could never imagine Tony even setting foot into her house, not even to pick her up.

Maggie totally adored Tony. She loved looking at him and kissing him and she really wanted them to be a proper boyfriend and girlfriend. The 'doing it' remained a bit off and she really wanted to ask Linda and Jude if it was normal, well Linda, it seemed that Jude and Stephen were courting and the nitty gritty of Jude's sex life with her brother was not at all appealing. But no one knew, so she would just have to figure it out all by herself.

Quarry's End would be closing when the Sharp's left for their winter break. Three whole weeks off. She was touched and a little bit embarrassed when Mrs West and Ann gave her gifts on their last afternoon before they broke up, Maggie hadn't even thought about it, but she had never worked in an office before so took the gifts with a hug and a promise that she would make it up to them the following year. It still amazed Maggie how quickly and how well she had settled in, any thoughts of working in the trendy hairdressers was well and truly out of her mind now. She loved being at the quarry and she was very fond of her two colleagues.

Tony came to see her on his last break. She hadn't asked too much about his holiday, he could tell her all about it when he got back. Perched on the end of the desk he whispered how much he was going to miss her and how he couldn't wait to get back and they could go for a drive. For some reason the ringing sound in Maggie's head seemed to rise an octave and it made her feel sick. Reaching in her desk she pulled out a couple of pain killers and swallowed them down wholesale, no water required. Smiling at Tony she told him that she was looking forward to that too, that she was going to miss him and that she hoped that he would have a nice Christmas. Unsure whether to lean in and kiss him, he took the situation into his own hands by jumping off the desk and pressing a little gift wrapped package into her hand.

Smiling, Tony made a big thing of hugging Mrs West and Ann in turn and wishing them a Very Merry Christmas, leaning into Maggie, he kissed her on the cheek, just like he had done on the first 5 driving dates they had been on, her stomach flipped. And then he was gone.

All that remained was for Maggie to wait patiently for her dad to arrive and for him to drive her home for Christmas.

Little did Maggie Hunter know, but she would never be returning to Quarry's End as a Junior Typist again. That the promise that she had made Mrs West and Ann earlier about making up for her lack of gifts that year with something huge the following year would never happen.

The pain killers weren't helping. The ringing alarm bells in her head were persistent and she kept getting little bits of sick in her mouth that she had to keep swallowing down. The journey home with her dad and his frosty silence seemed to take forever and by the time she arrived home, all she could manage was to make her way up into her bedroom and into her bed.

42

9) The Sun

Christmas was always very much a family affair. Auntie Joan, Uncle Ken and Tom would all come and stay on Christmas Eve, to date it was a tradition that continued, even with the kids no longer being kids there was the excitement of the families all being together.

When they were younger Maggie and Tom would share a bed, but as they got older Tom was moved into the boys room. Maggie always felt that Tom was happier in the boys room than with her, but it was a notion that both her mam and dad and her auntie and uncle would never have considered. Tom was more likely to get up to mischief with the boys if they were that way inclined than he ever would have been with Maggie. But it was always all boys together and that's the way it stayed.

Maggie was feeling better and enjoyed helping her mam prepare for the days of festivities they would be having. They cooked and cleaned and when Linda and Jude came over to exchange presents with Maggie, Doreen Hunter welcomed them with open arms; even Jude who miraculously seemed to be flavour of the month now she was Stephen's girlfriend.

It was a jolly household on Christmas Eves, jollier still when the Grey's arrived. The girls ended up staying much later than they had done on previous years and whereas the past couple of years Stephen had gone out and met up with friends, that year he stayed in. At ten the girls went home, Stephen insisting that he saw them home safely. Stephen was as smitten as Jude was!

Later lying in her bed, Maggie was staring at the ceiling. She could hear the noise coming from the adults downstairs, the laughter. There was always laughter coming from downstairs when the Grey's were there. It was a comforting sound.

The alarm bells ringing in Maggie's head weren't as loud, more of a drone. She wondered what Tony would be doing? Was he missing her? Was she missing him??? She couldn't be certain that she was. She missed looking at his beautiful face and she missed the kissing, but as young as she was, she knew that the relationship probably wouldn't be going anywhere. It had been months and they hadn't moved beyond driving dates, fumbling sex and Tony sitting perched on her desk. Tony Sharp was out of Maggie Hunter's league.

Maggie slept fitfully. Tony Sharp's beautiful face haunted her dreams and by the time an over excited Tom was bouncing on her bed shouting 'Santa has been' she felt like she had only just fallen asleep. But it was Christmas morning and she bounded down the stairs with her cousin Tom and waited for the arrival of the rest of the family to come down before they could open their presents.

She did well. There weren't the piles and piles of presents that would greet them on Christmas morning when they were all small. But still, she had new nighties, slippers and dressing gown. The customary new outfit that they all got every year that they would wear on Christmas day. Maggie got some new perfume and a record voucher. All in all, she was delighted.

And best of all, it was the first time that she had ever been able to buy any of her family decent gifts. On a whim she had bought her mam and dad a teasmaid, she had often heard them talk about getting a one, save them trundling up and down the stairs with hot cuppas they said, but it was one of those things they had never got around to buying. It had cost a lot more money than Maggie had intended to pay, but it was the first time she had a wage coming in, she could afford it and it was worth it just to see the look on their faces.

All in all, it was a nice morning, the music was playing, and the women made dinner, whilst the men folk dodged off to the local cricket club for a few pre-Christmas Dinner drinks. Maggie and Tom messed around whilst setting the table and Shaun shot off somewhere on his bike, Maggie thought he may have been in a huff as Stephen had been invited for a pint but there had been no mention of Shaun going. He would be back in time for his dinner, woe-be-tide him if he was late. There weren't many rules in their house, but Christmas Dinner was sacred.

At 1pm everyone was seated around the dining room table. The men were merry and Maggie was sure that her mam and Auntie Joan had been on the sherry, they seemed to be finding dishing the dinners up very funny.

Maggie had forgot to take her painkillers that morning with all the hustle and bustle going on, the bells ringing in her head were beginning to feel like Big Ben and she felt a little woozy. But no breakfast had been eaten and she had only had a couple of Quality Street chocolates since her tea the day before. It was nothing a Christmas dinner wouldn't put right. There was no Grace in their house, but the dinner wouldn't be started until every cracker had been pulled and paper hats were adorned on heads. Glasses were raised, toasts to absent friends and then it was time to tuck in.

It was Maggie's favourite meal ever. All her family around the table, everyone happy and smiling and because it was Christmas she was always allowed a glass of babycham as was Tom, Shaun would have a beer. It had always made her feel grown up. Delicious!

But half way through her Christmas dinner, something went very wrong.

Chestnut stuffing was always her favourite. She did that thing with her dinner which never really made sense but kept all her favourite bits until last. So, the stuffing, turnip and the roast potatoes were the last things on her plate. She had already demolished the rest. The stuffing was delicious, her mam always made it herself from Granny M's recipe and Maggie spooned it into her mouth by the forkful.

No sooner had she swallowed it though than she could feel it coming back up. Thinking that she had just ate it too fast she swallowed it back down again and stuffed a roast potato into her mouth for good measure. But it was no good, Maggie could feel it all coming back up again.

Unsure that to do and certainly not wanting to spit it all out onto her plate in front of everyone, she excused herself from the table and ran up the stairs to the loo. Only just making it in time, the whole of her Christmas dinner departed her body.

Shaking and exhausted Maggie clung on to the toilet bowl. She felt dreadful, she was cold but could feel her face flushed and touching her forehead she could feel little beads of sweat.

There was nothing else for her to do but to make her way into her bedroom and into her bed. She must have fallen asleep because when she woke it was dark and her room felt cool. She felt better, her body felt a normal temperature and stepping up out of the bed, the wooziness had gone.

Back downstairs everyone was still sitting at the table. The food had been cleared and they were having a game of cards, another of their customs for Christmas Day afternoon. Making her way back onto her seat, they all voiced their concerns as to how she was feeling, how it must have been something she had eaten that hadn't agreed with her and she was looking better than she had been looking that morning.

Munching on a mince pie, sipping lemonade, she asked to be dealt in to the card game. Whatever was wrong had passed, Big Ben had stopped chiming in her head, it was now more tinkling, no tablets required and the rest of Christmas Day passed without any disruption.

But sure as eggs were eggs, it wouldn't last.

10) Seven of Pentacles

It was eggs that would be Maggie's undoing. She woke early on Boxing Day morning and was lying in her bed staring at the spot on the ceiling that she had become so fond of. She wondered what Tony Sharp was up to. Had he had a good Christmas? Had he been thinking of her? She hadn't particularly thought much about him. She hadn't even opened his gift yet! It had been too busy and she had been ill and then she had slept and then she had been having too much fun playing cards with the family. No she hadn't really thought very much about Tony Sharp at all.

Thinking that she would get out of bed and see who was up and about, it hit her. Maggie could smell frying eggs and bacon. The nausea was on top of her before she knew what was happening, this time there was no time to make it to the toilet. The waste paper bin got what remained of her Christmas Day goodies. Cold and shaking, with the burning face and the beads of sweat, Maggie lay back in her bed and pulled the sheets and blankets up over her head. She felt dreadful and all of sudden very very tired.

Maggie's sleep was filled with strange images, not quite a nightmare but certainly not sweet dreams. She was woken by the sound of her bedroom door being opened. It was her cousin Tom. She didn't need to be told she looked dreadful, she felt it. But as she sat chatting with Tom, she began to feel better. The Grey's were off home, another of their customs, Boxing Day breakfast and then they would make for home. Tom refused to cuddle her, didn't want to catch her lurgy, but she was going to miss him and promised him she would call him on New Year's

Eve, like they had done every year since they could hold a conversation, he really was Maggie's favourite person in the whole wide world.

Whatever it had been that had bothered Tom at school seemed to have left him since he moved into 6th form. He seemed so much happier, in himself, in his skin. Maggie was under no illusion what her creative cousin was, what was it her Granny Hunter used to say about him??? A friend of Dorothy's!!! Maggie had always loved the fact that he sought her company out over her rough and tumble brothers, he would much rather spend time with Maggie in her bedroom designing hair styles and perfecting her make-up. She always wished that he lived closer.

But as even as close as they were, Maggie hadn't told him about Tony Sharp. There hadn't really been opportunity during his Christmas stay there and even now, as he sat on her bed, cockerling at the sick in her waste bin, it seemed a pointless exercise. Maggie felt sure that her dalliance with Tony Sharp would soon be over. Even with the driving dates and the lush kissing and the fumbles in the grass or the sand or where ever it was they could find five minutes to be intimate and despite the fact that he was the most beautiful boy that she had ever clapped eyes on, there would be no future for them. He was skiing in France, she had been sick in her wastebin. It said it all.

After the eggs and fried bacon, there was the furniture polish her mam had been using the day after Boxing Day, same routine, sick, bed and sleep. Then it was Turkey soup followed by chip pan fat, toilet cleaner. The toilet cleaner proved to be the hardest. She was being sick then sick again. And so, it went on.

The family stayed away from her. They all had plans for New Year's Eve and didn't want to catch the bug. So, her days were spent in her bedroom with dashes to the toilet and then down to the kitchen to find something to eat that didn't make her want to retch.

Maggie slept, a lot. When she slept she didn't hear the tinkle of bells in her head, or have the wooziness that made her stagger from one room to another. She slept in glorious colour, images of Tony, sometimes she saw faces she had never seen before in her life. It was a kaleidoscope of colour and images. Sometimes she thought her Granny Hunter was in her dreams, but she could never be sure. She would wake and remember Tony, what he had been doing, but images of her Granny Hunter would disappear as if they were made out of quick sand.

1985 ticked into 1986. Maggie saw it in alone. It didn't bother her, if she had been feeling herself, she would have been out with her mam, dad and Shaun at her mam's friend's house. They went there every New Year's Eve. But she hadn't felt up to it and had assured her mam and dad that she would keep the doors locked and even if someone came knocking trying to come and celebrate, then she wouldn't let them in.

Maggie watched Big Ben on the telly, listened to the bongs that would signal out with the old and in with the new and wondered what 1986 would have in store for her.

Surprisingly she found she loved her job. She was a good typist and even though Quarry's End wasn't really the job of her dreams, she liked getting her little brown wage packet at the end of every week and she had grown really fond of Mrs West and Ann.

Tony Sharp wasn't the man of her dreams like she had thought he was when she had first met him. But he was nice and her dalliance with him had given her a confidence boost. He was older, good looking and rich. And he certainly wasn't the only man in the world. When she was feeling better, she would start meeting up with some of her friends who ventured into Newcastle, she wasn't 18 but she certainly looked it, especially when she had her make-up and hair done. That would be good, spread her wings a little, she what or who else was out there for her.

Knowing her mam, dad and Shaun wouldn't be back for hours, she checked the doors, switched off the lights and made her way up to her bedroom. She was overcome with tiredness and as soon as her head hit the pillow, she was asleep.

11) Two of Cups REVERSED

The smell of the frying pan woke her, the nausea was on top of her before she could get her bearings. Then she did something that she hadn't done since she was a little girl, she was sick all over her bedsheets. There was something very wrong with Maggie Hunter.

Maggie Hunter was still too poorly to go back to work. Her dad looked disgruntled as Doreen Hunter told him that whatever the bug was Maggie had was still hanging on her and it would be ridiculous her returning to work, he would just have to bring her back home again.

The sickness and wooziness was still there, but because she had eaten so little, by lunchtime she would normally be feeling more herself and would venture downstairs and lie and watch the television. Maggie's mam didn't seem overly concerned, she had worked in a school for years and knew that in winter, all sorts of viruses ran ragged.

It was strange there just being Maggie and her mam in the house, even though Doreen Hunter had always had all of the school holidays off with her daughter, there would always be Shaun there and more often than not, her cousin Tom too. So just being on their own had a very strange feel to it.

They weren't very close. Maggie had always somewhat resented her mam for working in her school. Not that she wanted to be naughty at school or anything, but nothing got passed Doreen and if she said so herself, Doreen Hunter was very opiniated.

Pupils, teachers, admin staff, Doreen had something to say about all of them. Not always in a bad way, but what Doreen Hunter didn't know wasn't worth knowing about.

It always made Doreen's relationship with her daughter a little bit strained. Maggie tended just to keep 'mum' about most things. She envied her friends relationships with their mams, especially Jude's whose mam Carole was really cool. Having had Jude very young, she was still young herself and was always on hand to advise the friends about hair and make-up and boys. For the life of her Maggie could never remember an occasion when Doreen Hunter had talked about hairstyles with Maggie.

But it could have been worse. They managed. The moseyed along.

Doreen Hunter wasn't due back to school until the following week. So, while Maggie lay in her bed in a morning her mam would do the housework. By the time Maggie made it to the sofa in an afternoon, Doreen would plonk herself in a chair and they would spend their afternoon watching crap telly, drinking tea and eating biscuits.

At 5 Doreen would make her way into the kitchen and get tea ready for her dad and brothers coming in from work, Maggie would go to her room and stay there until everyone was home and their tea was on the table.

Maggie would manage to eat her tea, no matter what it was, even the fish on Friday didn't have her rushing up the stairs to hug the loo. But by the next morning, the slightest thing that had any type of smell knocked her sideways.

Linda and Jude were shocked by how Maggie looked when she saw them. She hadn't seen sight of them since Christmas Eve, even when Jude had been to the house with Stephen, Maggie would be in her room.

After the initial shock at how green around the gills Maggie was, the friends caught up on how their Christmas and New Year's had been. Maggie obviously had little to report, but Linda had been super excited about all of the Woolworth's vouchers her and Paul had been given and how they had loved getting bits and bobs for their home in the Boxing Day Sales.

Jude was loved up with Stephen. Maggie decided that she had to think about Stephen in the third person, it was all just too weird hearing her best friend talk about this amazing boy she was courting and Maggie having to try to be enthusiastic about it knowing her amazing boy was her brother!!

After having missed one week at Quarry's End, Maggie was sure that she would be able to go back the following Monday. She was starting to get a bit bored, especially in an afternoon when she began to feel more herself. Maggie missed Mrs West and Ann and she desperately wanted to see Tony Sharp and see how his trip had been.

Maggie was still uncertain about how she felt about her Adonis. She missed their driving dates and the kissing, missed 'doing it' less so and she missed looking at his beautiful face as he perched himself at the edge of her desk and tell her about his day. But Maggie wasn't sure if she was missing him, or she was just bored of being in the house day in day out. It had been almost 3 weeks,

So, on Sunday night, she hung up her work clothes, packed her bag and went to bed early. For a very long time she stared at the spot on the ceiling and thought about what the new year would bring her. The ringing in her head came and went. Sometimes it was quite noisy, other times it was more of a murmur, sometimes she didn't hear anything at all. When the bells were clattering loudly, Maggie resisted the temptation to pop painkillers, she had a feeling that it was the consumption of them on a regular basis that had made her feel so ill.

The gift Tony Sharp had given Maggie before he went to France still lay unopened in the bottom of her jewellery box; aptly seeing as without even opening the gift, Maggie knew they were earrings. Pointless really, if Tony had paid any attention, he would know Maggie didn't have her ears pierced and the fashionable plastic ones she was fond of wearing, were clip ons!

Typical bloke.

She dreamt of Tony Sharp. His beautiful face swam in front of her eyes. Perfect and then not perfect. Tony's face grew so hideous that Maggie woke up scared and sweating. Disorientated it took her a few moments to steady her beating heart. It was morning already, she felt like she had only been asleep 10 minutes, she was just so tired. But she would have to get up, get ready for work. No sooner had she put her feet on the floor when she got a whiff of something, what was it?? Hairspray maybe?? Whatever it was it had Maggie running for the bathroom where the toilet was waiting for her hug.

Maggie was still rolled up in a ball when she heard her dad leaving for work. Without her. She heard the boys leave and then Doreen Hunter popped her head around the door to see how Maggie was before she left for school. 'Think we may have to get you to the doctors if you're not feeling better soon' And then she was gone.

By afternoon Maggie was feeling better. She watched crap television and as it approached tea time, she headed into kitchen to make the tea. It was Monday so it was sausage egg and chips, just like every other Monday since as long as she could remember. Tuesday was pie and chips, Wednesday was mince and dumplings, Thursday macaroni cheese and Friday was whatever fish was in season and chips. If Maggie was abducted by aliens and then returned to earth any teatime, she would know what day of the week it was. It was the Hunter's way.

If the family were shocked that Maggie had made tea, they never said. They all just sat around tucking in. The eggs and the sausage and the chips hadn't made Maggie woozy at all, she was walloping her tea off. Maybe she was on the mend at last.

Talk was on how everyone's day had been, Maggie was especially interested of what was going on at Quarry's End. Jumping up, Leslie Hunter rushed out into the hallway then came running back in with an envelope in his hand. They had all been invited to a party! As was the way with the staff at Quarry's End, if there was an event happening in any of their families, then everyone at Quarry's End and their own family were invited.

Maggie was excited to see who was having a party. Before she worked there she would make every excuse under the sun not to go. But now working there it would be different, she wouldn't feel so out of place.

Leslie Hunter handed the envelope to Maggie, after all she was the only other person sitting at the table who knew who everyone at Quarry's End was.

Taking the invitation out Maggie began to read out loud.

Mr and Mrs Anthony Sharp request the presence of

Mr & Mrs Leslie Hunter & Family

On Friday 14th February 1986
To Celebrate the Engagement of their Son
Anthony Junior to Nichola Porter

7pm until Midnight

At The Swallow Hotel Gateshead

Maggie was trying hard to concentrate on the words. Surely Anthony Junior was Tony!!!! Tony had a girlfriend?? Tony was getting married??? All the time they had been on driving dates and kissing and 'doing it' and him sitting perched on her desk in his breaks, he already had a girlfriend!!!

The noise in her head was deafening. Clang, clang, clang. Maggie couldn't think straight. She just sat and stared at the invitation. And then the wooziness came and she couldn't hear and she couldn't see. And then it was darkness……

12) The Ten of Swords

There was a chink of light shining through her door when she woke up. The door was pulled to but not closed. She had no idea how she got into her bed, someone must have carried her. She was still in the clothes she had made the tea in. Her clock told her it was just after 9pm, she could hear the television downstairs, but had no inclination to go down and see everyone. What would she say?

So, she crept to the loo, closed her door and then lay back on her bed and stared at the spot on the ceiling.

The clanging in her head had stopped. In fact, it was silent. No ringing or clanging or even murmurings, just quietness.

Tony Sharp had a girlfriend, an almost fiancée! He hadn't told her. To be fair she had never asked. She had been so overwhelmed by his interest in her, the topic of was he exclusively hers had never crossed her mind. But on reflection, they had always met at his suggestion, when he was free! But there had been no talk at Quarry's End about his girlfriend. But maybe it was common knowledge and that was the reason why Mrs West grimaced when she saw them together! Did her dad know about her?? The questions whirled around and around her head. She felt silly.

Maggie slept well, no images of Tony Sharp's face either beautiful or grotesque. She slept soundly and very late. It was way after 10 when she opened her eyes and the house was silent. She felt a bit woozy but not sickly and for the first time in a while she pulled on her dressing gown and made for the kitchen.

At a loss at what to do, Maggie decided that she would tidy her bedroom, there were still piles of Christmas presents to be put away and it wouldn't harm to give the room a dust and a hoover. By lunchtime her room was ship shape and in Bristol fashion and she was dressed. A quick rummage under her bed to pull out anything she had kicked there and that would be her job down, she would be able to go downstairs, watch crap telly and eat biscuits. She would even make tea again, it was Tuesday so pie and chip night, Maggie had already seen the bag of potatoes on the kitchen bench. She had never chopped potatoes for chips before but she would give it a go. It was the least she could do after all the commotion she had cause the night before.

The funny thing was she hadn't really given Tony Sharp that much thought all day. After the initial shock that he had a girlfriend had worn off, she found that she really wasn't too bothered. Maggie had already established that there really wasn't ever going to be a future for them. The typist and the boss. It was the stuff that books were written about. No, she would go back to work, wish him well. She may well give the engagement party a swerve, but she would see.

Pulling out a collection of socks, knickers and sweet wrappers from under her bed, Maggie was surprised to find her diary there. When she had been at school, she had written in her diary religiously, nothing major just things she had to do, thoughts etc, but flicking through it she thought it seemed childish. Even the handwriting seemed childish, working in an office had changed a lot about Maggie Hunter.

The last thing she had written in it was her second driving date with Tony Sharp, after that there had been nothing. It seemed weird reading it now, like it had been written by someone else. There was her party along with the invitation list. There were exam dates and times, a dentist appointment, there were even the dates of her periods so she could work out when her next one would be and be ready for it. She had seen for too many girls at school caught out and the tell-tale sign on their skirts, Maggie could think of nothing worse. Thankfully she had always known within a day or two when her 'friend' would come and have something in her bag ready.

Pushing the diary back under the bed, Maggie made her way down the stairs, made a cup of tea and plonked herself onto the sofa chomping away on biscuits. The crap telly must have bored her because the next think she knew it was getting dark and there was the distinct clanging of bells in her ears. So much for her peace and quiet she thought to herself.

As she attempted to peel the spuds for chips, Maggie thought about the ringing in her head, were they really something to do with having second sight like her Granny Hunter had said. They were certainly loud leading up to the invitation reveal. But why now? What had brought them back?? What had changed since this morning when all was still and silent.

Maggie had tidied her room, she had ate biscuits and then peeled the potatoes for tea.

The ringing was so loud in her head. Maggie was struggling to think straight. She thought that she was going to pass out again. Tensing her body she did her best to keep lucid, in a moment or two it would be over and she would be able to go and lie down. A pain in her hand snapped her back into reality. Looking down there was blood everywhere, her hand was still wrapped around her mam's best sharp knife that she had been using to peel the potatoes.

But it was more than that. Reality was really hitting home. Dropping the knife and wrapping a tea towel around her bleeding hand, she left the carnage of the kitchen and with the deafening clattering in her ears, Maggie bounded up the stairs two steps at a time.

Scrabbling under the bed, she found her diary and began to turn page after page after page. She found it, the last symbol entry she had made. September 3rd. Maggie sat on her bed staring at the diary. Her head had fallen silent; the alarm or warning bells or whatever they bloody well were had stopped. There was no need now. She knew. She did a quick rekey, there had been no need for any further symbols. There had been no interruptions to the driving dates and the lovely kissing and the fumbles.

Her hand was throbbing, she was going to have to remove the tea towel and see how deep the cut was. But it could wait. She hadn't needed to put a symbol in her diary since the beginning of September, it was now mid-January. Maggie Hunter was stupid. Maggie Hunter was pregnant.

13) The Ten of Wands

She felt calm. Calmer than she had done in weeks. There were no bells ringing and clanging. There was nothing to warn her about. Maggie knew. In the bathroom she untied the tea towel and ran her hand under the tap. Once the blood had been rinsed away the cut wasn't as deep as the blood loss had signified, a large Elastoplast out of the bathroom cabinet covered it.

Back in her room, the diary was once again flung under the bed, a fresh set of clothes was put on and all the bloodied stuff was bundled up and taken downstairs to put in the washing basket. Maggie cleaned the kitchen and washed and chipped the potatoes.

By the time everyone arrived home, the table was set and Maggie was dishing up the tea onto plates. Everyone was concerned about her cut finger and joked about how bloody awful the chips were. But there were 5 clean plates, her first attempt at chips couldn't have been that bad.

Maggie said nothing. She needed time to take everything in. She needed to think what she had to do. She certainly couldn't face Tony Sharp yet. There was no way she could go back to work. So, after sitting watching the news and Eastenders, Maggie excused herself saying she was feeling tired and a little bit off again.

Back in her room all she could do was lie on her bed and stare at her spot on the ceiling.

She thought she had done enough to get tomorrow off. If need be she would swoon in the morning, but she thought it wouldn't be necessary. She couldn't believe how calm she was, everything that had been knocking her off balance the past few weeks seemed to have abated. No clanging bells, no wooziness or nausea. She felt normal.

Placing her hand on her flat stomach she found it hard to believe that there was a tiny little life growing there. She didn't know much about babies, there weren't really any in her family, she was the youngest of her lot, on both sides of the family. Her friend Jude had little brothers, they were only about 3 and 5, they were cute, but the only time Maggie saw them was when she went around to Jude's to babysit. They always smelled of talcum powder and were shiny and clean. Maggie knew that they weren't always like that, they were normally a two man demolition team and liked nothing better than destroying anything that belonged to Jude if they could get to it.

So as far as Maggie was concerned, babies were aliens.

But she couldn't ignore what was happening to her. She would have to talk to someone who would know what to do. Not her mam, Doreen Hunter was the last person that Maggie wanted to talk about her predicament to. Well maybe not the last, that would be Tony Hunter. All that fumbling and pushing and pulling had done its damage, he had done his damage.

Obviously Maggie knew about the birds and the bees, from school not from any chat Doreen Hunter had sat down and had with her. She had known some of the nitty gritty off her friends who had 'done it' long before she had. She still felt underwhelmed by the whole experience, it had been nothing like what Linda and Jude had said it was like. Though she had to admit, she did like the kissing.

She didn't particularly know how not to have a baby. Obviously. She hadn't really given it much thought when she was in the throes of kissing Tony Sharp's face off, even when he was 'doing it' she had sort of assumed that he would be doing something. Lordy he had a girlfriend who was soon to be his fiancée and then his wife. Surely Tony Sharp didn't want his Junior Typist at Quarry's End having his baby, seemed like a silly risk to take. Nevertheless, he hadn't done anything and now Maggie was in a predicament and there was only her that could sort it.

No one came to see if she was ok. She had kept her bedroom light and lamps off, they would assume she was asleep. Hopefully they would leave her be in the morning. Her eyes became heavy and sleep was starting to wash over her. Somewhere in her in between state, she knew what she needed to do. Second sight? Maybe!! A moment of clarity?? Probably!!

Maggie would go and see Jude's mam Carole. She had been about Maggie's age when she had got pregnant with Jude. She would know what to do, where to go, who to talk to. Maggie didn't even know what options she had. But what she did know was whatever she decided she needed to act fast.

Hopefully she would be left to lie in the morning. But this time she would get up and get dressed when everyone left for work. Carole would be taking her eldest boy to school but would be back with the little one about 9.30. Maggie wanted to be there for when she got back.

It was Wednesday, there would be mince in the fridge for tea. When she got back she would make the mince and dumplings, well she would if she could find her mam's Bero book; she had no idea how to construct a dumpling…..

14) The Four if Swords REVERSED

Carole Todd looked concerned when she found Maggie Hunter sitting on her wall, Maggie could see it in her face as she made her way along the road with a toddling toddler. Maggie had almost given up and went back home, but just as Maggie thought that Carole had maybe gone somewhere else, she spotted her inching along the road, carrier bag in hand and her smallest son dragging along behind.

Maggie felt crap, she couldn't remember what Jude's little brother was called. While she waited for Carole to arrive at her gates, Maggie made her way through the alphabet. Adrian?? B??? C??? D?? Was it David?? Maggie was sure one of Jude's brothers was David, but this one?? E??? F?? G?? Then she had it, he was Marc – with a C! She thought.

'Is everything ok Mags? Has something happened with Jude?' Smiling weakly at Carole Todd, Maggie reassured her that it wasn't Jude, but she would appreciate five minutes of her time. Letting Maggie into the house, Carole put on a video on of some cartoon and David or Marc instantly plonked himself in front of the telly and was mesmerized.

Following Carole into the kitchen, she took a seat at the table. 'I've no one else to talk to and I don't know what to do' Unexpectedly tears started to fall down Maggie's face. Since she had found out the possibility that she may be having a baby, Maggie had felt nothing. For some reason saying it out loud was unravelling her, she was trying her best to keep it together but as she told Carole Todd the reason for her visit, massive stomach heaving sobs overcame her.

Carole had her arms around her, she didn't say anything as Maggie tried to control herself, she just held on tight and rocked Maggie as she would a baby.

When the sobs became little whimpers, Carole let go of Maggie, put the kettle on and made the girl some sweet white tea. After checking on David or Marc, Carole sat at the opposite end of the table and sipped on her own tea, encouraging Maggie to do the same. 'Tea is good for the soul'. Maggie smiled, Carole sounded like her Granny Hunter.

'I think first things first and before you do anything else we need to find out if you are pregnant. Let's not go into details, you can tell me everything if you want, but it's your choice Maggie. But we don't have to do that today. I think what we I will do is put a sample in at the doctors, wee sample! I will call and pick a sample bottle up on my way back from school in the morning. If you meet me again like you have done this morning, you can do the sample and I will drop it in on my way back to school. They usually quick, we should know in a day or two. They will assume it's for me. Again!'

Maggie didn't exactly feel like a weight had been lifted off her shoulders, but she felt better just talking to someone, even having a cry. Carole Todd was right, until they knew for sure that she was pregnant, there was nothing they could or should do.

The following day she wee'd into a sample bottle and Carole Todd took it away with her to drop into the doctor's surgery. It was Thursday. Macaroni cheese day. As she let herself into the house, she thought she might give it a go. She still didn't want to go back to work the following Monday, so she was going to have to be careful, if she looked too well then, she knew for sure that her mam and dad would and insist she went back. Pregnant or not, there was no way she could face Tony Sharp and his imminent engagement party.

She felt well, there were no bells ringing in her head and she didn't feel woozy. She was going to have to pretend, as much as she didn't like the idea, she liked the idea of Quarry's End even less. She would make tea as she had done all week and then head to her bedroom. A few more days and she would know for sure, a few more nights staring at her spot in the ceiling.

Going into the kitchen, she reached to the shelf with the recipe books on. How hard could macaroni cheese be???

15) Temperance

Maggie was sitting on Carole Todd's wall waiting for her return from dropping David off at school on Tuesday morning.

She knew which boy was which now. Marc had clambered onto her knee the previous week when she had gone back to Carole's to do her sample. She had been so embarrassed, the little bottle of wee was still warm as she handed over to Carole for her to hand back in at the doctors. What a lifesaver Carole was. Maggie was unsure what she would have done without her.

It had been a very quiet and insular few days. The majority of the time she had been in her room. Where normally she would listen to music, a constant complaint of her mam's that the volume was too loud, her recent days had been in silence, feigning that she was sleeping. In reality she had lain under her blankets and stared at her spot on the ceiling.

Maggie thought of lots of things. She thought of Tony Sharp, she still didn't know what she thought of him, she had certainly been flattered by his attention. He had a nice car and he always had the smell of expensive aftershave. He was always complimentary towards her, but beyond the driving dates, the kissing, fumbling and perching, there wasn't much else. No wonder, Maggie thought, it must have been hard keeping the two females in his life happy, exhausting.

She thought about her mam and dad. How would they react if she was pregnant? In truth, Maggie had no idea. They certainly wouldn't be happy. Their youngest child, their only daughter. Nope, Maggie could not even think about it, she wouldn't until she had to, until she knew for sure. The thought of telling them brought bile up her throat and into her mouth. She couldn't cope with being sick again. And then there was Stephen and Shaun, her big brothers. So, Maggie changed track and thought of things that wouldn't make her throat burn.

The thought of reading a book was unimaginable, even though she constantly had a novel on the go, lines and lines of words just didn't appeal to her. No music in case her mam and dad thought she was well enough for work, she was at a loss as what to do with the hours and hours of nothingness.

She drew a typewriter key board on some card and practiced and practiced her touch typing. First, she would watch her hands to see what 'key' she was hitting. But as her confidence grew, she typed away with the sure knowledge that her hands were positioned correctly and her speed and her accuracy was improving.

How Maggie missed Quarry's End. Not Tony Sharp and all the stuff that went on with him. Even if she was lucky enough to be able to return, she wasn't sure what she was going to say to him. 'Hi Tony, I've just had a really big pregnancy scare and congratulations on your engagement'. It was all a bit daft. But she did miss the work. She missed Mrs West and Ann and their daily chatter. Maggie wished she had appreciated them both a bit more when she had been there. She wished that she hadn't been so distracted by Tony Sharp and his desk perching. But what was done was done. She could only hope.

And hope had her sitting on Carole Todd's wall waiting for her return with little Marc on tow.

Maggie waited patiently. Carole was calling at the doctor's on her way back from school. She had felt for sure that the result would be back. Maggie would wait, she had nowhere else to be. Her 'pretend' fatigue had done the trick. The only mention there had been of Maggie retuning to work had happened at Friday tea.

Leslie Hunter had come home with the customary fish and chips that he called for on his way home from work every Friday night. He told Maggie that everyone at Quarry's End was asking after her and that they hoped that she would be back soon. Leslie Hunter had said that she would no doubt be back in a couple of weeks when the colour had returned to her cheeks and her bug had well and truly gone. Maggie sighed with relief. She would still have to get through the weekend, but she knew that unless she said that she wanted to go back to work on Monday morning, her dad wouldn't ask.

'Who had been asking after her?' Maggie wondered. Certainly, Mrs West and Ann, but had Tony?? She wouldn't ask. She didn't want to know.

Maggie spotted Carole and little Marc Todd coming along the road. Snail's pace or more like Marc's pace with his little legs and tottering steps. She couldn't look at Carole. She didn't want to see the look on her face until the very last possible moment. She just wanted to have a feeling of being normal for a few more minutes. Because in her heart of hearts, Maggie didn't need to be told. It wasn't her second sight. It wasn't the sickness. It wasn't any tell-tale signs her body was giving her. She just knew. Taking in great gulps of air, she watched for Carole's feet passing her on the way up the garden path. She stood up and followed her, in through the door and into her future!!

16) The Sun

Maggie ended up spending most of the day with Carole Todd. It wasn't until she jumped up to get Marc ready to go and collect his big brother from school, did Maggie stir herself to go home and make Tuesday nights pie and chips.

Surprise, surprise she was pregnant.

She hadn't been shocked and neither had Carole. By Carole's reckoning and if Maggie's diary symbols were right, then she was about four months pregnant. Too late for options.

Whether she felt sorry for Maggie or wanted her to know that there was light at the end of the tunnel, Carole Todd told the young girl about her own experience. About Jude!

Carole had been younger than Maggie was. She hadn't quite reached 16 when she found out she was in trouble. Her mam and dad had been very bohemian, they were parents of the sixties so were fond of having parties, going to parties and generally partying their way through their lives. Often people would arrive at their house after school on a Friday; both of her parents were teachers, and they would be there until Sunday afternoons when they would be politely told to go to their own homes so that her parents could get ready for the school week ahead. Carole always thought Sundays were funny nights. Her parents would have hangovers and would have to spend their night marking homework.

Carole had an older sister May, both girls were named after the time of the year they had been born. Carole's birthday was Christmas Eve so she was named after Christmas Carols, though they had been good enough to add the E on the end so she wasn't quite a Christmas Carol. May had been born on May day, hence may. Thank goodness neither girls had been born around Halloween or Lord knows what they would have been named.

The girls were never really involved with the parties. If the party was at their house then they tended to just stay in their rooms, just venturing down to the kitchen when they were hungry. The air was always thick with marijuana; the house used to stink. It was better if her parents went to someone else's house for the weekend. Then they wouldn't see them from when they left from school on a Friday morning until they returned sometime after lunch on Sundays when they would sit like bookends at the dining room table drinking copious amounts of coffee and trying to concentrate on the homework of their respective History and English Literature pupils.

Carole and May had an awful amount of freedom. Not so much through the week when their mam and dad were role model parents, but at a weekend they were mainly left to their own devices. Both popular, their house would be party central when the parents were away.

Martin Cunningham was Carole's boyfriend. They had been that way since they had attended Junior School together. They weren't inseparable, they both had their own group of friends, but if there was anything happening and they were both there, then ultimately they would end up together by the end of the night. And of course Martin would stay the weekend at Carole's when her parents were away. They shared bed and they had been having sex for a while.

Carole's mam and dad liked Martin and would welcome him with open arms when he came over when they were there. If they thought that Martin was staying in their absence they didn't say, though May would often say that Carole was too young to be having that type of relationship, but no one really stopped them.

No one noticed that Carole was piling the lbs on. Her mam was voluptuous so maybe everyone thought that her younger daughter was heading in the same direction. It wasn't until one day lying on the sofa with her feet over her mam's legs and her tummy did a complete somersault, so large that not only did her mam feel it, but she saw it happen.

A trip to the doctors, Carole was told she was having a baby and that was that. That night she heard loud voices from downstairs, her parents were having a very heated discussion. Then silence. In the morning Carole was told that she wasn't going to school and in no uncertain terms was she to leave the house, then she was left.

She knew she was having a baby. What she didn't know that the baby would arrive in a matter of days. What Carole also didn't know was that it was going to feel like it was ripping her body apart and the pain was almost unbearable. Her mam delivered the baby in Carole's bedroom.

They baby arrived, a girl. Her mam took her away with her and Carole was left to sleep. The following morning Carole, her mam and dad and

May all went in the car to the local hospital where Carole was checked out, down below much to her disgust. The baby was there too. It was prodded and poked too.

Then they all trundled back into the car and went home. The baby stayed in her mam and dad's room with her. The parties stopped. For a while anyway!

Carole went back to school the following week. She hadn't seen Martin, but he knew all about the baby. Everyone knew and looked at her as if they had never really seen her before. The following weekend Martin and his mam and dad arrived at the house. There was much discussion about what to do with the baby, all the while Martin nursed it in his arms making funny cooing noises which Carole found very weird. But she sat and listened to them as they all decided that the baby would stay where it was, and they would all help look after it.

'Hey Carole what should we call the baby??' Someone shouted. Carole had the funny third person feeling as she sat there. She was there but not there. Considering what had just happened, their 16-year-old children had just had a child, they were in a very jolly mood. 'Hey Carole, earth to Carole' they shouted again. Snapping out of the trance, Carole looked at them all! 'What is it?? The baby, is it a boy or a girl???' They were all looking at her. Obviously, she had just landed on the planet after all. The baby must have been over a week old now and she didn't know what sex it was!!

'Hey Carole, it's a little girl' the voice said again. It was Martin's dad who Carole had no idea what his name was! What was with all the 'Hey!!!'

He wasn't American. They were all looking at her, wating for her to say what she wanted to call the baby, which she now knew was a girl. In her head she was humming a song. 'Hey Jude, don't make it bad …….' They all continued to watch her. She didn't know what to call her, at that moment she didn't really care. She hadn't even touched the baby, at that moment the baby meant nothing to her. But they continued to stare. Not just stare but smile. It was like they had just bestowed the greatest gift on her, naming the baby.

Carole had no idea. What did you call babies?? Could she follow her parents rule of thumb, but it was March, that didn't seem like a very kind thing to do, even to a baby she had no attachment to. March?? The staring and the smiling continued. She said the first thing that came into her head. 'Jude' I would like her to be named Jude!!!

So Jude it was. The new daddy and the grandparents all nodded and smiled. Carole sat in her third person mode humming her little song, in the detached state she would be for the foreseeable while the rest of the group in the room bonded over the baby and became its family.

17) The Ten of Cups

Carole Todd remained on the outer edge of the baby's life for the next couple of years. She would help when asked to, but that didn't happen often, she couldn't remember one occasion when she had been left alone with her child. There was always someone else.

Whilst her mam and dad went to school, Martin's mam would take the baby, Martin would usually bring the baby back after tea and bath and settle her down. He was even allowed to be with her on his own. Between the baby's family, every single one of its needs was cared for.

Carole's life went on much as it had before the baby had come. She went to school, she met her friends, but there were no parties, no empty houses at weekends for her to be able to have people stay over.

There was no more Carole and Martin. The baby seemed to have drove a wedge between them, they were still friends, but there was no more sleeping together, no more boyfriend and girlfriend. Martin was very much the baby's daddy, but Carole didn't think herself as its mammy. May was the more maternal sister, and as the baby got older, it seemed to sense that Carole was clueless about its needs and would cry its eyes outs if she tried to care for her.

After leaving school, with what was to be fair quite decent qualifications under the circumstances, at least that's what everyone told her, Martin's mam had kindly nominated her for a job as a trainee cashier at the bank where she worked. Carole had gone for the interview and remarkably had got the position.

It was strange, it was a small branch and she was very much the new girl, but they were like one big happy family. They all knew about the baby, after all it was Martin's mam's grandchild, but no one mentioned the fact that it was Carole's baby. She wasn't sure if Martin's mam hadn't told them or they simply thought it was something that couldn't be mentioned, whatever it was, when there was mention of the baby, Carole would revert to her third person syndrome and zone out.

But she liked her job, she wasn't particularly good with numbers, but she always tried her best, had a ready smile on her face for customers and became part of the bank family. Carole went out with friends, had her first girls holidays and generally lived the life of any other girl in their late teens.

May got herself a serious boyfriend, Carole was happy for her, he was nice, nice for May anyway and he seemed to like the baby too and didn't mind it tagging along with him and May when they went on outings. The baby continued to adore May.

Carole couldn't think of having another relationship. It had been far too much and far too young with Martin, she would flirt on nights out, but if anyone got a bit fruity, then that was that, she would simply walk away. Maybe she would never have another relationship? It was no big deal. Even when Martin got himself a new girlfriend, Carole wasn't bothered. There was no jealousy, no thinking that should have been her, if anything she was pleased for him, having a baby at sixteen wasn't exactly what every girl would look for in a boyfriend, but Jackie seemed to take it all in her stride. Embraced the baby so to speak.

Everyone had their titles as far as the baby was concerned. Auntie May, Grandma, Grandad, Nanny, Grandpa, Daddy and of course Carole was Mammy, but it was in title only. She certainly wasn't the baby's main care giver. If she was left holding the baby, it would be restless and wriggly and always seemed to be looking around for someone to come and save it from this person who they called Mammy.

But as the baby became a toddler and became more independent she sometimes totter her way over to her Mammy and garble something or other or hand her a toy that she wanted them to play with. May had moved out to live with her boyfriend and although she was still a frequent visitor and the toddler had even been to have sleep overs at their place, with only Grandma, Granddad and Mammy the majority of the time, the toddler had little choice but to try and make Mammy play with her.

And little by little they began to have a relationship.

The toddler became known by her Mammy as Jude and whereas when Carole got in from work she would leave the bedtime routine to one of the other care givers, she found that she began to look forward to it. The nightly splash around in the bath, the bottle of milk and biscuit and the reading of a bedtime story, before carrying a sleepy Jude up to her bed.

She started to buy her little outfits, toys and books out of her wages and would look on with glee as Jude's little face lit up when she handed her a new plaything. Carole hadn't taken much notice at the baby when she had cried, there was always someone else to soothe her, now if she was in another room and she heard her whimpers she would be sprinting to see what was causing Jude such distress. At almost 3 years old, Jude Todd had eventually managed to wrap her Mammy around her little finger, just like she had done from the moment she was born with everyone else.

As late as it was, Carole took to motherhood with relish. She arranged Jude's 3rd birthday celebration, even baking and icing in a fashion her birthday cake. She might have been on the outside looking in for Jude's previous birthdays, but no more. This birthday was both of their day, it was like Jude had just been born.

No one said anything about Carole's new found maternal streak, they had never said anything about her lack of it. They had just all rallied around and made sure that Jude had the best possible start in life she could. Carole would be forever grateful to them. Jude was perfect. Happy, sociable and above all else, healthy.

When Carole suggested that she may take Jude on holiday to Pontin's, just the two of them, no one objected. They all brought little outfits, no one lectured her about what she should or shouldn't be doing. Martin even borrowed his dad's car so he could take them to the train station, promising he would be there to collect them the following week on their return.

And what a week they had. They fit together like a hand in a glove. It was fun but it was more than that, it was when Carole grew up and realised that this beautiful, funny little girl was her daughter and she had to take responsibility for her.

Returning back off their holiday, Martin was waiting for them when the disembarked the train. Jude ran into his open arms and covered her daddy with slobbery kisses. It made Carole's heart swell, most boys Martin's age would have ran for the hills and far far away, but he hadn't, he had taken responsibility for Jude from the first time she had been placed into his arms. Carole refused to feel glum about not having had that attachment, she could only think about how she felt for Jude now, how she would feel about her in the future.

Carole was going to move out and take Jude with her, it was time. And she did with the blessing and support of the rest of the family and Martin and his parents and all of the extended family that had become such a big part of Jude's short life.

And like she said to Maggie, the rest was now history.

18) The Moon

Maggie knew that she couldn't end up giving birth 5 minutes after telling her mam and dad. It had to be done sooner rather than later. Friday night, Stephen and Shaun never hung around long after their fish and chip supper, it was pay day so they would clear their plates, have their baths and then disappear to where ever they were going, Stephen with Jude and Shaun with his mates.

Friday night would see Maggie left in the house with just her mam and dad.

She hoped against hope that her mam and dad would take to her news somewhat like Carole's mam and dad had. They had just jumped into it with both feet and welcomed the baby into their home and into their lives, from what Carole had said, there hadn't been any repercussions, only lots of love. It had been strange for Maggie hearing Carole's story. Jude had been her friend forever and even though she knew that the dad that she lived with wasn't her real dad and that her real dad lived on the other side of town, she didn't really know that much about her. It had always just been school girl stuff.

So, Friday night arrived, her dad arrived home with the fish and chips, they boys walloped theirs off and disappeared to get ready. They were both out of the door before the three left at the table had finished drinking their tea.

Maggie had struggled eating her tea. There was a lump in her throat and she had to chew what was in her mouth for a very long time so she could swallow it. And there was ringing her head, great big clattering. The warning alarm bells of impending trouble. Second sight?? Fear factor? Whatever it was there was a definite pattern to its coming and going that Maggie was beginning to recognise. It warned her of trouble ahead.

The chatter over the tea table had been menial, what had happened at their jobs that day! What time they were going to go shopping the following day! Should they have beef or chicken for Sunday lunch! Maggie felt terrible, their world was going to be blown out of the water, they wouldn't give a shit what they had done at work that day or what time they were going to go shopping and they certainly would not give a shit if they were going to eat beef or chicken on Sunday.

Before she knew what she was doing and with more of a shout than she had intended thinking that they could hear the bells clanging in her head too, Maggie blurted out 'I'm pregnant!!!!'

If there was silence, Maggie couldn't hear it, the ringing was now a siren. She looked at her mam and dad staring at her. It was the look of loathing. The look of disgust. She had nothing else to say to them. So, she sat and stared back at them, scared that they would say something and she wouldn't be able to hear them if she dropped her gaze. They all just stared, and the siren blared in her head.

Her mam was the first to speak. 'How do you know?' Maggie replied as calmly as she could 'I put a test in at the doctors!' obviously, that wasn't strictly true, the doctors would have Carole Todd recorded as having had a positive pregnancy test, but that was one thing that Maggie wouldn't be telling Dorothy and Leslie Hunter, Carole's involvement.

'Who did it?' her dad asked. Maggie thought about lying and saying she didn't know but was uncertain if that would make a bad situation worse. So, she just sat staring at them. Her dad raised his voice. 'I asked you a question, who did this???' Taking a huge gulp of air Maggie said the name!

Her dad pushed back his chair, left the room and within minutes she heard the front door slam. Then there were two.

She looked at her mam and her mam stared back at her. The combined look of loathing and disgust was hard to take, but what else could Maggie do but sit and wait.

What happened next happened in a split second. The plate in front of Dorothy Hunter was in the air and crashing into Maggie's head. The pain was horrific. She could feel the blood running down her face. She looked at her mam, Maggie couldn't make out the look. Dorothy Hunter was off her chair and making her way towards her, Maggie thought to comfort her for what she had done. But as she reached Maggie's side of the table there was more pain.

Dorothy Hunter pulled Maggie by the hair up off her chair and away from the table. And then she laid into her. She punched and kicked her daughter like a wild women. Maggie tried to curl up into a ball, but that didn't help she was kicked in the head, in the legs and in the back. She could feel her mam pulling great lumps of her blonde hair out and all the while she screamed and yelled like a wild woman. It was relentless. It hurt. And then it was over. Dorothy Hunter stopped, walked out of the door and up the stairs.

Maggie was hurt. Very hurt. She couldn't stay where she was, her mam might come back. Getting up best she could, she staggered to the front door, she was going to have to get out of there. There wasn't a part of her body that didn't hurt. The blood was running into her eyes, but she was sure that one of her eyes was just about closed. Her head was throbbing with pain and her mam must have kicked her between the legs because there was definitely something going on there.

She had no coat, no nothing. The only place she could think of to go was to Carole Todd's, she was the only other person who knew why this would have happened to her. It was dark as she made her way around the streets to where her friend lived. Maggie tried her best to walk straight, not draw attention to herself, if anyone saw her they would call the police. When she saw a couple walking towards her, she ran across the road the pavement on the other side.

It was cold, but her body felt red hot, she was in big trouble. It would be a miracle e if the baby had survived, but she couldn't think about that then. All she could do was put one front of the other best she could and get to Carole's.

It seemed to take forever. Every step hurt. And then she was there. Maggie knocked on the door and stepped back away into the shadows, she didn't want David opening the door and seeing her like that, it would have to be Carole.

The hallway light went on and the door opened. Carole Todd. Maggie stepped forward just enough for Carole to see her. She could do no more, all she could do was hope that Carole would catch her before she fell to the ground. And then it went black and it was over …

19) The Three of Swords

Maggie was unsure what happened next. Weeks later Carole Todd filled in the blanks for her, it had been a long journey. A long and painful one.

Carole Todd had caught Maggie before she hit the floor. Carole's boyfriend Glen had been in the house so she had screamed for him to help get Maggie into the house. She had been a dead weight and they had been frightened that they were hurting her even more bundling her into their house, along the passage into what was known as their best room.

Luckily both the boys had been shattered and were tucked up in bed, it would have terrified them seeing a broken and bloodied body being carried into their home. Though they wouldn't have recognised it as being Maggie's body, she looked like a piece of cattle, almost unrecognisable.

Lying Maggie on the sofa, the couple tried to ascertain what her injuries were, how serious and what could they do. Glen was all for ringing the police, it was obvious to him that she had been terribly attacked by someone and that person needed to be brought to justice before they hurt someone else. Chances were she could have been raped.

Carole Todd knew different. This was the result of the news that she knew Maggie was going to break to her parents that night. As they pulled a blanket over the still unconscious Maggie, Carole told Glen of the recent events concerning Maggie Hunter. No, the police weren't the answer, there was no crazed attacker running the streets of their town. Someone Maggie loved had done this.

But Maggie did need medical attention. She needed to see a doctor. So going to the telephone in the hallway she put a call into their local doctors, yes there was a doctor on call and he could be with them in ten minutes. Until then Maggie shouldn't be left on her own and if her condition deteriorated then they had to call 999 and an ambulance would be sent.

Dr Graham arrived at Carole Todd's house in what seemed like minutes. The look of concern on his face when he went to attend Maggie terrified Carole. The condition of the young girl was much worse that Carole had feared and Dr Graham made the same suggestion as Glen had done earlier, to call the police!!

Some instinct in Carole though made her feel that a police involvement was something that Maggie wouldn't want. She would do her best to stop the police arriving until Maggie was at least awake and could decide for herself what she wanted to do. This hadn't been a random attack; Carole knew that if it had been she would have made her way back to her own home and not seek out Carole who was probably the only other person on earth that knew she was pregnant.

Carole Todd explained to Dr Graham as clearly and concisely as she could about Maggie coming to seek her advice about her predicament, the pregnancy test that hadn't been her own and the knowledge that Maggie Hunter had said that she would be telling her parents that very evening that she was pregnant and more than likely about four months.

Dr Graham was using smelling salts to bring Maggie around, she woke but was still very much not of this world. As the doctor examined her injuries, he voiced his concerns that Maggie really should be taken into hospital, he didn't think that there were any broken bones, but he couldn't be sure, especially around her ribs which were very bruised. There was a huge gash on her forehead, which he said needed stitches, her head was bleeding where the hair had been pulled out at the roots, both her eyes were closed, her lips bust open top, and bottom and he said he couldn't even begin to count how many bruises there were all over her body.

It had been a frenzied beating.

As Carole stared at Maggie, Dr Graham applied butterfly stitches to the cut on Maggie's forehead, how could Maggie's dad have done all this to her. She might have been in trouble, but she was still a child. She didn't deserve any of this.

Dr Graham left her a list of instructions as to what they would need to do. How to clean her wounds and apply the salve he was leaving. Especially her scalp, which was going to be really sore. He was going to go straight to his surgery and make out a prescription for some painkillers, antibiotics and some more ointment. When Carole asked about the baby, Dr Graham said he didn't know. He hadn't seen any bleeding but doubted whether a baby more than likely in the first trimester would survive a kicking like what Maggie had sustained. All they could do would be wait and see.

After Dr Graham left, Carole despatched Glen firstly up the stairs to check on the boys and then off to the local to get Jude. Maggie needed a friendly face and Carole was sure that Jude had mentioned a darts match Stephen was playing in. But she couldn't be sure.

With Glen out of the way, Carole got a bowl of water and a towel and started to clean up Maggie's body. She had bile in her throat as she did it, how anyone could do this to their own child was beyond her. Almost 20 years ago her situation with Jude could have been like this, she thanked God that her family had stood by her. Carole physically shuddered.

Maggie was sleeping. Dr Graham had given her a shot of something before he left. He said it was best if she got as much sleep as she could, let her body start to heal. He would be back in the morning to check on her, maybe give her another sedative. What a mess it all was. Should she get a message to Maggie's mam and dad and let them know that she was there? Carole didn't know Mr & Mrs Hunter at all, they had passed in the corridors of their daughters schools, been at the same Nativity Plays and sports days, but they had only ever said hello. She would wait until Jude got home, she would have an idea about what the best course of action would be.

Carole found a nightie in the ironing pile, it would do. As she struggled to get Maggie out of her clothes and into the nightie, she heard a commotion outside. The door was shut so she shouted that she needed 5 minutes. Happy that Maggie was looking as good as she could, she left her sleeping in the room, the lamplight lit beside her so that if she did wake she wouldn't panic, it wasn't ideal her having to sleep in their best room, but at least she had peace from the boys, because woe betide them if they ever went in there unless it was Christmas.

Glen, Jude and surprisingly Stephen were sitting in the kitchen. Carole wasn't sure what to say. 'Hi Stephen, how did your darts match go?? By the way your sister is in our best room, sedated because she is pregnant and your dad has smacked the living daylights out of her and she is probably going to lose the baby anyway!'

But Glen had saved the day. He had explained to the young couple what had happened. Carole didn't know what to say to him, he looked as white as a ghost. For months he had been a regular visitor at their house, Carole liked him, he was a good influence on her flighty Jude, she was so what was the word her own mam used to describe her? Wanton!! Jude was a born flirt, anyone in a pair of trousers really and Carole did used to worry about her. She herself had been a one woman man, well apart from Jude's dad Martin, but that had been a childish relationship, so she never quite grasped why her very pretty daughter would constantly crave attention from most of the male population.

However, Stephen Hunter had arrived, Jude was doe eyed and all was well in the world, for now anyway. Stephen was older than Jude, 4 years which when you are 16 is a big gap. But it had been so far so good, and Carole was grateful.

Carole took Jude and Stephen into the best room to see Maggie. She was sleeping peacefully, but the bruising on her face seemed to have swollen in the 5 minutes that Carole had left her and the butterfly stitch gash on the forehead looked grotesque. She was a sight.

Leaving Maggie's best friend and brother in the room, Carole made her way back to the kitchen and into the waiting arms of Glen. It felt like a safe haven in a storm.

20) The Five of Pentacles

Stephen Hunter left Carole Todd's house in an almighty rage. Jude refused to leave her friend and spent that first night and every following subsequent night in the best room with Maggie.

Dr Graham returned the next day and once again examined Maggie from top to bottom. He brought all the bits and bobs that they would need to care for Maggie when he thought it would be best to take Maggie off the sedation. Until then he would like her to rest. The police once again got a mention, but Carole once again stressed that she wanted it to be Maggie's choice, that she had been through enough without waking up to find a big burly police officer poking his nose into her life.

So, for now she would remain in the best room and the Todd's would take care of her best they could under Dr Graham's supervision.

Stephen Hunter also returned the following day, he looked like he hadn't slept a wink. He also brought his brother Shaun with him, a younger even whiter version of Stephen. Carole had met him lots of times over the years, he was in the same year as Jude, so he had often been over with Maggie for play dates in the garden. He was a nice lad. But this whole business had shaken him and as he sat with his baby sister, Carole was sure he was crying.

One day turned into two and Dr Graham thought it was time to start reducing the sedation. Maggie had taken quite a beating and he had to determine if there had been any long term damage. She hadn't uttered a word since she had arrived on their doorstep, but then again, she hadn't been given chance to. There didn't seem to be any sign of the baby departing. But then again, she hadn't really moved so once she was on her feet, there would be a good chance that the baby would just come away. Sad, but maybe for the best in the long run. And they needed to know what had happened.

Mr and Mrs Hunter obviously knew where Maggie was, Stephen would have told them. But there had been no contact and Maggie had now been with them almost three days. It seemed a very strange affair indeed.

The sedation was stopped. Maggie still slept an awful lot and didn't seem to want to talk about what had happened. Not to Carole or to Jude or Dr Graham. When her brothers turned up, she would be asleep, or at least pretend to be. She didn't utter a word to them.

By the end of that first week, the bruising was starting to go down. Maggie looked jaundiced with all the yellowing bruising. Maggie mainly spent her time sleeping. She was on painkillers and antibiotics, and they seemed to be taking it out of her. Carole spoke to her, but she rarely received an answer. It was early days. But there was still no sign of her mam and dad!

All Carole Todd could do was continue to care for Maggie the best she could. Jude spent the nights with her, Glen picked up helping with the boys and Stephen and Shaun came every night after work. Dr Graham called every day. He too was concerned that Mr & Mrs Hunter seemed to have so little care for their youngest child.

There was no sign of the baby leaving.

On one of his nightly visits, Stephen brought a letter from home. Maggie was doing her usual sleeping façade, Carole was convinced that she was never asleep when her brothers were there, when any of them were in the best room with her. In the beginning yes, with all the sedatives followed by the mix of pain killers and anti-biotics. But now Carole had the distinct feeling that in-between people entering the best room, Maggie was awake and alert.

But if she didn't want to communicate yet that was her choice. It wasn't every day you got a good hiding off your dad, time Carole would give her, she would speak when she was ready. So, Stephen and Shaun never stayed long, just long enough to see that their sister was on the mend. The letter was propped up beside the lamp on the cabinet went to check on Maggie before she made her way to her own bed. Of course, Maggie was already asleep, if she had seen the letter, she certainly hadn't opened it.

Carole Todd was woken from her sleep by a scream. At least she thought she had heard a scream. She lay in the bed and listened. It wasn't the boys, they would have kept on screaming until either her or Glen had gone to them. But there was no sound. Wide awake she made her way downstairs to make herself a cup of tea, it was pointless lying in bed tossing and turning, a cup of tea, a digestive biscuit and a load of washing sorted and in the machine would do the trick. She would be back in the land of nod within an hour. She was an old hand at broken night's sleep with both of the boys when they were babies.

Passing the best room on the way along to the kitchen, Carole stopped, she could hear crying. Making two cups of teas, one with sugar, she made her way back to the best room opened the door and went in. Maggie was sitting up on the sofa, her yellow face soaked with tears. Her battered eyes had been starting to open, but as she sat crying, they were almost closed again. Carole took the teas and went and sat at the opposite end of the sofa and waited.

Maggie was going to talk, she could sense it.

But she didn't. what she did was pass the content of the envelope that Stephen had left for Maggie earlier for Carole to read.

Margaret

As far as myself and your dad are concerned this is no longer your home.

You have brought us shame and embarrassment to us.

Any belongings that are here will be brought to Miss Todd's house by your brothers.

My only hope is that I kicked you hard enough to kick the bastard out of you.

I have a respectable job. Your father works for the alleged father, and I say alleged because I think that was a lie and it is some snotty boy. Either way you have brought shame to us both.

You are no longer our daughter and will no longer be welcome here.

D Hunter

The sob was out before Carole Todd had chance to do anything about it. Maggie's mam had done the beating. She had admitted that she hoped she had kicked the baby out of her. What type of mother was she?? All Carole could do was bundle Maggie up gently in her arms and cry with her. How would Maggie ever get over any of this. The beating and the letter were intolerable. The baby was probably no more. Carole had never felt rage like it. If it had been Jude, yes, she would have been disappointed but she wouldn't have disowned her or even raised a hand to her. Maggie could have died. It was a ten minute walk from the Hunters house to her own, she had no idea how Maggie had managed to get to her door.

One thing she did know was, she wouldn't cast this girl aside. If Maggie had no one else, she would have Carole Todd and her family. She would help her heal. Carole continued to rock Maggie, holding her tight, she stroked her hair, or what was left of it, there were more bald patches than hair, it would grow back strong though, just like Maggie would!!

21) The Star

Maggie Hunter had never thought that a broken heart was a real thing. But she had found out the hard way. Whatever she had thought her mam and dad's reaction would be about the baby, she hadn't been expecting that. Leslie Hunter walking out of the house, well yes. She had seen her dad remove himself from dramas lots of times. Never known to raise his voice, even when Stephen or Shaun had pushed all of his buttons, he had never raised his voice at them never mind hit them. He would just give them all a disappointed look and leave the room and ultimately the house. They all hated the 'disappointed' look.

Dorothy Hunter was a screecher. When she was Annoyed with them, she would go up at least 10 octaves. Maggie had been expecting lots and lots of screeching and a lot of name calling, her mam had never been shy telling them what little shits they all were. Maggie would find 'angry mam' amusing. At school she spoke like she had a plum lodged in her mouth, another thing that made Maggie smile, where did she get her work voice from? To Maggie it sounded ridiculous, they weren't posh, but her mam always said that the voice was just her telephone voice and it made it easier for people to understand her. Dorothy Hunter was like two people!

But the attack had taken Maggie by surprise. Many a time she had been clipped around the ear off her mam, which was her thing. The screeching and the clip and then it would be over and normal service would resume.

When Maggie had started to wake up after the attack, she had lain in the bed and waited for her mam and dad to come and collect her. No one had said whether or not they knew she was there. But as unresponsive as she had seemed to be to everyone, especially after Dr Whatshisname had taken her off the sedation, she had heard everything that anyone that was in earshot had said.

Carole Todd had done so much for her, and she hated that she couldn't speak to her, but she didn't know what to say. Maggie wasn't sure if they knew it had been Dorothy Hunter that had done the damage, she suspected that they thought it had been her dad, either way, Maggie didn't want to talk about it. Not even to Carole. She was so ashamed.

So, if there was anyone around, she would pretend she was asleep. It was easier.

Carole must have known that she hadn't been attacked by some random. If there had been talk of the police being called, they hadn't materialised. Carole Todd was the only person that knew Maggie had intended to tell her parents of her pregnancy that Friday night. She must have put two and two together and decided that whatever had happened, it had happened within the confines of the Hunter's house and bringing the police in would only make a bad situation worse. Something else to be grateful to Carole for.

But her mam and dad hadn't come to get her.

They would know where she was. Stephen and Shaun had both seen her, lots of times. There would have been discussions at home about what was going on. How Maggie had sustained her injuries. Her brothers knew she was pregnant, she had heard them talking. Was the baby alive still??

Was it?? Maggie didn't know. She hadn't been up off the sofa since she got to Carole's. There had been some sort of bandage thing put on her. She knew that her mam had kicked her between the legs, quite a few times if she remembered correctly. Dr Whatshisname had examined her, she did remember that even in her delirium, Carole had been there too. Even now her face burned with shame. She hadn't been to the loo, she barely drank and she barely ate. She had not had an urge to wee or poo. From the overheard conversations, Dr Whatshisname was due back to examine her thoroughly the following day.

When Stephen left the letter from home Maggie resisted the urge to snatch it out of his hand and tear it open. She knew it would be off her mam. Leslie Hunter was no writer. Maybe Dorothy Hunter was testing the water, maybe she was too ashamed to come to the house to collect her and was asking her to make her own way home and they would sort it out, her family, not the Todd's.

So, she pretended she was dozing. When Carole came in for her final check of the night, she kept her eyes tight shut and her body still. She kept so still that she did actually fall asleep, for a little while anyway. The lamp had been left on, the envelope propped up against it. Pulling herself up on the pillows, Maggie grabbed at it. Her mam's handwriting. Margaret?? She never called her Margaret, she had been Christened Margaret but named Maggie.

Reading the neat secretarial handwriting, Maggie screamed. Just the one piercing scream before she placed her hand over her mouth and sobbed.

The words were written in pure hate.

Maggie cried and cried. She read and reread the letter. It could not have been made any clearer. Dorothy and Leslie Hunter had washed their hands of their only daughter.

The door opened and Carole Todd came in wearing a nightie and holding two cups. It made Maggie cry more. The only thing she could do was pass the letter over and wait to see what Carole would make of it. Even though her eyes were still almost closed with the bruising, she could see the rage on Carole Todd's face. It made Maggie cry more, then the arms were around her and she was being rocked like a baby. There were no words. Just the gentle rocking and the feeling of Carole's hands on her back and her hair.

When the sobs subsided, Carole lay Maggie down on the pillows, pulled up the blankets and sit herself at the bottom of the sofa. Maggie had no idea how long Carole stayed there for, exhausted she had fallen asleep. When she woke in the morning Carole was gone and so was the letter. If it hadn't been so awful and beyond all comprehension, Maggie would have thought it was a nightmare.

Carole came in with more tea and some toast. They didn't need to say anything. They both knew that today was going to have to be the beginning of not only Maggie getting well, but the rest of her life. For once Maggie looked Carole in the eye. A joint understanding. Carole said that Dr Graham was calling that morning, after he had been she thought it may be a good idea if they tried a bath, got some off the dried blood off her, did something with her hair.

Maggie nodded in answer. She knew she couldn't spend the rest of her life on Carole Todd's sofa, she had to start making an effort. But of all the injuries she had sustained, all the pain and discomfort, the thing that hurt her the most was her heart. She could feel it as she sat sipping her hot sweet tea, if felt like a stone, a stone that was cold, like it was made of glass and would shatter at any moment. But somewhere deep in her she knew that despite the beating and how broken her body and her heart were, she would fight on. She was loved, her brothers loved her, or at least she thought they did, they had both been to see her every day since she had got there, they must care!! And Carole Todd cared about her. She wasn't alone.

The tears were there again, trickling silently down her face. The letter may have gone, but the words would never leave her, ever. They were etched across her glass made heart, etched in ice. Cold and callous, she vowed that if she ever had children, even the one that may still be growing inside of her, she would never made them feel the way her own mam had made her feel, the words had hurt her much more than the beating had.

What was that old saying 'Sticks and stones may break my bones, but words will never hurt me!' Well, that was rubbish. Words did hurt. Maggie Hunter aged 16 had been disowned by her family.

The funny thing was, as she sat there, there were no warning alarm bells ringing in her head. No warnings of trouble coming like there had been. Whatever it was that lay ahead was not going to hurt her. Or was it that there was nothing that could be done to her now that would hurt her more than she was feeling now! A broken heart was a very real thing.

Maggie heard the knock on the front door and the sound of Dr Whatshisname. He didn't come directly in to see Maggie, she could only assume that Carole was filling him in on the nights events. Her body still hurt, she couldn't touch her ribs, but after Dr Whatshisname had been in and prodded and poked and checked everything, she could have a bath. The thought of submerging herself in clean water, washing her hair and getting rid of the smell of dried stale blood off her made the whole thing of with Dr Whatshisname that much more bearable.

Carole Todd helped Maggie to the bathroom. The house was a big old terrace house and the bathroom was downstairs at the back of the house. Getting off the sofa had been a bit of an ordeal, Maggie's legs felt like jelly. But they had shuffled and stopped then shuffled a bit more and eventually they had got to the bathroom where a huge bath waited for her filled with bubbles. Pretty Peach!! It smelt of cleanliness and innocence, if a smell could do that.

If Carole was shocked at Maggie's body as she helped her undress she didn't say. The bandage contraption thing had been removed by Dr Whatshisname. There had been no blood, no sign that the baby had left Maggie's body, but he said they weren't out of the woods yet. Maggie had no idea what was supposed to happen when a baby died inside you, she barely had any idea how a baby lived and grew. She wasn't bothered.

Maggie couldn't look Carole in the eye. She sat on the toilet as Carole pulled the nightie over her head and revealed Maggie's bruised body. Her shins were black and yellow, the inside of her thighs the same and as she glanced down, her stomach was still black and purple, especially around her ribs. Holding on to Carole for dear life, she pulled herself up, over to the bath and stood, the water was hot, the sort that you had to ease yourself into and knew that even if you got straight back out of the water, your bum would be red like one of those baboons.

Down she went. The smell and the bubbles were pure heaven. Carole said she would leave her for a little while, she would be back she said and she would wash her hair, it didn't matter that there was soap in the water, at least it would be cleaner than it was now.

Carole Todd had been so lovely to Maggie. Lying in the hot bath covered in bubbles, she felt a tiny fragment of ice melt from her heart, it was for Carole. She had no idea what she would have done without her, it didn't bear thinking about, because in truth aside from her mam, dad and brothers, she really didn't have anyone. Friends yes, she was squatting in one of her best friends best rooms and she wasn't sure if Linda even knew, but that was about the extent of the people in Maggie Hunter's life who cared for her.

Not even that many now. Her mam and dad had made it abundantly clear how they felt about her. She had Tom, her cousin, but again, did he know where she was? Did he know what had happened to her. One thing she did know, she couldn't pretend to be asleep any more. She needed to communicate no matter how embarrassing it was. She wasn't sure what was worse, the being pregnant or the having the shit kicked out of you and ultimately disowned.

But lying the bubbles she began to feel a little bit normal. Her hand went down to her tummy. 'Are you still there baby?? Are we going to do this together??' Of course, there was no answer, even with her second sight she couldn't know if her baby was alive or dead, but she felt warm and she felt calm, she actually felt peaceful. Somehow Maggie had the feeling that the baby was nestled in her tummy feeling the same way. She had no idea what tomorrow would bring, or the next day or the day after. She had nothing. No home. No money. No hope really. The lump of ice that had replaced her heart seemed to expand and contract. Panic!!

But before she had chance to wallow in her own self-pity, the bathroom door opened and in came Carole, jug in hand. 'Hair wash time Miss' she said with the same tone that she had heard her talk to David and Marc with. She didn't mind. Just having a hair wash seemed like a very good idea.

22) The Tower

Carole left Maggie in the bathroom to brush her teeth. She was wearing a clean nightie, socks and one of Jude's dressing gowns. Her hair was still up in a towel and Carole had gone off to fetch a brush and hair dryer so they could have a go at making her hair look decent.

The shampoo had stung her scalp, not painfully but she was aware that there were many gaps of hair on her head where her mam had pulled clumps out. Carole said it would grow back, it would take time, just like everything else would.

Shuffling their way back to the best room, Maggie was shocked and touched to see that a bed had been brought in. The sofa had been pushed to the other end of the room and in its place as a little single bed. More than that though, her belongings were all neatly stacked beside her bed.

Stephen and Shaun were in the kitchen, they would like to see her if she was up to it. But they would sort her hair out first, make her look more like herself. So, she sat on a chair while Carole Todd gently brushed her hair, dried it for what seemed like forever, keeping the hair dryer as far away as possible so as to not hurt her sore scalp even more. Carole changed the side for her parting to hide some of the bald patches and when it was done, she looked at Maggie and smiled.

Maggie knew she would have to see her brothers. She wanted to. She had no idea what life would be like for them at home, she needed to explain. So, Maggie told Carole she would see them, but Carole said that before she did she wanted to have a little word with her herself.

As Carole Todd spoke, Maggie tried to hold it together. Carole had spoken at length to Glen and Jude, and she had also spoken to Stephen and Shaun. They all wanted her to stay there at the Todd's, for Carole to be able to look after her, at least until she was well, at least until they had a plan about where Maggie could go. There would be no rush. The best room was hers for as long as she needed it. Make it her own. They would work through it all together.

The tears were back. Maggie could feel them dripping down her face, sitting there still she could feel something else begin to drip, the ice around her heart was beginning to thaw, she could feel the ice cold drips running through her body. That was twice Carole Todd had touched her heart that day. She felt stronger than she had done in months, since the days of driving dates and the kissing and the fumbling and the perching on her desk. Since Quarry's End. Since Tony Sharp. She was ready to see Stephen and Shaun.

The Hunters weren't a cuddly family. Even on Birthdays or at Christmas there were no kisses and cuddles. There had been when they were all little, but as the got older it was mainly a comforting arm around the shoulders. Maggie could remember her mam and dad snuggled up together watching television when she was younger, but that hadn't happened for a long time. They sometimes held hands when they were out walking anywhere but that was about it.

So, Stephen and Shaun holding on to her for dear life had taken the wind out of Maggie sails.

They were both visibly shocked and upset about Maggie's condition. Both parts of it.

Both the brothers began talking at once and it very quickly became a jumble of events. So, Maggie told them they would have to take turns or else she would never know what was going on. Her stomach was in knots. Even though it had only been little over a week since that ill-fated Friday night supper, it felt like a life time ago. Not a distant memory, Maggie doubted that she would ever be able to forget it, she thought that she would never be able to eat fish and chips from the chippy again. The thought of them brought bile up into her throat.

And she would never be able to forget her mam's grotesque face as she stared at her across the table or the image of her dad leaving the room. Every other image that she had ever had of her parents were supressed by them on that Friday night.

Stephen said he had come back to Carole's house when Glen had come to the darts match to get Jude. All he had said was that Maggie had turned up at the house and someone had given her a good hiding. Stephen said he wasn't too concerned as he made his way back, teenage girls had fights all of the time, especially over boys. The only thing he had thought of was why go to Jude's and not home, unless it had something to do with Jude.

So, he hadn't been prepared at all for the sight of his baby sister. Carole hadn't had chance to say, before he bundled into the room expecting to tell her she best get herself home before mam and dad had a dicky fit. Even just lying on the sofa she looked tiny, something she wasn't, she was almost as tall as him. Battered and bloodied, she barely resembled the girl that had sat at the table earlier in the evening with him.

The doctor had been called and Carole as doing her best to keep Maggie awake. Stephen's first instinct had been to call firstly an ambulance and then the police. He stood stock still unsure what to do, he should go and get his mam and dad, but as he made to leave Carole Todd asked him if he would wait in the kitchen until the doctor had been.

So, he waited with Glen. They did small talk. They did what men did and not talk about the obvious. They heard the doctor arrive. They heard someone running up the stairs and then they heard them running back down. Glen went to check on the boys and then got a couple of bottles out of the fridge for them when he came back. They talked about football and work. If it wasn't under such strange circumstances, it would have been canny. Stephen hadn't really spent, much time with Jude's mam and step dad, if he was at their house, he would usually be up in Jude's room while she got herself ready.

Jude had been unexpected. They hadn't been together very long, not long after Maggie's birthday party. She was his first serious girlfriend. There had been girlfriends in the past, but none of them could hold a candle to Jude. She was young, 4 years younger than him, but in many ways so much older. She was a born flirt, he had seen plenty of her over the years when she had been at their house with Maggie, but as flirty and flighty as she had been, there was something really sweet about her. They just clicked and though he wouldn't tell Jude, he was the happiest he had ever been.

They both glanced at the door when they heard the doctor leave. More footsteps up the stairs and then about ten minutes later, both Carole and Jude came in. Both as white as sheets. Carole said that Maggie was sleeping.

And then she brought them all up to speed. Maggie coming to see Carole because she thought she might be in trouble. The subsequent tests and the knowledge that Maggie had decided that she was telling Dorothy and Leslie Hunter that her suspicions had been right and that she was pregnant. Stephen couldn't believe it. His sister was pregnant. She was only 16. And he thought a young 16. He didn't even know that she had a boyfriend, even Jude hadn't mentioned it. Then she revealed that she hadn't known. Jude said that she had been so wrapped up in Stephen that she hadn't really seen much of Maggie, especially with them not going to school together anymore. Jude smiled a weak smile at Stephen, she had given away a bit too much he thought to himself. Wrapped up in him?

Maggie was all that mattered then though. His and Jude's mutual appreciation society could wait for another day. So, if she had been to tell his mam and dad that she was pregnant, who would have literally kicked the shit out of her. Surely not his mam and dad, his mam liked to give a slap now and again, he himself hadn't felt the heat of his hand for years, but he knew Maggie and Shaun had, but if Maggie was as hurt as much as Stephen feared he had, he thought it unlikely that Dorothy or Leslie Hunter had done it. What about the boyfriend??

No, he hadn't known about the baby as far as Carole knew. Maybe Maggie had gone to tell him after she had told his mam and dad. Yes, that would more than likely be the culprit. Maggie had gone to tell him and he had flipped!

Who was the boyfriend?? Someone at her work Carole said. Maggie hadn't named names, but he had a car and he worked at Quarry's End. Stephen tried to think of people that his dad and Maggie had chatted about, he knew there was an apprentice, but he couldn't imagine him being Maggie's bloke, he sounded a bit on the thick side!

Maggie was very still on the sofa as Jude and Stephen crept in to see her. Carole said the doctor had sedated her, but she was so still she could have been mistaken for dead. Stephen felt sick, her hair was caked in blood and her could see that her face was bruised. 'Who the fuck did this to her??' he whispered to Jude. She didn't answer, glancing at her, he could see the tears rolling down her face.

Taking her hand he led Jude back into the kitchen, to her mam and Glen. Putting on his coat he said nothing, just left. He needed to find out what had happened. His dad must have some idea who she had been hanging around with at work, there weren't that many working there. And Maggie travelled backwards and forwards with his dad, they must have talked.

The house looked like it was in darkness, strange. But as he opened the front door he could see a light coming from the kitchen, his mam and dad must have been in there. Making his way in he found his mam sitting at the kitchen table alone. The remains of the Friday night tea were still on the table and his mam was sitting in exactly the same position she had been when he left.

He was just about to ask whether she knew where Maggie had gone when she went out when he notice the state of the table. There was a broken plate, mostly the pieces were on the table but there were fragments around where Maggie sat. Stephen looked at his mam. She was as white as a ghost. She was looking miles away, as if she wasn't even there. Stephen was at a loss at what to say, if his dad had been the one that hurt Maggie, which was unimaginable; why hadn't his mam tried to stop him.

It was obvious that something had happened in their house. And where was his dad?? Was he out looking for Maggie??

Stephen opened his mouth to ask what had been going on, when he stopped. As Dorothy Hunter sat, she was weaving something in and out of her hands. What was it??

It was hair!! It was Maggie's long hair and his mam was moving it in and out of her hands as if she was weaving wool. Surely not!!!

Once again he went to ask what had happened but Dorothy Hunter beat him to it. 'Maggie has gone. No idea where. Good riddance is what I say. Did you know that she was pregnant??? That slut of a girlfriend of yours must have known and she would have told you?? Did you?? Did you know?? Anyway she left and she won't be coming back!!! I want nothing to do with her and neither does your dad. Showing us up! What will they say at school when they find out??? What do you think that

they are going to say??? What are they going to say, Stephen????
'You must be so proud Mrs Hunter, what credit to you she is!!!' Pregnant at 16!! And what about your poor dad?? He has to go to work, because let's be honest, where else is he going to get a job at his age and that place is all he has ever known!!! He has been there most of his working life!! Then she goes there, is there 5 minutes and throws herself at the young boss!!! He has no interest in her, he's getting married. She has made her bed she can lie in it!!!!

Stephen could taste the hatred, it hung in the air like the fish they had eaten for tea! This woman who he had called mam was just so full of malice; at least at the minute. And no matter which way he looked at it, the disappointment and embarrassment of Maggie being pregnant, she didn't deserved to be lying on Jude's mam's sofa, beaten and sedated. Her mam didn't even know where she was. Who was this woman in front of him?? This woman that was pulling her own daughter's hair backwards and forwards through her hands, hair that she had pulled out by the root in a frenzied attack!

And where was his dad?? Where was Leslie Hunter when all this had been going on. Had he taken himself out on one of his huffy walks, the ones he always did when things got a bit heated with his kids. Stephen understood that it was shocking Maggie knocking about with his dad's boss's son and obviously her being pregnant was crap, but it wasn't life and death. Though thinking about Maggie lying still and ghost like on the sofa not ten mins away, it could well have been.

With nothing left to say and unable to stay one more minute in the kitchen with his mam, Stephen made his way up the stairs to the bedroom that shared with Shaun. His brother wasn't home, it was after

10 so he would be back any minute. What the fuck was he going to say to him. At least by the time he himself had arrived home that night he had an idea what was going on, not his mam's involvement, but he had known Maggie was having a baby and he knew that she wasn't there. Shaun was walking into a scene from a disaster movie.

Stephen stripped out of his best clothes and pulled on a pair of shorts and a t-shirt. He kept the door open a little bit and waited for the sound of the front door opening heralding his brothers return, he would shout him upstairs before he had chance to find the shadow of their mam in the kitchen, playing with strands of their sister's hair.

He heard the door open. Shaun!! Going to the landing at the top of the stairs he shouted for Shaun. No, he wasn't coming up, he was starving and wanted crisps and a drink from the kitchen. But whether it was the seriousness of the tone in Stephen's voice or the fact that as well as being starving, he was desperate for a wee, he turned on his heel and bounded up the stairs and made straight for the toilet. Stephen waited at the bedroom door for him.

'In here, now!!'

Shaun followed closing the door behind him.

It took less than 15 minutes to bring Shaun up to speed in what was going on. The first thing Shaun wanted to do was to go and see Maggie, pointless Stephen said, she was flat out, they could go together the next day. And then he wanted to go and confront their mam, see why she thought it was ok to kick the living daylights out of Maggie. Another fruitless exercise, Dorothy Hunter was full of hate and malice sitting there in the kitchen. Best thing they could do was leave her there to stew. She still had no idea where or how Maggie was, surely at some point she would come out of her stupor and start to panic.

So, they sat and waited for their dad's return. He would talk some sense into his wife after he discovered just what she had done. While they waited, they talked about Maggie, her condition, what would happen to her, who the lad was that had caused all of the trouble. And just when they thought that he was never coming back, they heard the door go and Leslie Hunter return home.

Stephen and Shaun sat on their beds, just like they had done when they were little and had been naughty for their mam and she would threaten them that she would be telling their dad when he got home. Their dad would never smack them for their shenanigans, he was a quiet man, but they hated to disappoint him and when he called them down to apologise to their mam, they hated that look on his face. His disappointed in them face. So, sitting there, felt like they were little boys all over again.

They waited for the shout up the stairs telling them to go down and sort the trouble out. But they waited and they waited, and the call didn't come. Stephen went to the loo, standing on the landing and trying to hear what was being said. There was no noise coming from the kitchen apart from the sound of plates being clattered together as if the table as being cleared.

Back on the beds, Maggie's brothers waited some more.

They heard footsteps on the stairs and someone going into the bathroom. The bathroom door opened and whoever it was made straight for the bedroom. More footsteps, into the bathroom again. Out of the bathroom, landing light off, the sound of the bedroom door closing and that was that.

It was just like any other Friday night. It was just like any other night of the week. But it hadn't been. Maggie Hunter wasn't in her bedroom as she would normally be. Stephen couldn't hear the hum of the music playing softly from the room next door. She was lying on a sofa in the best room at his girlfriend's house. Battered, bruised, knocked out and knocked up. By all accounts beaten up by their mam. It was nothing like a normal Friday night, but Dorothy and Leslie Hunter had taken to their beds without explanation or any sign of remorse.

Shocked, both Stephen and Shaun talked quietly into the night. Neither of them sure what the hell was going on, what was going to happen and how they would get over it. Because the woman they had called mam, who had loved them all unconditionally, affectionately had flipped her lid. He couldn't get the image of Maggie lying on that sofa out of his head. The battered face, the raw skin on the scalp where her hair had been pulled out at the roots. For the life of him he couldn't see his mam doing this to Maggie, but she had. He needed to talk to Maggie, when she was ready, he would speak to her and see what had happened. As he fell into a fitful sleep, one thing was sure, he wouldn't tell anyone, not even Jude. Just as he was about to hit the land of nod, he knew what it was he was feeling. Ashamed!! Of Maggie? Of his mam?? Of his dad?? He wasn't sure, he just knew it was an emotion he had never had to deal with before and it was one he didn't like.

23) The Moon Reversed

The following days in the Hunter house were strange. Their lives were going on as normal, without Maggie. It was the same weekend as always for Dorothy and Leslie Hunter, the shopping the Sunday lunch, all without Maggie. Stephen tried to talk to his mam and dad about Maggie, together, separately, but they ignored him completely and would change the subject. It was like Maggie had never been there.

Her washing remained on the fifth step of their stairs just like it always was. Every Sunday after his mam had ironed all their freshly washed clothes, she placed them on the stairs waiting for reach of them to collect them and take them to their rooms. Leslie Hunter was on the bottom, Dorothy Hunter the second and so on. Maggie's sat on the fifth, alone and untouched. In the end Stephen was sick of walking past it, picked it up and threw it onto Maggie's unslept in bed.

Both he and Shaun had been to Carole Todd's to see their sister. Each time they went she seemed not to have moved. Her face was white and purple, and her hair remained a bloody tatty mess. Stephen was grateful that the Todd's seemed to be taking such good care of her. No one had said anything about getting the police involved, they had every right to, after all if anything happened to Maggie and she was in their home, there would be questions asked.

Jude pushed Stephen about what his mam and dad had said. Just like his parents did at home, he dodged and avoided giving a direct answer, if she thought it strange his mam and dad not appearing at her house, she never said.

Shaun had been livid when he first saw Maggie. They were so close in age that they had one of those love hate relationships. Most of the time they acted like they couldn't stand each other, but they had moved in the same circles at school and were much closer than they ever let on. Shaun was visibly shaken at the sight of his sister and as they left the Todd's house the first time, he wanted to fight the world. He was as confused as Stephen was that his mam was even capable of hurting anyone that much, nevertheless her own daughter. And just like his older brother, he said he felt ashamed.

Sausage egg and chips for tea on Monday, everything the same as always, just no place for Maggie. Chit chat between his mam and dad about their work days. The brothers said nothing. And so, it went on. Their lives without Maggie. Strange and a little disturbing in Stephen's mind, how could they not even ask if he or Shaun had seen her!! Did they not care about her at all? What if it had been him or Shaun, not pregnant of course, but did something that was going to show their mam and dad up, would they be outcast without a second thought too.

One thing was for sure, Stephen could not stay in that house. He could not live with the people he loved most in the world while they continued to act the way they did. Would you say that they were burying their heads? Definitely! But that wasn't how families carried on as far as he was concerned. Look at Jude's mam and step dad, they were caring for Maggie even though they barely knew her. They were putting up with the disruption of having her live in their best room despite having two small children to care for and the added intrusion of having him and Shaun and even that doctor on their doorstep all of the time.

Stephen had no idea where he would go if he did leave home. It was something he had never really thought about, though that was not strictly true, recently he had been thinking about how he would feel about spending the rest of his life with Jude. She had come along and totally taken the wind out of his sales, but even with all that thinking, he assumed if he left home, it would be on the morning of his wedding, wearing a nice suit and the full support of his mam and dad. But even with all that had happened with Maggie, now he knew exactly what his mam thought of Jude. The word slut would stay etched on his mind for a very long time. So, there would be no wedding morning in the Hunters house, for him and Jude anyway.

So, he was at a bit of a loss about how he even went about getting somewhere to live. The Council?? He was going to have to ask some questions, maybe Carole Todd would help. He would need something with 2 bedrooms, he wasn't going to leave Shaun there. He was 16 and could leave home, if he wanted to anyway. Even if he decided to stay with mam and dad, it wouldn't harm to have somewhere where he could go if need be.

The thoughts would go around and around in his head. He went to work, he went home had tea and then went to see Jude and Maggie. Sometimes when he sat with Maggie, he had the feeling that she wasn't asleep, Carole Todd had told him that the doctor had taken her off of sedation, she slept now with shock and exhaustion. Stephen wasn't convinced.

When Dorothy Hunter asked Stephen to give Maggie a letter he was both shocked and hopeful. He had assumed that his mam would know Stephen knew where his sister was, but she had never said, and she had never asked how she was. So, the letter somewhat made him think that his mam and dad had begun to thaw. After all it had been almost a week now. Perhaps there would be a way that they could somehow work through all of the mess. That they could be a family again, that Stephen wouldn't need to move out so soon, because to be honest, although he played the big man, he was barely 20 and the thought of taking total responsibility for himself terrified him. Better he left home on his wedding morning, with or without his mam's blessing.

So, he left the letter for the sleeping Maggie and hoped that by the following week, the world would be back on its axle and all would be relatively well again.

As if!

24) Queen of Swords Reversed

Both Stephen and Shaun were woken early on Saturday morning by a strange banging sound. It was hard to see what time it was, but it was still dark as winter mornings are. Shaun was moaning on about being woken so early on his day off, he had been working at their local Presto for a few weeks, packing shelves, but it was a job, and he hadn't seemed to mind working the early mornings. But being disturbed on his day off hadn't gone down well.

They lay and listened. The noise seemed to be coming from Maggie's room. Maybe their mam was giving it a spring clean ready for Maggie to come home. Stephen heard the door opening and then what sound like a thud, then another. There was a nothing else to do but get up and see what all of the noise was about.

Stephen made his way onto the landing. There were piles of black bin bags outside Maggie's door and Dorothy Hunter was systematically throwing them down the stairs. 'What you doing mam??' Shaun asked from behind him. 'Your sister is gone, and she won't be coming back, she has until this afternoon to get her stuff or they will be out with the bin in the morning!!'

The brothers were flabbergasted. Surely the letter was to put things right. Stephen went back into the bedroom and got dressed, he had to go and see Maggie, see what had been said in the letter. Shaun was back in his bed by time Stephen was ready, pushing past his mam, dodging the black bin bags on the stairs and out of the door in minutes.

By the time he got to Jude's he has breathless and a little bit shaken. Thoughts of being able to stay at home until his wedding day scuppered once again. If his mam was having some sort of mental breakdown, he couldn't be around to see it. It wasn't him being shallow, it was self-preservation and saving his relationship with Jude, because Dorothy Hunter was like a loose cannon, it would be the end of him and Jude if she let her tongue loose.

Glen let him into the house and told him that Carole was in the kitchen and would want to see him. Glen busied himself making teas as Carole Todd went to one of the kitchen cupboard and took out the envelope he had left for Maggie the previous evening. Taking the letter out he read it, read it again and then read it again. This wasn't his mam, not the mam that had brought them all up, this was something else. There was no way back for Maggie. Even if Dorothy Hunter came to her senses tomorrow Maggie couldn't possibly forgive her not just for the beating and the humiliation of been cast out of the family, but the letter. That would be enough for Maggie to never speak to his mam ever again.

Carole said she was going to keep Maggie with her for the time being. Since she had the letter, she had been awake and alert, obviously distressed, but talking so that had been progress. Stephen told Carole and Glen what had happened that morning with Maggie's belongings, how her mam had black bin bagged everything up and threw them down the stairs, they had hours to collect them, or they would be out with the bin on Monday.

As they sat, they made a plan, there was a spare bed in David's room, it was ready for Marc, but he was still in his little bed in Carole and Glen's room, a bit longer wouldn't hurt him. They would bring that down to the best room and Maggie could use that. Dr Graham was popping to check on Maggie soon and as soon as he had been and he thought it was all right, Carole was going to get Maggie into the bath and get her cleaned up. While she was out of the room, they could have a change around and bring the bed down. In the meantime, why didn't they go and get Maggie's things. Jude and Glen would help.

When the doctor knocked on the door, that was their cue to go. Stephen let himself into the house while Jude and Glen waited in the garden. The house seemed empty and apart from all of the black bin bags in the hallway, it would just be like the other hundreds of times he went home. He ran up the stairs, Shaun was getting dressed, telling him to come with them, the four of them managed to carry all Maggie's stuff, telling Shaun what was going on as they walked.

Stephen hadn't given a shit about piling all the black bin bags outside, let the neighbours talk. His mam was so concerned about what other people thought, let her deal with that one because those neighbours of theirs missed nothing.

Returning to Carole Todd's she said that she had managed to get Maggie into the bath. Stephen knew by the pained look on Carole's face that her body must have been as bad as her face and hair. They all worked effectively, and the bed was down the stairs, fresh sheets put on and the bags and bags of belongings dotted around the room.

All happy that they had made the best of a bad job, they went to the kitchen. Carole was going to help Maggie out of the bath and back into the best room. Once she was back and settled, they would talk, maybe try and make a plan as to what to do next. Stephen put himself on the list for what to do next, he didn't want to be at home. Dorothy Hunter was beginning to feel more of a stranger than his mam and he couldn't handle it.

25) The Hermit

The weeks following Dorothy Hunter's letter were the most peaceful of Maggie's life. There were no noises in her head, no warning alarms or second sight. Just the sound of silence. All was calm though not so bright. Her life was still full of uncertainty and fear, but for the first few weeks following the letter, when there was nothing for Maggie to do but heal, were, well bliss.

Carole Todd took good care of Maggie. Day by day the bruises faded, her scalp was still sore and Maggie would run her hands over the bald patches feeling for any sign of life, there was none. Her appetite began to come back and she found smells no longer sent her running to hug the toilet. Her heart was still broken, though she did feel that around the edges where it had thawed, she could feel a steady beat.

Stephen and Shaun had been amazing with her too. There wasn't a day went by when they didn't pop their heads in, even just for 5 minutes. She never asked them about home and they never said. It was like her mam and dad had been abducted by aliens and disappeared off the face of the earth. Stephen was moving out. Some bloke he worked with had a room in his house that he let out, it was at the top of an old house and apparently was enormous, with its own little bathroom, the only thing he would have to share was the kitchen. Stephen was chuffed, the room was for 2 people so there was room for Shaun too, if he wanted it. Maggie asked neither of her brothers how they felt about everything. The banter was always just general, nothing was spoken about that would cause any of them upset.

And then there was Jude. She had been a little star. She made Maggie feel normal again. She would come and lie on the bed and they would chat about nothing just like they had always done. Who Jude had seen on her travels, old school friends and what they were doing. She said the only person she had told about what was going on was Linda, who was desperate to come and see her but would only come when Maggie was ready. She wasn't, not yet.

Jude would rub some oil thing she had bought from Boots the Chemist for hair, it alleged on the bottle that it would simulate hair growth, the box showed a picture of a bald middle aged man on one side and on the other the same man with a full head of bushy hair. Maggie didn't have much hope, but Jude was excited about it so just went with the flow and checked all of the time for the emergence of the full bushy hair!

Dr Whatshisname had paid her one last visit, it was just a few days after the letter and she was still a bit shellshocked, but he was happy that she seemed to be on the mend, didn't press her about what had happened to her and said he would like to see her a couple of weeks later in his practice and they would have a chat then. He seemed nice.

The baby seemed to still be there in her tummy. She hadn't seen any blood loss and Dr Whatshisname said if there had been something wrong, then by then she would know about it. Maggie knew that the baby was fine, she could feel it. Not feel it feel it like it was moving around or kicking or anything. She just knew. This baby would arrive in not that many months' time, she would be a mam at the tender age of 16. Lost a mam, found a mam. It was all a bit ironic.

The very thought of her mam and dad hurt her. The number of times she wanted to put her clothes on and go and see them, the feeling was sometimes overwhelming. But the she also knew that the rejection would be even more painful a second time. The first time had been an adrenalin fuelled experience, physically and mentally. There had been the fear of the build up to telling them that she was pregnant, then the shock of everything that happened after that.

The hurt had taken over her whole being. Maggie couldn't go through even a fraction of that again. For the time being she was on her own. Not on her own, she had Carole and Jude and her brothers and Glen. But she didn't have her mam and dad like any other normal 16-year-old, but what was normal about the situation.

Carole had been helping her formulate plans, things she would need to do, she had no money, so she was going to have to get some from somewhere. Maggie assumed that she no longer had a job at Quarry's End, not that she would ever have gone back, but she didn't even know what happened when you left a job. Realistically she had only been there a matter of months, they were hardly going to miss her. But she had liked Mrs West and Ann and would always feel a flush creep up her neck when she thought of them. They must have thought she was a very silly little girl.

She was a very silly girl. She had been so flattered by Tony Sharp and his nice car and the driving dates and the very nice kissing and the not so nice fumbling and him perching on the edge of her desk making her feel like she was the only girl in the world. Getting pregnant had never crossed her mind, he was way older than her and she assumed that he would have taken care of that side of things. She obviously knew there had been no condoms, she would have known that, but she thought he had done something, and it made her feel even more stupid now to know that he certainly had not.

Maggie wondered how his engagement party had gone! Had her mam and dad gone?? It would have looked very strange if they hadn't, Leslie Hunter had known Tony Sharp all of his life. Maggie wondered if Tony had asked her dad where she was, why she hadn't returned to work. Maggie knew without any uncertain doubt that her dad would not have told Tony Sharp the truth, because that would be far too revealing for the Hunters. They may have told him about Maggie being pregnant, but the good hiding her mam had given her had put paid to that. They would not risk losing face, especially in front of the Sharps and then ultimately the staff at Quarry's End.

Maggie knew that there would have been no mention of her pregnancy and some cock and bull story would have been invented to satisfy the curiosity of people questioning Maggie's absence. No doubt she had run away with some boy she had went to school with. It made no odds to her. Tony Sharp didn't need to know, what use would telling him be anyway. They would never be together, they might have tried to make them get married to give the baby a name, but this was 1986 not 1966 and there was no need to the charade of people not having sex until after marriage.

Tony Sharp had been a cheat, and would no doubt always be a one as long as he could get away with it. Maggie had been so upset when the invitation had arrived for his engagement party, surely he would have known that she would find out about his girlfriend. There had been no warning, he had never once hinted that he had a girlfriend, he had made

Maggie feel like she was the only one, that she was special. But she had been the toy of a spoilt young man, who thought he could have anything he wanted.

As much as Maggie was hurt, she knew that she couldn't wallow in whatever it was she was wallowing in. She had been dealt a shit hand, she had no idea how to look after herself or a baby, but she was going to have to learn fast and feeling sorry for herself wasn't a luxury she could afford. Carole Todd was happy for her to stay with them as long as she wanted, but even Maggie knew that the sooner she could get herself sorted the more chance of surviving all this she had.

Carole said she would ring the council on Maggie's behalf, she was technically homeless, it was something Cariole had never had to do, her predicament although similar was also very different, her family had been supportive and had money. Maggie had neither of these things, so they were going to go to the council to see what options there were and then take it from there.

The thought of living on her own filled Maggie with fear. She had never even stayed at her mam and dad's for one night on her own. She was always hearing things go bump in the night, she would wake and lie and lie and lie and listen to whatever it was moving around. It would only be the sound of her dad's snoring that would lull her back to sleep again. What would she do if it happened and there was no dad snoring? She would die of fright. But she didn't have anywhere to live on her own at the minute so she would put that thought out of her head until it was a reality and, in the meantime, concentrate on the things that were happening.

Like the council, Carole had gone to pick some form up. Maggie would start there. Somehow Maggie knew that she was on the right path. There were no noises in her head, no alarm bells ringing like they had been when she had been with Tony Sharp and the subsequent months on the lead up to Dorothy Hunter flipping her lid. There was no second sight. Where ever it was she was going, it was somewhere that she needed to be. Somehow knowing this gave Maggie a bit of courage, she had little choice but at least knowing that the God's seemed to be on her side made things a little bit better.

26) The Two of Pentacles

Maggie Hunter was due to give birth in the middle of June.

By then she would have been left school a full year. Not exactly how she thought her first year of being a school leaver would have entailed. She had hopes of being a hairdresser, maybe having a boyfriend and certainly having lots of nights out in town with her friends. None of the above had happened.

Maggie had no job. She had no boyfriend and she had never been into town for a night out. She had a house and a huge bump that had a life of its own. But as her Granny Hunter had always instilled in her, she had to always keep her glass half full.

So, Maggie had a house that on a daily basis was becoming a home. She had good friends in the shape of Jude and Linda. A new 'family' in the shape of the Todd's who she had no idea what would have happened to her if she hadn't had them. Probably dead. And she had her brothers; Shaun and Stephen. And she had her baby, who had become her new best friend. The bump that she talked to day and night, telling all her utmost secrets and fears to. Who in a matter of weeks would no longer be a bump and be a babe in arms.

She had been living in her house for a few months. It had been the third one the council had offered her, and it was the one she had walked into and knew it was it. The first two had given her the willies. The first not only had a horrible smell but felt cold and unwelcoming, the alarm bells weren't ringing, but they didn't need to, it just felt wrong.

The second looked and smelled nicer. But again, Maggie didn't think it felt right. There was a sadness about it that she couldn't put her finger on. Carole Todd looked at her in disbelief when she had said hadn't wanted it. Carole stressed to her that she would only be given a choice of 3 and then she would be back to the bottom of the list or in a hostel. But Maggie said no to Mr Pearson from the council and waited patiently for the next offer.

The doctor had confirmed Maggie's pregnancy. Like she hadn't already known, but they had done some sums based on the little symbol in Maggie's diary and assumed that the baby would be putting in an appearance around the 17th of June. He gave her a couple of envelopes, one for council and one for benefits and made her an appointment to see the surgery's midwife a couple of weeks later.

Both of Dr Whatshisname's envelopes had turned out to contain vital and magical pieces of information because the council said that she would be made priority with regard to housing and the benefits people arranged for her to be given a book so she could collect money from the Post Office every week. They made a note when she had last been paid and had kindly told her that her money would be back dated until then. The rent on a house would be covered and there would be an allowance paid to her for decoration and some vital essentials for her new house. To Maggie it seemed too easy. But she would take everything, because she had little choice or help coming from anywhere, financially anyway.

The book duly arrived at Carole's house and she made her way to the Post Office to cash the first part and was amazed to be handed over a mammoth amount of money in back payments. More money than she had ever seen nonetheless had in her life. After arguing about giving a chunk of it to Carole for all the time she would be living there and losing the argument on the grounds that she was insulting Carole, she took the money and placed it into her jewellery box in preparation for whatever came next. Though she did manage to sneak 2 x £5 notes into David and Marc's money boxes without the beady eyed Carole seeing her.

And she continued to wait patiently until the call came informing Maggie that there was another house available for her to view. It was literally around the corner from where she was staying at the Todd's and even before they had officially been to view it, Carole and Maggie had been around, peered through the bare windows and evaluated the garden. It was the one. Maggie had known it would be. It didn't exude happiness, it was just a house, but it didn't have the weird sadness that the previous two houses had and which Maggie had picked up on even before entering them.

Mr Pearson was delighted that she wanted it as Maggie and Carole explored the house a few days later. It was bigger than they had thought it would be, it had 2 decent sized bedrooms and a small box room, very similar to the Hunters house in layout. But Maggie couldn't think about that or compare, this was going to have to be her home and she couldn't take any demons with her. Mr Pearson assured Maggie that she would have the keys in the next few weeks, he would bring them himself after some essential work had been carried out. He was just so relieved she liked this one, because he certainly didn't want to have to refer young Maggie to social services to be housed, she was a nice young girl.

So, as they waited for the keys, Carole took Maggie to buy paint, her house her choice of colours. It was to be a joint effort for them all to go there and get a lick of paint on it, she had been given more money for decoration and there was another lump for a cooker, washer and anything else she may need on the way. Maggie struggled to get her head around not just the money but the fact that she was buying stuff to furnish her home.

Maggie had eventually seen Linda, who had cried when she saw Maggie. Jude assured her that the current version of Maggie was a far improved one than the one that had arrived on their doorstep months earlier. The bruising had all but gone, but there was still the scar on her forehead which would never go, fade with time obviously. But if Maggie was ever feeling particularly homesick, then she would run her finger over the puckered skin and know that she could never return. Dorothy and Leslie Hunter had outcast her and there she would have to remain.

But it was lovely the three of them being together again. Talking about other people's lives instead of her own was a treat. She never wanted a house of her own at 16. Though it was something that Linda still wanted very much. Linda and Paul had set a date. The wedding was to be in July the following year, on Linda's 18th birthday! The girls joked that it would give Maggie plenty of time to get skinny again, especially if she was going to be a bridesmaid, which Linda mixed into the conversation without them noticing. Jude and Maggie bridesmaids! It was just too lovely. It gave Maggie a modicum of hope that when the baby had arrived and she was all settled into her house and surviving to tell the tale, that she could maybe have a bit of a normal life again. That she might even get to go on a night out with her friends in town!

Maggie told her friends about Tony Sharp. How he had made a friend of her from day one, how he had been perching himself on her desk. And then how there had been driving dates and lush kissing and then the fumbling that came later. She had even laughed with her friends because she didn't get what all the fuss was they made about it! And how she had thought that Tony was taking care of her but clearly hadn't been. How the invites for the whole family to attend his engagement party had been brought out during tea. Her friends were outraged. Tony Sharp was a sleaze bag of the highest level.

But the Jude and Linda both disagreed with her underwhelming sex experience. Maggie put her hands over her ears when Jude went into full throw about how amazing it was; Stephen was her bloody brother, she didn't want to know. But it was lovely that the three of them were back together. Maggie didn't mind that the girls would pop in for their hair doing if they were going out, it was nice to see them and if she had pangs of jealousy about her not being able to go out, she just swallowed them down.

She wasn't good at going out. She always had the fear factor that she would bump into her mam and dad. Even if she was with Carole, she would scour the shop to make sure that there was no sign of them, even in shops that she knew Dorothy and Leslie Hunter had never set foot in. it was always a relief to get back to the Todd's' and back into the best room. It was a feeling that she would have until her end of days, even after her mam was long gone.

People looked at her. She may have looked older than her 16 years before she got pregnant. But now that she had bald patches all over her scalp she tended to just tie her hair up to hide them. And she had cut herself a fringe in to cover the raw scar on her forehead. Even when wearing a smidgen of make-up, the whole look made her look young. Like a 16 year old. And that made people stare, especially with the huge bump that she tried to keep zipped up and hidden under her coat. It didn't and she would see people take a double take and then the look that would cross their faces. 'Slut!!' Because in a small town that what people thought of young girls who got pregnant, no matter what the circumstances!

So going out was always a bit of an ordeal. When Carole suggested that they started to buy things for the house, Maggie was reluctant. But then it was Carole Todd to the rescue again. She had a catalogue, it was the never never kind, but there was no reason why Maggie couldn't get what she needed and pay Carole the money. There would even be some commission to be had when it was all paid for and they would maybe be able to get a few extra bits. It was a perfect solution, Maggie knew that her anxiety would be through the roof and she would panic buy, the catalogue was perfect. She spent hours and hours working out what she needed for each room, making lists, checking prices. But then she would find herself flicking through the pages and pages of women's clothes and pick out what she would buy if she wasn't fat and pregnant and had no life!

But what was done was done and as long as the alarm bells didn't start again in her head she would keep moving forward.

27) The Eight of Wands

Mr Pearson met her at the new house with the keys. Maggie signed all of the paperwork and the house was hers. Mr Pearson sheepishly handed her over a package and said that he hoped that she didn't mind and that his wife had made it. Puzzled. Maggie ripped open the package and there was a beautifully hand knitted baby set in the softest of wools. Maggie was flabbergasted, it was the first thing that she had been given or bought for the baby. She was over 7 months pregnant!!! Instinctively she reached out and hugged Mr Pearson. He must thank his wife, what a lovely gesture. Mr Pearson obviously knew what had happened to Maggie and her family, it was such a thoughtful thing for him to do, and his wife. In her head she promised that she would get word to Mr Pearson when the baby arrived, it was the least she could do.

New house, new baby. That was one of her Granny Hunter's sayings. She had only taken ownership for the house 5 minutes earlier and already the baby was making its presence known. She had been right to hold out for the house. For some reason had the feeling that the house had been waiting for her, just like she had for it.

The next few weeks were frantic. Paint was sploshed on all of the walls and the place was cleaned to within an inch of its life. Carpets arrived thanks to one of Carole's neighbours who worked for a large company but did his own little thing on the side, so they were purchased and fitted at a knock down price. Still a small fortune in Maggie's eyes who had no concept whatsoever with regard to how much money setting up a house would take.

Everything else started to arrive thanks to the catalogue company who delivered everything direct to the house, so Maggie found herself spending most days at her new home and only spent her nights at the Todd's until the bed arrived.

And then the last delivery arrived and the last lorry pulled away and it was time. Maggie didn't have many belongings. Just black bin bags full of clothes that she had no idea if she would ever fit into again. She felt like she was the size of a semi-detached house. But they trundled them around to the new house and she hung them in the new wardrobe and the new set of draws which had arrived and Glen had assembled in her bedroom.

Maggie hadn't meant to cry when she left Carole Todd's house. But it had been such an emotional time and they had all been so supportive. She had even grown fond of David and Marc who seemed to love to have Maggie read to them or play a game. Carole had saved her life and then saved her sanity. They had forged a bond over the past months and Maggie was sure that it was a bond that would remain there until the end of days. Maggie would often shudder at the thought of not having Carole Todd in her life, she most likely would have ended up dead, because there would have been nowhere else for her to go!

So, she cried and cried as she made that last trek from the Todd's house to her new home. Carole held her hand all of the way around and Jude said she would stay the night with her if she wanted. But Maggie wouldn't hear of it. She had intruded enough in the home and in their lives, she had to do it on her own or else she would never do it. But she knew they would worry if she didn't get a grip. So, by the time she put her key in the door, she had put some steel in her back and a smile on her face.

And an hour later she was on her own in her own home. For the first time in her whole life there was no one. Carole and Jude had left with a look of concern on their faces, Maggie knew that they would both have a restless night, Maggie would be along at their home tomorrow assuring them that everything was fine and that they could stop worrying.

But looking around her living room she was unsure. This was all new, everything was new. Being on her own. The house. The furniture. She had a few of her own belongings dotted about, but if she was honest, they looked childish in such a grown up setting, nothing like they looked in her bedroom at home with its posters on the wall and the beads and bangles dangling off every orifice.

She had made her bed though, she was just going to have to lie in it.

Maggie checked all of the doors and windows and made her way up to the bathroom to run herself a bath. There was a spider running around in the bath. Her first instinct was to turn on the tap and flush it away to its fate down the plug hole, but then Granny Hunter was back in her head. 'They bring you luck Maggie, never kill one!' So, Maggie scooped it up in her hand gently, made her way back down the stairs and opened the back door. The weather was warm, even if it had been a house spider it would be fine outside until it found itself another home. 'Goodbye Good Luck' and with that he was off scuttling into the garden.

Jude had bought her some bubble bath and it felt a luxury lying in the bath in a bath full of bubbles. There would be no one knocking at the door asking her how long she was going to be. She could lie in the bath until the water went cold or her skin went wrinkly, whichever came first. The lump was too big to be completely submerged, Maggie found herself pouring water over her tummy, the baby liked it. Anytime she got in the bath she would feel the baby wiggle about. There was no one to hear her here so she talked, and she sang to her bump and in return it kicked and wriggled about and seemed to be enjoying the sound of its mam's voice.

No matter how she felt, she wasn't alone. And God willing she wouldn't for a long time. Maggie and the baby were in this together. This was their home. They had a roof over their heads, they were lucky. Money may be an issue but after the baby was born, she could work, she wasn't sure what she could do or who would look after the baby but she would do something.

Maggie slept fitfully. Things went bump in the night. There was no reassuring snoring coming from the next room, but there were also no noises in her head heralding any danger. So, she would strain her ears and when all was silent again she would fall back to sleep. It happened a few times, but it didn't bother her too much. It was a new house to her with new sounds. All houses had their sounds, she would eventually not hear them, they would just be the house.

When she woke she was surprisingly fresh. She was dressed and was out of the door in no time. It was Saturday so she knew that the whole family would be in the kitchen having breakfast and had promised that if she could she would be there too.

The relief when she walked through the door was tangible. David and Marc sprang off their seats and bounded towards her as if they hadn't seen her for months instead of hours. But it was a lovely feeling. This was home!

28) The Ace of Cups

Maggie Hunter gave birth to her baby on 21st June 1986, just a few days after Dr Whatshisname had estimated.

To say Maggie had been unprepared for childbirth had been an understatement. No matter how many pamphlets she had read, there was no way that they could ever convey the inscrutable pain that having a baby would be.

In the last few weeks of her pregnancy, she had moved from the size of a semi-detached house to simply a detached house. She couldn't see her feet!! It took her ages to get up and down her stairs and sleep for anything longer than an hour was a luxury, because if it wasn't finding a comfortable spot then she would need to wee!

Stephen and Shaun had clubbed together to pay for her to have a telephone line to be put in just in case and the front door was ever evolving with visitors making sure that she was ok.

There had been enough commission from the catalogue to buy a pram and cot, the latter was already assembled and, in her bedroom, the former was at the Todd's, another of Granny Hunter's wise words about not having a pram into the home until the baby was born.

Carole had supplied baby grows that she hadn't thrown out from her two youngest along with some essential bits like towels and sheets and they had another shopping spree in the catalogue for any other bits that she didn't have. The thought of going to the shops hadn't abated in the past few months and Maggie couldn't decide whether this was because of the size of her or in case she bumped into anyone she knew.

Jude and Linda had both insisted on having sleepovers, but where they thought they would all fit into Maggie's bed, it only happened once and the next time they came they brought sleeping bags with them and slept downstairs, Maggie was just too big and too restless. But it was nice them sleeping and Maggie was sure that they were trying to make her laugh the baby out of her.

If only that was how it worked.

Just when Maggie thought that the baby was never going to come, her waters broke. It was like a waterfall all over her bedroom carpet. She waddled herself downstairs and rang Carole who could only have been sitting on top of her phone because she answered it in one ring. She was at the house in a matter of minutes, took one look at Maggie and rang for an ambulance.

Her case had been packed for weeks in the hope that the baby would arrived early, and Carole grabbed it from her bedroom after she had managed to soak up most of the water Maggie had left there earlier, just before it stained, she said!

In hospital they were happy for Carole to stay. They assumed that she was Maggie's mam, and no questions were asked. Maggie thought that it was all going swimmingly, she could do this, but realistically, she hadn't really gone into labour. She had herself a little doze, she hadn't slept properly for weeks, but then she was woken by bells ringing. She thought it was the fire alarm and looked at Carole, who was sitting on a chair next to her bed emersed in a Mills and Boon book, but she didn't seem to be alarmed by the impending fire.

The penny dropped just as the first pain hit her. It wasn't a fire alarm, it was the alarm bells in her head, it was the warning that there was trouble coming, just like it had in the past. But she hadn't listened, again and the pain that ripped through her was horrific. It took the breath out of her body and made her pant like a dog. Mills and Boon was on the floor and Carole was holding her hand giving Maggie her full attention and everything she knew about giving birth. Breathe, pant, don't push.

The pains came in waves. Just when she thought that it was over another one would replace it, bigger, stronger, longer. They moved her into another room and offered her some gas and air which she sucked on greedily. Maggie had no idea if it helped or not, but it gave her something to bite on as the pains got worse, if that was even possible.

She was hot, she was cold. She wanted to stand up but as soon as she sat up, she was sick. And the pains would just not stop. The noise in her head made it hard for her to hear the midwives or Carole and had to rely on their facial expressions and hand gestures. It went on for what Maggie thought was hours. How could anyone do this more than once.

Dorothy Hunter ran through her head, had she gone through this to have Maggie?? Surely not with Stephen or Shaun because no one in their right state of mind would do this if they knew what it was like. The pain ripping through her were like red hot swords; and somewhere from deep within her came a piercing scream, she thought it must have been 'Mam' because she could see the midwife gesturing towards Carole, as if saying its fine your mam is here! The pains were fierce and cascading, relentless, how could one small thing give so much pain.

Then just as she thought it certainly couldn't get any worse something else came along, the urge to push. Maggie had never felt anything like it. It was so all consuming that she everything else paled into insignificance. The ringing in her head, the pain ripping through her, the faces of the midwives and the continuous hand squeezing by Carole. All she wanted to do was to push and push and push. The burning between her legs was felt like a furnace and as she pushed, she would feel the heat creeping up her body. She could feel the drops of sweat running down her face. And still the urge to push was overwhelming. So, she pushed and she pushed and it continued to burn, there felt like an all mighty wooosh and it was over.

Tipping her head back into the pillows Maggie took in great gulps of air. There were no sounds, no alarm bells ringing in her head. The danger had passed. She could see Carole at the end of the bed, her back was turned away from Maggie and she seemed to be talking animatedly to the midwives, who also had their backs turned. Maggie tried to focus, what was wrong? For the first time since all the pain had stopped, she thought of the baby. What was wrong??

One of the midwives turned and came back towards her. She smiled. This time when her mouth opened to speak to Maggie, she could hear every word. 'You did really well Maggie, especially for your first baby, it will be easier next time. Baby just needs warming up, came out in a hurry in the end. Just going to tidy you up while we waiting!! It's a beautiful morning mind ……' Her chatting went on and on, while she fiddled about at the bottom of the bed between Maggie's legs.

The door opened and a woman came in with a cup of tea and some toast. Maggie didn't normally drink tea, but it was strong and sweet, and she found that once she started sipping at it she couldn't stop, it tasted like nectar; though she didn't touch the toast, her appetite was well and truly out of the window.

The first midwife finished whatever it was she had been doing, the sheets were pulled off and a new set put on as quick as a flash by the woman who brought in the tea. With the sheets tucked in around her body, Maggie was surprised to see that she still had a huge bump, surely the lump that had been there was now gone, why did she still look so pregnant. She was about to shout for Carole, when she looked up and the second midwife was making her way towards her with something wrapped in a blanket.

'Maggie meet your daughter!!!'

So there she was. 8lb 1oz of gorgeousness.

Carole was crying, she had never seen a baby born before and was overcome with the joy of the occasion. And it had been a very long night. She sat cradling the baby in her arms, not wanting to leave Maggie but knowing that she was needed at home and that they would all want to know that Maggie and the baby were fine. She had thought of telephoning them, but it was still early and didn't want to wake the little ones if she could help it.

She would have 5 more minutes and then make her way home, with the promise of returning at visiting time along with anyone else who wanted to go. She was so proud of Maggie, despite everything that she had been through, the emotional strain as well as the awful beating her mam had given her, Maggie had kept the beautiful baby girl safe and well.

Maggie couldn't stop staring at her daughter. 'Daughter!' She kept saying daughter over and over in her head. Towards the end of her pregnancy, she had the feeling she was having a girl. If the truth be known, she only picked a girl's name, but didn't tell anyone just in case she was wrong. But she had known her baby was strong, they had been through so much together. Maggie would have been just as pleased with a boy, she was used to them having two brothers and she had spent so much time playing with David and Marc at Carole's that she wouldn't have minded at all. But she was delighted to have a little girl. 'You have a daughter you have a friend for life' Another of Granny Hunter's little sayings.

It was funny, Granny Hunter had been dead for a long time, but she was still very much alive in Maggie's life. Her sayings, her ways, her funny little superstitions were as much part of Maggie's life now as they had ever been, if not more! And it was Granny Hunter's name that Maggie had decided to name her daughter. Well not exactly the same, she was shortening it to something a bit more modern.   Her Granny Hunter been Evelyn Hunter. Maggie's daughter was going to be Eve.

'Im going to call her Eve. Eve Carole Hunter!' Maggie said to Carole. 'I will never be able to repay you for everything that you have done for me, I hope giving Eve your name as part of hers goes some way! Welcome to the world Eve Carole Hunter!'

29) The Ten of Cups

Maggie ended up spending 4 more nights in hospital. She had ended up getting a bit of a temperature, which felt nothing in comparison to the heat she had endured during the labour, but still the doctors wanted to give her anti-biotics and insisted that she remain in hospital until they knew they were taking effect.

Eve went in to the nursery every night with the rest of the new born babies and Maggie was able to sleep and recover.

Maggie couldn't stop looking at her and touching her. She was perfect and for some reason looked very familiar, though as hard as Maggie looked at her, she couldn't see anything of Tony Sharp there, though her eyes hadn't been open much, so maybe that would be a tell-tale sign once they opened properly. Maggie wouldn't have loved her any less even if she had been the spit and dab of her daddy. She was her baby and hers alone.

Eve was being bottled fed, Maggie had never thought for a minute about feeding her herself, she wouldn't know where to begin. But once the infection had kicked in, there was no choice anyway, the anti-biotics had put paid to that. So, Maggie's nights were uninterrupted as Eve was fed in the nursery and only brought back to her mammy at breakfast time.

Every visiting time she had visitors. Her bedside table was covered in flowers and cards, and she had lots of little gifts in her bag ready to be taken home and opened there. Eve had two very smitten uncles, Maggie could see them melt before her very eyes the minute they saw her. Carole came in every chance she had, and Glen even popped in with her one afternoon. Jude and Linda came in and coo 'ed, Maggie had the feeling that Linda would have a family of her own as soon as she got married. She was a natural with Eve.

And then it was time for them to go home. Carole would go to her house to meet her, but she was going to have to get a taxi from the hospital, another first for Maggie. But if she could give birth, then she could certainly manage to get herself and her baby home in a taxi, bags and all.

Maggie dressed Eve in a baby grow and then the coat, hat and mitts that Mr Pearson from the council's wife had made. One of the midwives carried Eve to the foyer and Maggie took her bag and flowers. The taxi was waiting and as she bundled their belongings into the car, she heard someone call her name.

It was Mrs West holding onto the arm of a quite elderly lady whom Maggie assumed was her mam. There was too much distance between them to hold a conversation, so Maggie waved and jumped into the back of the taxi. The midwife handed Eve to Maggie, the door closed, and they were off heading home. The taxi crawled along the lane in front of the hospital, right in front of Mrs West who was standing with her mouth wide open in shock. Whatever Leslie Hunter had said at work about the absence of his daughter, it hadn't been that Maggie was having a baby. There were no alarm bells ringing in Maggie's head, Mrs West wasn't a threat.

Carole, Jude and Linda were waiting to meet Maggie and Eve as the taxi pulled up. She had only been away from her house for 5 nights, but it felt so good to be going home. To her house! It was basic, she only had the bare essentials, but still it was somewhere safe for her and Eve to live.

And that was that. Maggie Hunter was 16 years old, she was mother to a new born baby girl. This was her life. Outcast by her mam and dad and befriended by her best friends family, things could have been so much worse.

Those first few days at home with Eve were both terrifying and amazing. Eve had some lungs on her when she wanted something, and Maggie would panic thinking that she wouldn't know why she was crying or what to do about it. Carole helped her loads, showed her how to feed her and how to help her with wind when she got a little pain. Carole even stopped the first few nights, but she needn't have, as soon as Eve stirred Maggie would be awake and tending to Eve's every needs.

Maggie waited for the blues to arrive, her mam had often told her that after giving birth to each of her children she had spent days weeping and wailing and not being able to deal with their day to day care very well. She had called it the baby blues and luckily, they had passed. But she had been sure that her own mother had been suffering with them for the rest of her life after the birth of her children. So, Maggie waited for the tears, but they did not come. There were no alarm bells ringing in her head and the only second sight she seemed to have was to know instinctively why Eve would screech.

Eve Hunter became the focus of not just her world, but that of her brothers, the Todd's' and her friends. Eve had brought them her own kind of love, she bonded them together. Eve made them some sort of dysfunctional family. For Maggie it made her feel so much more not alone.

With each day Maggie grew more confident. As a mother and in herself. She had been so disappointed when she went to put on a pair of her pre-pregnancy jeans and she couldn't get the zip up, her tummy had shrunk but there was a good five inches stopping the zip from sliding up. Back into her baggy pants and a vow to keep off the biscuits and crisps.

Eve became Maggie's comfort and safety blanket. If she was feeling a bit lost and alone, cuddle Eve. If she was scared and afraid, cuddle Eve. If she wanted to go out anywhere, then Eve would be in the pram and there was an invisible shield around Maggie and she could cope with going to the supermarket or to pick up her money from the Post Office. There were no longer stares. There were no longer looks on people's faces that said 'slut' without them even having to open their mouths. No one probably thought that the baby that she pushed around in front of her was even hers. They no doubt thought that it was her baby sister, or she was babysitting. The people who did engage with her never asked who the baby belonged to, they just coo 'ed and would often ask how old.

And Maggie coped. She cared for Eve, and she kept her house as clean and tidy as she could. Mistakes she made, like putting something coloured in with Eve's delicate whites and turning them a funky shade of grey, she learned from them and was more careful next time. She could make herself meals, usually basic stuff if it was just for her, she was a dab hand with omelettes and the like. But if someone one was coming to tea, Linda or Jude or more her most frequent visitor at teatime Shaun, she would get out the recipe book and try something a bit more daring. Shepherd's Pie was a favourite.

Her 17th birthday came and went. There was no party like there had been the previous year. It was hard to believe that it had only been a year. It had been nice though. Carole had put a little buffet on for them all and they all sat in the sunshine in the garden while David and Marc played in a paddling pool and Eve slept in her pram in the shade. Maggie really did not know what she would do without Carole.

Stephen had moved out of her mam and dad's house, there was only Shaun there now. He spent the odd night at Maggie's and other nights at Stephen's. Maggie never asked about her mam and dad, she didn't want to know what the answers were. But she did wonder if they knew that they had a granddaughter. Surely natural curiosity would have led them to ask one of her brothers. But they never said. No one spoke of Dorothy and Leslie Hunter.

Jude and Stephen remained as smitten as ever. Jude was so different to the sassy flirt she had been at school, she was most definitely a one man women now and Maggie had loved watching their relationship grow. Stephen was no longer shy and awkward. The thought of him picking Jude up, throwing her over his shoulder and into the little ones paddling pool would have been unthinkable 12 months earlier, he would have died of embarrassment, but now it came as second nature to show his adoration for Jude. Maggie had a feeling that the Todd's and the Hunters would be a proper related family at some point in the future. And she wasn't using her second sight, just her eyesight.

Linda and Paul turned up at Maggie's garden party. They too were as together as ever. Wedding plans were well under way and in a few weeks Jude and Maggie would go for their first fitting for their bridesmaid dresses. Maggie was pleased it was an auntie of Paul's making them, she still had her wobbly tummy, but the removal of the biscuits and crisps and the added walks she had been having with Eve in her pram was starting to make a difference, but still. When Linda had first said about the fittings Maggie had thought they were going to some posh shop in town, thinking she would have to explain to some snooty woman in a shop that she still had a baby tummy made Maggie feel sick, but Linda had already warned Paul's aunt that her friend had just had a baby.

All of the love around her sometimes made Maggie feel lonely. A single mam at 17 was hardly the type of girl any lad would want to take home to meet his mam and dad. The future looked bleak, on the love front anyway. Tony Sharp had hardly filled Maggie's head full of longing for 'doing it'; underwhelming was the only lasting memory of that dalliance, maybe the lush kissing, she liked kissing. Oh and Eve!

Eve always made her feel better. She could cope with a loveless life as long as she had Eve. Every day she amazed her, a look, a windy smile, a hiccup, a grasping hand around her finger as she fed her. And the sheer joy on Eve's face at bath time. Maggie would talk and sing to her just like she had when she was a bump, only now Eve would kick and splash in the water and make noises that to Maggie sounded like the sweetest singing.

Maggie walked further and further each day with the pram. There was a park on the outskirts of town which had a duck pond, and she would walk there, feed the ducks and sit on the bench and while away an hour watching the world go by. She made hay while the sun shone. It was nice to get out of the house and she had the safety blanket of the pram with her.

In her own way she was content. A job would be nice, she had loved her job at Quarry's End, or had she just loved it because of Tony Sharp?? No, she had been a surprisingly good typist and she had really liked Mrs West and Ann. But she couldn't go back there, and she had no idea where she could have Eve looked after while she went out to work. But she would love a job and thought maybe she would ask Carole Todd, she had worked when Jude was little, it was only when she had David and Marc close together when she met Glen that she became a stay-at-home mam. But someone must have looked after Jude.

30) The Tower

Summer turned into Autumn.

Maggie was recovered in all aspects of her life. The only remnant of her mam's good hiding was the scar on her forehead, Maggie continued to cover it with her fringe, but it was still pink and it was still raised. Carole thought maybe she should have had it stitched, but it was too late now, it was just something that Maggie carried from her previous life into her current one.

Her scalp was better. The tufts of new hair had begun to appear and the bare scalp was no not as obvious. If Maggie was going anywhere she still tended to tie it up, but at home she let it fall in the hope that the new hair would take itself off in the same direction of the old hair.

She still saw as much of Carole Todd as ever, Saturday morning breakfast and Sunday lunch were a regular occurrence and Maggie still had visitors for tea in the shape of her brothers and her best friends. Jude and Maggie had been taken for their first bridesmaid fitting and Maggie was pleasantly surprised that her baby tummy had almost vanished, and she was nearly back to her pre-pregnancy size, though the jeans that hadn't zipped up stayed firmly in the drawer until Maggie knew herself that they would be zipping up without a struggle.

Maggie took Eve out for a walk most afternoons. It had helped her get back into shape. She didn't always go as far as the park, sometimes she would just make a loop around the town and then head home, it usually depended on having visitors for tea.

The days were growing shorter. The park was a luxury she would keep up for as long as she could, she liked watching the wildlife on the pond. Mainly ducks but there were swans and geese too, but soon they would go, and she wouldn't see them again until they returned in springtime, it was just what happened. So, she would leave the house earlier and head across to the park, feed the ducks and sit on the bench. But the days were growing colder and although Eve was well wrapped up, Maggie did worry about her catching a cold. So, she would sit for a short time and then head back home.

It was as she was heading out of the park it happened. The sound terrified her, the familiar shrill of the alarm bells ringing in her head. Danger. But what and where. She looked around, there was nothing out of the ordinary but still. As she made her way home she stayed alert. There was something amiss.

Maggie was careful crossing roads, kept an eye on a sleeping Eve to make sure there was nothing wrong with her and all the while the alarm bells rang and rang. She still had about 30 minutes left until she got home, it was going to be a long laborious task keeping an eye on Eve and stray cars and people. But as long as the alarm bells rang in her head, she knew that there was something that was going to hurt her physically or mentally.

The stupid thing was that because of all of the noise in her head she didn't hear the danger coming. Maggie was so intent on keeping Eve safe that she didn't see the car. She didn't see it and she didn't hear it until it was by her side.

If she hadn't had all of the noise in her head, she would have heard the car. She would know the sound of that car anywhere, she had sat and waited for it enough times. But she hadn't heard it and she hadn't seen it flash past her. Maggie didn't know it was there until it was at the kerbside next to her.

The driver was staring at her. Tony Sharp!! They locked eyes for a moment! Then Tony Sharp dragged his eyes away from Maggie's and she saw him looking at the pram, the little pink teddy bear dangling off the hood giving away the fact that there was a little girl lying in it. Tony Sharp looked away. The car went into gear, and he roared off down the street. This time Maggie heard him, the alarm bells had gone. The danger was over but as Maggie almost ran the remainder of the way home pushing the pram, she had the dreaded feeling that the danger had only just began!!

31) The Hermit

Seeing Tony Sharp had totally taken the wind out of Maggie's sails. He wasn't stupid, he would have known that the baby inside the pram was his. It all tallied in with her disappearance from Quarry's End and his life.

For once she decided that she wasn't going to keep Tony Sharp a secret.

So, she told Carole and Jude and then her brothers. If Tony Sharp decided to turn up on the Hunters' doorstep, at least Shaun would know who he was.

The weather turned and even though Maggie had no compulsion to walk to the park on the outskirts of town or even the shops for that matter, it was no fun in the wind and rain so tended just to stay at home. Carole kindly took her shopping list for her weekly trip to the supermarket and got whatever Maggie wanted there.

Self-enforced isolation.

Shaun said all was quiet at home and he didn't mention Dorothy or Leslie Hunter mentioning Tony Sharp, but even if her mam and dad did talk about her, she doubted Shaun would tell Maggie.

The catalogue came back out for Christmas courtesy of Carole. Eve was far too small to realise what was going on, but there were David and Marc and the rest of the Todd's, Linda and Paul and of course her brothers. Catalogue shopping really was the way forward, not because she could make weekly payments, but the whole shopping thing had never been Maggie's thing and now with the added worry of Tony Sharp maybe looking for her, it was just easier.

Maggie ordered herself a little tree so by the time 1st of December arrived, she had her tree up in the living room and all her gifts were neatly wrapped and hidden in the spare room upstairs. Eve was almost 6 months old and would coo and laugh and kick her legs if Maggie placed her near the tree so she could watch the twinkling lights. Maggie made a Christmas cake, not for herself she didn't like it, but it would a nice little extra to take to the Todd's' on Christmas Day, she had also tried mince pies, but they hadn't been quite as successful.

It was going to be a very different Christmas from the year before, the thought of a Hunters Christmas brought a lump to Maggie's throat. She missed her cousin Tom Grey so much, they had always been so close. He must be really disappointed in Maggie because she had heard nothing from him or about him. Surely, he would have asked Shaun where she was and what had happened, but there had been nothing. He would love Eve, he would have been a great uncle. She had picked her telephone up lots of times, she knew his number by heart they had called each other so much. But she couldn't do it, she didn't know what sort of reception she would get, and she couldn't face another rejection, especially from Tom.

Maggie's heart had almost completely thawed, mainly thanks to Eve, but also Carole and Jude and Linda and the support of her brothers. She might have made her bed, but she had the prettiest sheets and the softest of pillows thanks to the dysfunctional family she and Eve seemed to be front and centre of. A year on from Quarry's End and she was very much glass half full, it could have been so much worse.

She thought living on her own would have been lonely. But she enjoyed locking her front door on an evening, getting a bath when Eve was settled and maybe reading a book or watching a bit television. She didn't particularly feel like she was missing out on anything, she hadn't really had it to miss. Linda and Jude were loved up so weren't doing the whole going out places thing. She got that, when she had been doing the driving dates with Tony Sharp, she hadn't really given her friends a second thought. She was lucky they both liked having nights at her house, she could quite easily have been forgotten about.

Christmas Eve was a busy one. She had ventured out of the house and done one of those special shops like her mam and dad always did at Christmas. Nice nibbles, fizzy pop, some cakes and some nice cold meats. Maggie and Eve were spending Christmas Day at the Todd's, but she would still be at home quite a bit and the shops would be closed, so it wouldn't harm to treat herself and anyone who might call in for a visit.

After Eve's lunchtime nap she bagged up all of the gifts for the Todd household and made her way around. The little ones were out at a pantomime with Carole's mam and dad, so she knew the coast was clear and could have gifts placed with the rest that Santa Claus brought.

It was a very jolly house indeed and Maggie found herself swept along on the excitement of Christmas Eve and ended up staying much longer than she had intended to. Back home, she gave Eve her nightly bath, fed her the final bottle of the day and put her down to sleep in her pram in the living room, which was her usual nightly routine. Eve would go up in her cot when Maggie went up to bed.

Dressed for bed, Maggie switched on the tv and watched the 9 o'clock news, though she found it difficult to concentrate, she found her mind wandering back to Christmas Eves past with Shaun, Stephen and Tom at the Hunters house. It was hard not to. It was such a poignant night of the year. A little ripple of what she could only think of was loneliness washed over her, but it passed and with the warmth of the heat from the living room fire, she dozed off.

Something woke her. Had something gone bump in the night? No, she could hear distant bells and glancing firstly at the pram with the sleeping Eve in and seeing all was well, she looked at the television and saw that there was a carol service playing and carols being sung.

There was the bump again though. And the bells?? The bump was someone knocking at the door. It was little after ten. It was chance to be Jude and Stephen calling on their way back from the pub making sure that she was all right. Making her way towards the door the bells were getting louder, they weren't the jingle jangle of Christmas carols, they were the alarm bells ringing in her head.

But by then she was at the front door, the only thought running through her head was that something had happened to someone. Her mam or dad? Her brothers?? Maggie couldn't get to the door and open it quick enough.

Only to find that the danger was staring her in the face. Tony Sharp. He had found her! He had found them!!

32) The Knight of Swords

Maggie had no choice but to let Tony Sharp in. The total shock of seeing him standing there had knocked her off kilter and she didn't want him to see her under pressure on the doorstep. Better to give herself a couple of minutes to compose herself while she showed him into the living room.

He made straight for the pram and the sleeping Eve.

Maggie was given a lot more than the couple of minutes she thought she was getting by letting him in. He must have stood looking into the pram for a good five minutes. At a loss what to do she made her way into the kitchen, flicked on the kettle and made a cup of coffee. She didn't have hot drinks herself but remembered from the perching on desks at Quarry's End that Tony Sharp was fond of a cup of coffee with milk and two sugars.

Back in the living room she handed Tony the cup of coffee and beckoned him to have a seat.

This was it she thought to herself. Time to come clean. The carol service was still playing on the television, but the alarm bells in her head had vanished. The danger was over, and Tony Sharp was going to be no threat to her or to Eve.

'She is beautiful Maggie!' Tony said perching himself on the edge of her living room chair. He looked strange being in Maggie's living room.

There was only the flickering light of the television and the twinkling of the lights on the Christmas tree lighting the room. He looked out of place, awkward. He looked scared. The alarm bells in her head remained silent.

Maggie had the strangest of feelings. He was as handsome as ever, more handsome if that was even possible and Maggie felt another little piece of her heart thaw and the tempo of her heart increase for a moment or two. 'Would you like to hold her?? Her name is Eve!'

It was gone midnight when Maggie Hunter closed the front door on Tony Sharp.

He had held Eve in his arms for the whole time. At first, he had been nervous in case he dropped her, but as they talked his confidence grew and he kept kissing her forehead and smelling her. Maggie talked first, there was no point hiding any of it, so he got the whole story, warts and all. The sickness, the beating and how Carole Todd had saved her life.

Tony apologised. He had been in a relationship with his girlfriend for a long time before Maggie had come along. He said he couldn't be sure if he had thought Maggie was his last hurrah, whatever she had been he said he was very fond of her. Said Quarry's End wasn't the same place without her. But his engagement party had gone ahead and yes, her mam and dad had gone! Maggie felt her tummy contract as if she had been punched at the mention of her mam and dad.

He had asked Leslie Hunter if Maggie was poorly, at first, he had said she was, that she had picked up some viral thing. Tony had asked each week that Maggie hadn't materialised until one week Leslie Hunter had looked at him as if he was scum. Tony had no idea why and then he was even more perplexed when Leslie Hunter had told him that Maggie wouldn't be coming back at all.

Mrs West had no idea what had happened either. She had obviously known that Maggie and Tony were close, but she said that she was as puzzled as he was about Maggie's illness and the news that she would now be returning to her post. Tony said that Mrs West was quite upset about the whole matter, she thought Maggie a very good typist. This news made Maggie smile.

Tony said that they hadn't particularly stayed long at the party. He couldn't even recall what her mam had looked like, just that she had been there. Leslie Hunter had barely spoken a word to him since Maggie worked there and it had crossed his mind whether he knew about their relationship, so he had sort of avoided them at the engagement party, it hadn't been the time or the place for revelations!

And that was all he knew about Maggie until the day he had passed her in the street when she was making her way back from the park pushing a pram.

Then everything had made sense. Tony said that he knew instantly that the baby in the pram was not just Maggie's, but also his.

Maggie was going to ask him about why he hadn't taken care of things. If he had, then none of this would had happened. But then what was the point. Eve was truly the best thing that had ever happened to her. It didn't matter that she was only 17 years old, what mattered was the love that this baby had brought with her, the contentment that she felt. Her sense of achievement, because Eve was thriving. So, she said nothing. There was no need for blame. It had happened. Shit happened.

Tony told Maggie that from then on in, he couldn't get the image of her and the pram out of his head. He had to find her.

He obviously couldn't ask Leslie, he didn't think he would have told him anyway, he hardly passed the time of day with Tony anymore. So, he had taken matters into his own hands and parked down the street from the Hunters in the hope of seeing Maggie coming or going. He obviously hadn't. He had seen Dorothy, or who he assumed to be Dorothy Hunter and Leslie travelling backwards and forward from the house. But there had been no sign of Maggie.

Tony Sharp knew that Maggie had brothers, there was a young lad that went in and out whom he assumed was the younger one. So, he started following him when he left. Maggie laughed when he said he had followed him to the shop twice, the chippy once and to some mates house.

Then one day he had struck lucky. He had followed Shaun to Carole Todd's house. Tony had sat outside and waited to see what fruitless journey he had made this time. He hadn't had to wait long, within 5 minutes Shaun was leaving the house, this time with a girl and another young lad. Tony knew that this was Maggie's older brother, he was identical to the other one apart from being slightly older and slightly taller. So, Tony followed them, kerb crawled he described it as.

Anyway, they didn't see him, luckily he had started to use the works truck and not his own car. Within 5 minutes they were walking up a garden path and into another house. Maggie's house.

Tony still wasn't sure at this point who the house belonged to. After an hour or so and there still being no sign of them leaving, Tony gave up, but made note of the address and vowed to come back another day and see who the occupant was.

The first opportunity had been that afternoon. Christmas Eve. The little house had been in darkness, but Tony had been determined and unless the occupant of the house was away for the festive season, his hunch told him that if he was patient, they would return.

He had been right. He had seen Maggie pushing the pram along the street, up the garden path and into the house. It was when she had returned from her afternoon at the Todd's' when she had been delivering the gifts and having a very jolly afternoon.

Tony had left, he had an Christmas Eve tea to attend, it was the first time in years they hadn't been abroad for Christmas but there had been a slump in business, they had to let a couple of lads go and it didn't seem right for them to do that and then gallivant off on holiday, so it was Christmas at home for them that year, but as soon as he could he had made his way back to Maggie's house. He had been sitting outside Maggie's house a good hour before he had plucked up the courage to knock on her door.

The rest as they say was history!

But he was so sorry. Sorry for everything that had happened to Maggie since he last saw her. Sorry about not telling Maggie he had a girlfriend. Sorry for seducing her. He was just sorry. To Maggie he was a sorry sight, and her heart went out to him. To be fair to Tony she could have contacted him at any point. It was her own choice not to, maybe she had been cruel to him not letting him know about Eve.

They had both made mistakes from beginning to end.

In the midst of all of the madness though, they had made the most beautiful little girl. The little girl who was sleeping peacefully in her daddy's arms for the first and maybe the last time.

Maggie had left the room at that point, she was shaking. It had been a most unexpected turn of events. She made another coffee for Tony and a cup of tea for herself, the same as the one she had been given in hospital the morning that she had given birth to Eve. She didn't normally do hot drinks, but this felt like a whiskey type of moment but seeing as she didn't drink either, a hot sweet cup of tea seemed like the most nerve calming solution available.

So now what??

Tony Sharp was getting married the following Spring. Obviously, a big lavish affair, both of the families were well heeled, so it was one of those big whistle and bell type weddings. It wouldn't do to upset the apple cart, Maggie's suggestion not Tony's!! His name hadn't been put on the birth certificate, there was just the words 'father unknown.' There was less than a dozen people who knew the truth, Maggie knew with certainty that none of her 'dysfunctional family' would spill the beans, her mam and dad wouldn't, they wouldn't want to lose face and if the whole sorry tale got out, then they would look far worse than Maggie or Tony would, especially Dorothy Hunter. It wasn't every mother who tried to kick the living daylights out of their daughter. No, the secret was safe if that was the way they decided to do it.

Much to Maggie's surprise, Tony was really upset. She had no idea what he thought was going to happen. Did he think that Maggie was going to beg him to be with her and be a family together? That was never going to happen. Even before Eve even existed Maggie's interest in Tony Sharp was beginning to fade. She had loved the driving dates and obviously those lush kissing sessions and she really liked his attention when he sat perched on her desk at Quarry's End. But the physical part of their relationship hadn't really worked, not if it was supposed to be how Jude and Linda said it should be like. No Maggie Hunter didn't want to go riding off into the sunset with Tony Sharp. He had been her first, but she was certain he wouldn't be her last. There was plenty of time for all of that when both she and Eve were older.

So, what to do??

There was no way that they could have regular contact, that wouldn't be fair on any of them. Tony and his new wife, Maggie and any future relationship she may have. Or Eve. She didn't want some once in a blue moon dad. This had to be it. For the foreseeable anyway. This had been a one off. A Christmas miracle in some respect. But Maggie knew in her heart that Tony would be back, he may not knock on the door or make his presence known, but she had the feeling that he would sit in his truck in the street and watch for them. She just had a feeling.

And for some reason she thought that Tony knew what he would do too.

He had a look of peace on his face as he placed Eve back in her pram, leant over and kissed her one last time. It was time for him to go!

At the door she put her arms around his neck and cuddled him in. He smelt gorgeous and memories of the lush kissing flooded her mind, but it wasn't going to happen. That part was all over now. There would be no more Maggie and Tony. But she was fond of him and they had made the most beautiful baby and it was Christmas so giving him a cuddle seemed to be fitting.

Closing the door behind him Maggie leant against it until she heard the sound of his car starting up and the familiar roar of the engine as he hustled off down the street.

It was Christmas Day, and it was time for Maggie and the little lady in the living room to go to bed. Santa wouldn't come if they stayed up any longer.

Later settled in her bed listening to the steady breathing of Eve in her cot, Maggie focused on an invisible spot of the ceiling just like she had when she was in her own bedroom at the Hunters. A million memories were running through her head like a movie. There were no ringing alarm bells in her head. All was calm and for some reason Maggie thought that for the first time in a very long time, all was bright.

33) The Page of Cups

Tony Sharp was the first of Maggie Hunter's Christmas surprises.

The second came after lunch at the Todd's' house. It had been a lovely day, she had slept later than she had expected to. It had been late to bed and late to rise, Eve had even slept on later than she would normally do, probably due to the late night visitor.

They had opened the gifts that had been left under the tree for them. There were toys and clothes for Eve and jarmies and smellies for Maggie all from the Todd's and Linda and Paul. Shaun and Stephen had said they wanted to give them their gifts when they saw them and she was excited to see what they had bought them, she couldn't ever remember even getting presents off them before.

Maggie and Eve both had new outfits to wear for the special day and just before 12 they were dressed and, on their way, around to the Todd's' where they would stay for the rest of the day!

David and Marc were so excited. Santa Claus had been, and the house was full of toys in all shapes and sizes. And it was also full of people. As well as the resident Todd's, there were both Carole and Glen's mam and dad, Carole's sister May and her husband along with two teenagers who Maggie seemed to think were twins, but looking at them she wasn't sure, one was a red head and the other a blonde so maybe there weren't. There was also Jude's dad, and he had his wife with him.

The best room which Maggie had spent all of those months staying in was back being the best room again and there was a huge dining table, which Maggie had never seen before all dressed ready for them all to sit down and share Christmas Dinner.

Shy at first with so many new faces and the usual feeling of what people would think of her having a baby when she was so young, she was happy when she didn't once see that look of 'slut' cross any of their faces. There were only smiles. And Eve was ruined. Everyone fussed over her, and she gurgled away and kicked her legs with joy at each and every one of them that showed her any attention.

By the time they all sat around at the dining room table, her brother Stephen had arrived. Maggie hadn't been sure if he was going to be there. But he had been asked by Carole Todd and not by his mam so to the Todd's he did go. It made Maggie feel a little sad, what was Christmas Day like at the Hunter's house??

But she was determined that she was not going to be glum. She hadn't seen them for almost a year. They had made no effort to see if she was ok. No effort to see their grandchild and no effort to see how they were living. The beautiful people who sat around the dining table were her family now. They were the ones that had given both Eve and herself gifts, but more than that, they treat her like she was one of them. That she had always had her place at the table.

After dinner they all sat stuffed in various parts of the house. Eve was having a much needed afternoon nap in her pram, there had been so many people and so much attention she had started to get over excited and tired. Maggie sat with Jude and Stephen, Shaun was coming at some point that afternoon and as they waited the three of them had a game of cards, just like Maggie and Stephen would have done if they had been at home. It had a surreal feel about it which Maggie was sure that Stephen felt too.

At some time in the afternoon Shaun turned up bearing gifts. There was a big box for Maggie, but better than that was the surprise that followed him into the best room. Tom Grey was standing in the doorway, Maggie was up off her feet and flinging herself into his arms in seconds, she was just so pleased to see him. As he was her. They had always had a special bond. It was neither the time or the place to talk, but as she cuddled in Tom said he was going to go back to her house with her, they would talk then! Maggie felt the drip drip drip of her heart as it thawed a little bit more. The familiar tempo as it sped up and thumped a little bit harder for the next few minutes. She was most definitely almost back to her normal self, there was only a fragment now that remained frozen. The part that belonged to her mam and dad. That part may never thaw, but she could live with that. The rushing of the blood around her body was enough, she could love and be loved with what she had.

The huge box turned out to be her record player from home, along with her collection of records and some new ones that Shaun, Stephen and Tom had bought her. How she had missed her music. She would listen to the radio at her house, but her collection of records had been built up over the years, it was the best present they could have given her.

By the time they had all had more food, played more games and generally had a really nice time, it was dark outside, and Maggie decided that she would get Eve home before it got too dark and too cold. Eve had sent most of the afternoon with her Uncle Tom who had taken to Eve as much as she had taken to him. Even when Eve was somewhere else in the room, she craned her neck to see where Tom was, the silly man that made noises and didn't seem to be the slightest bit embarrassed that he was communicating with a 6 month old baby, generally in her own language.

Again, Maggie could not thank Carole Todd and her family enough. She left with an abundance of left overs and kisses on her cheeks from everyone. Shaun had decided he would stay, Linda and Paul were due sometime early evening and they were going to be having a bit of a party. Maggie didn't blame him, by now Tom's mam and dad would have left the Hunters and she couldn't imagine it being much fun.

But Tom was going home with her. She pushed the pram and he carried the gift the few minutes' walk from one house to the other. As they walked, they talked. It was just so lovely to see him and be with him.

34) The Sun

Back at Maggie's he said how impressed he was with the home she had made for herself and Eve. They busied themselves putting food away, sorting Eve and generally tidying everything up. By the time Eve was having her supper bottle, Tom had set up the record player and was busy choosing what they would be listening to.

Eve settled and asleep in her pram, the cousins each took an end on the sofa, placed sweets and crisps between them and began to fill in the missing pieces.

Maggie told her news first. It was clear to Tom what the majority of her time had taken up doing. But she went back to the beginning. Back to when she had wanted to go and work at the hairdressers, ending up at Quarry's End, Tony Sharp and the perching on desks. Followed by the driving dates and the lush kissing and the bit that she thought that he was taking care of and obviously wasn't. She told Tom about being so sick and the alarm bells ringing in her head. Her absence from Quarry's End and then the realisation that she was in trouble. How amazing Carole Todd had been and how she had encouraged her to tell her mam and dad what was happening.

She did think about omitting the good hiding she got off Dorothy Hunter, after all her mam was Tom's mam's sister, but she had gone so far, and it was a very important part of what had happened and why she was where she was now! So, she spat it all out, showed him the scar on her head where the plate had cut her. She told him of how she had nowhere else to go and Carole Todd and her family had taken her in, cared for her, helped her to heal and helped her just survive.

Maggie tod Tom about the night that Eve had been born, that Carole Todd had been with her every step of the way, how her whole family helped, including Jude and her friend Linda and then there was Shaun and Stephen.

She finished her tale with the story of the time that she had been walking back from the park and Tony Sharp had stopped at the kerbside and looked at her and Eve and how nervous it had made her feel after that. And then she told him of the night before, of Christmas Eve and the visitor who had arrived at her home in the shape of Tony Sharp and the subsequent conversation after that.

Maggie had told no one about Tony Sharp coming to visit her and Eve. It wasn't the type of conversation she could have had on a boisterous Christmas Day with the house bursting to the rafters, she would tell Carole Todd, but when there was just the two of them and they could talk quietly. His appearance had still unnerved her a little bit, the sight of him sitting in her living room nursing his daughter was an image that she would remember for all time. She had no idea if there would ever be a 'father-daughter' relationship, she doubted it, but it would be a story to tell Eve one day, if she needed to. The Christmas Eve that Eve's dad had spent with her.

And that was basically all of Maggie's news. Obviously, there were other bits and bobs that Tom would find out over the course of the night.

But for now, that was it and it was time to find out what had happened to Tom Grey in the year that had passed since she had last seen him.

'Well, I've obviously not had as dramatic a year as you, but still I think I may have caused my own form of drama!!' Tom started.

Tom Grey had not been given the chance to make roads to university. There was no sponsorship and there had been no art degree, not the way he had planned when they had last spoken. Tom had left school the same year that Maggie had and had gone into 6th form in preparation for A Levels and then University. But Tom hadn't settled in 6th form, he was taking art at A 'Level but the course was taking him far far away from where his talents lay, and he said that he was not only putting himself under pressure but he was becoming a nervous wreck. It was a different set of school friends and he felt that he just didn't quite fit in.

So, in a dramatic change of events, after the last Christmas they had spent together, Tom Grey left 6th form and took on a full time position working at the same factory as his mam, on the production line of a toilet roll making manufacturer.

Hardly the job of his dreams, but just like Maggie had at Quarry's End, he enjoyed receiving a little pay packet every week and the more he got to know the people he worked with the more he liked it. Tom enjoyed the banter at work, the production line was predominately women, and he was good with them, his soft side which had made him different at school was embraced in his work place and he quickly became one of the 'girls!'

Not following his dream of University and a degree was softened by the fact he could now afford to buy art materials, so his spare time was spent creating lovely pieces which he took into the factory and sold to his workmates, the more he sold the more his confidence was growing. He became the go to man when anyone was looking for a little gift for someone. He said he had more money than he knew what to do with. And it got better!!

When he was in the art and craft shop buying supplies, he spotted a notice for a fine art class starting at the local technical college one night a week. Tom could do what he could but needed more training so found himself signing up for the course and that was how he now spent his Monday evenings. These had been his type of people. He had found his place. The Monday nights soon turned into Friday night suppers and Sunday afternoon walks. Describing them it made Maggie think of Carole Todd and her family, how they had been while Carole had been growing up. Was bohemian the word she would use to describe them? Whatever it was, Maggie was so pleased that her cousin Tom had found them!

And there was more!!

Tom Grey had met someone. It was the lecturer at his technical college. His name was John, and he was a lot older than Tom. Way older. But Tom said that the minute he walked into the art room and saw John standing there, he knew not only what he was, but he knew where he wanted to be and who he wanted to be with.

By all accounts it had been a slow burn. Weeks and weeks of classes and Friday night suppers and Sunday afternoon walks as a group, but slowly they started to gyrate towards each other. They would sit next to each other at Friday night supper and walk together on Sunday afternoons, sometimes oblivious to everyone one else in the group.

Until it was Tuesday night cinema, Saturday night takeaway and Sunday morning breakfast.

As Tom Grey spoke his whole face lit up. Granny Hunter had been right, Tom certainly was a Friend of Dorothy's and Maggie could not have been happier. And she couldn't wait to meet this lecturer John that was making her cousin shine like a beacon.

Tom spent a lot of time at John's house. As far as his mam and dad were concerned it was on the pretext that he had an art studio which he let Tom work in as and when he wanted. But Tom said that they weren't daft, it was just something that they wouldn't talk about. He never took John home and he kept conversation about him at a minimum and spoke mainly about work when he was at home, which was becoming less and less. The good thing was though, Auntie Joan and Uncle Ken didn't banish Tom from their lives whatever life style he was keeping. They would rather not know about it than not know him. But then unlike Maggie's very public shame in the form of Eve, Tom could live a kind of double life. But still, it irked Maggie that two sisters could have such different views about being liberal.

So, Tom Grey apologised. He had been so wrapped up in his own life he hadn't noticed that there was something very wrong in his cousin's.

He knew that something had happened. His mam and auntie Dorothy hadn't spoken for months. There had been no family Christmas that year. For the first time in his living memory, Tom had spent Christmas in their own home, just the three of them.

Hand on heart Tom went on, he hadn't realised that he hadn't spoken to Maggie until he started working at the loo roll factory. He said something funny would happen and he said he would make a mental note to tell Maggie, then he realised that he hadn't actually spoken to her since the Christmas before. So, he had rang the Hunter's house just to be told off his Auntie Dorothy that Maggie wasn't there. And then he rang again and again and got the same line. 'Maggie wasn't there!' Which was strictly true, Maggie wasn't there, but Auntie Dorothy hadn't elaborated and said she wasn't there because she wasn't living there and not just not actually out of the house at that time.

Tom had asked his mam. She had also been vague, there had been a fall out or something. So, he got sly and started ringing the Hunter house on a Saturday when there was a chance that his Auntie Dorothy and Uncle Leslie would be out shopping. Surely at some point Shaun or Stephen would answer and he might get some answers, Tom was beginning to worry.

His persistence paid off and he eventually managed to speak to Shaun, who was equally vague but agreed to meet up with his cousin in town the following weekend and he would explain everything.

That had only been at the beginning of December!! Tom and Shaun had sat in a café in Newcastle and Shaun had told him the whole sorry tale.

Shock after shock. Maggie, his Auntie Dorothy and Uncle Leslie, Stephen leaving home. He knew nothing about any of it. How had Maggie gone through so much and he hadn't known about it, it was well seeing that the second sight that Maggie had ran through her dad's side of the family and not her mam's! Tom had felt like absolute crap, he had been so wrapped up in himself he had never given his cousin a second thought.

But as he told Shaun, he would put it right!

Tom's mam and dad weren't shocked at all. Dorothy Hunter had given her sister the gist about what had happened with Maggie, omitting some of the most dramatic parts and basically implying that Maggie had taken herself off to God knows where. Joan Grey had been furious that her sister had no idea where her niece was and had said as much, from then on in Dorothy Hunter cut the Greys from their life. To all intents and purposes, the Hunter family consisted of Dorothy, Leslie and Shaun, even Stephen stretching his wings and moving out hadn't gone down well and he too was cast aside, though not as dramatically as Maggie had been!!

It made Maggie smile when Tom said that his mam and dad would like to see Maggie, and they were excited to meet Eve, there would always be a welcome at their house for her. It gave Maggie a little shiver down her spine, her little family was growing by the minute.

And that basically brought everything up to date. Tom was loving his art, more so now that he was encouraged and taught by John. The same John who had picked him up from home after Christmas dinner with his mam and dad and drove him from their town to here, picked up Shaun and the gifts and dropped them off at the Todd's' earlier that day. The same John who would be collecting Tom tomorrow and taking him to spend Boxing Day with their friends from the art classes, Friday night suppers and Sunday afternoon walks.

In Maggie's mind, Tom Grey had eventually found himself. He was the happiest she had ever seen him, he seemed to be happy in his own skin and with the people who got him. She didn't think for one moment that her Auntie Joan and Uncle Ken would cast him aside, no matter where his preferences with regard to who he fell in love with. They might not have been singing it from the rooftops, but they would certainly not risk losing the son over it.

It was hard to believe it was almost midnight, again. Maggie had a spare rooms, but they literally empty apart from the stuff that Maggie dumped in them, but she had spare blankets for when people had sleepovers and Tom would be doing what Jude or Shaun or Linda did and sleep on the sofa.

It wasn't until she was heading back down the stairs that she noticed a Christmas card at the front door, she was positive it hadn't been there when they had got home earlier, she would have run over it with the pram. But there it was larger than life on the mat, it was actually large, not a big card but it was a very bulky one.

Dumping the blankets on Tom she tore the envelope open. 'Merry Christmas to Someone Special'. There was another envelope inside the card, sealed and very bulky. The card itself had no name on, it hadn't been written in at all, but there was a note.

> *Maggie*
>
> *Im not sure where to start or what to say. Apart from I am sorry, for everything. You are the bravest person I have ever known, and I know that you will be an amazing mother to Eve with or without my help.*
>
> *I know that this goes nowhere near what you will need but I hope that it helps a little for now.*
>
> *Thank you for letting me spend time with you and Eve, I will be forever grateful. I have no idea what the future has in store for any of us but for now I think I need to be a coward and say goodbye. There are just too many other people that this would hurt.*
>
> *Merry Christmas Mags – kiss Eve for me.*
>
> *Tony xxx*

Maggie opened the envelope and there was a bundle of cash, an amount she had never seen before. Handing the card, note and money over to Tom, she said goodnight, lifted a sleeping Eve out of her pram and made for bed.

Sleep didn't come easy, she stared at her spot on the ceiling for a very long time. But there were no noises, no alarm bells, no feeling of dread. If she strained her ears, she could hear the sound of Tom Grey snoring on her sofa. She quietly got out of bed, spent a penny and as she returned to her room she left the door open behind her, The noise of Tom Grey's snoring downstairs was like music to her ears and within minutes she was fast asleep. Tony Sharp had been some sort of Christmas apparition. He was like Santa Claus. He had turned up on Christmas Eve, left a gift on Christmas Day and then was gone, until the next year…????

There had been £2000 in the envelope off Tony Sharp. A massive amount of money. Tom Grey had it all counted into little piles by the time Maggie and Eve came down in the morning. The note had been placed in the card and was placed beside the money. She didn't want to read it again, it would go in the bottom of her jewellery box with all the other things she couldn't face.

Tom left her mid-morning, he was going to walk back around and wait beside the Todd's for John to pick him up, then it would be party party party. Maggie was sad to see him leave, it had been an emotional few days and she could have really done with keeping his company, but he had plans of his own and in the bigger picture, she was just so happy she had him back.

With nothing else to do, Boxing Day turned out to be like any other day of the week. She could have gone around and saw Carole or Jude, but she felt a little bit wired and thought a day of just doing her own thing would be better for her.

So, she did her washing and hoovered around. She played with Eve and while she had her afternoon nap, she counted the money that Tony Sharp had left for her. Sure, enough there was £2000, a fortune. Hush money?? Maybe, he certainly wouldn't want her Announcing him the father of her baby and scuppering his wedding plans and probably his future. A leg up?? Probably. Maggie did feel that Tony Sharp wouldn't want Maggie or Eve to be short of money. But what to do with it.

Eve didn't particularly need anything. Maggie would maybe decorate the spare bedrooms, especially the bigger one in readiness for Eve needing it. But in truth that was months away, Maggie liked having Eve close by so she could hear her, they would probably end up in bunk beds at some point and more than likely sharing a bedroom forever.

Maggie would talk to Carole Todd about it. She was always the voice of reason in her mad world. For now, it would go in her infamous jewellery box with her other keepsakes.

Record player on, it was time to get lost in music. Until nap time was over anyway!

35) The Three of Pentacles

The New Year brought new opportunities for Maggie.

She had been right to go and speak to Carole Todd, she had known what to do. The money had been deposited in her Post Office account, it was a nice little nest egg to have, something for a rainy day.

Carole had come up with an idea though. Maggie had turned out to be a very proficient typist, Carole said that she had often seen little adverts for 'home typists' in the Post Office and local shop, maybe it would be a good idea for Maggie to use some of the money she had got to buy herself a little typewriter and take work in to do at home!

It was a perfect solution for Maggie. As much as she loved being mam to Eve, she needed to be doing something for herself too beyond housework. And joy of joy, they sold electric typewriters in Carole's catalogue, and desks and chairs. The year had barely began and all the items were delivered and she set herself up a little work place in her living room.

The first thing she did when she was set up was to type out some little cards offering her services along with her telephone number, followed by a morning of visiting various shops, the library and local college pinning her cards up. All she had to do was wait for the telephone to ring.

Carole Todd hadn't been surprised that Tony Sharp had shown his face on Christmas Eve. She had always felt that it would only ever be a matter of time once he had seen Maggie pushing a pram around the town. What had taken her by surprise was the money, he hadn't needed to. He could see for himself that Maggie was coping very well on her own. But he seemed to be a better man than she had first thought and as long as he left them alone and didn't mess with Maggie's head, then her opinion of him would remain as was.

Maggie was beginning to think that she had wasted her money buying herself a typewriter out of the money. No one rang as she thought they would have when her little cards went up.

But she would wait. If that failed then she would talk to Carole about something else, she had an answer for everything. She needn't have worried though, a girl rang and asked about typing up her dissertation for University, Maggie asked her to bring her work to her home, a price was set, and Maggie had her first paid typist job.

A playpen was purchased for Eve out of her first pay, she was a proper little wiggler and could get herself off her back and onto her tummy and then keep going, Maggie needed her to be safe whilst she worked, so the playpen was set up next to her little desk and she could keep an eye on her whilst she played.

Maggie enjoyed the work. After the first telephone call, there were others. It was always something different. She did work for individuals but also for companies too. Soon she was having to keep a little diary with deadline dates on.

After the playpen came the baby monitor. If Maggie was going to keep up with her work load, she would sometimes have to work into the night. Though the tap tap tap buzz of the typewriter didn't seem to bother Eve sleeping, she didn't want to disturb her, so she would often put Eve up to bed, turn the baby monitor on and get on with her tasks.

In the beginning she spent more time running up and down the stairs to check on her than she did typing, but she got used to it and although she found she couldn't not check on her every now and again, she would rely on the baby monitor to listen out for her waking or crying.

36) The Star

Winter turned to Spring.

Preparations were well under way for Linda and Paul's wedding in the summer. There had been another dress fitting and Maggie was delighted that the remainder of her baby bump had all but disappeared and her bridesmaid dress fit her perfectly.

Maggie and Eve also made their way to see Auntie Joan and Uncle Ken. It was quite a trek on two buses with a baby and a pram, but she had managed, and they had been over the moon to see her and to meet Eve. There had been no mention of Maggie's mam and dad which was a bit strange because the two families had always been so close, but to Maggie it seemed that her aunt and uncle had also been cast out by the Hunters.

She saw Tom a lot more. He would often pop in for his tea, his good friend John would drop him off and then return to Maggie's house to collect Tom a few hours later. At first, he would just sit in the car waiting for Tom who always did the longest goodbyes. But on Maggie's insistence, after about the 6th visit, John was brought in for a coffee. Maggie wasn't surprised that he was older than Tom, he was a lecturer after all, but what did surprise her was that he was quite a bit older, well a lot older. He sat awkwardly on Maggie's sofa sipping on a coffee and listening to Tom regale him on all Eve's progress in the time since he had last seen her.

Maggie instantly liked John. There was just something about him as he sat drinking his coffee. She knew it wouldn't be good, she didn't drink coffee at all and always struggled with how much to actually spoon in and had a feeling that she over did it. But John was drinking his as if it was the best cup of coffee he had ever tasted. There was just something about him, Carole Todd had the same sort of effect on Maggie. Whenever she was with Carole, Maggie felt like she could take on the world. But that was a trust thing, she had literally trusted Carole with her life. John had only been sitting on her sofa for 10 minutes.

It was his aura. Maggie could see it. She was taken aback, she had never seen an aura before, but there it was as clear as day. There was a purply/blue mist all around him and Maggie instantly knew that not only was he a kind and gentle man, but he was as connected to the spirit world as much as she was. It was something she would find out about him another time. She couldn't just say 'Hi John, do you get alarm bells ringing in your head when something bad or dangerous is going to happen?' Not five minutes after meeting him anyway.

But it made her feel happy that Tom was with someone that would care for him. It didn't matter that he was older, a lot older. What mattered was someone knowing Tom Grey inside and out, making him happy and keeping him safe. Maggie knew without a shadow of a doubt that the lovely gentleman, yes gentleman because that was what he was, would be the person to do that.

After seeing John's aura, Maggie began to see them everywhere. She didn't particularly look for them and she didn't see them around people she knew, but she saw them around people who called to her house to deliver and collect typing work, or a shop assistant. She also knew what the colours meant even though she shouldn't do. Red – passionate, orange – adventurous, yellow – creative. And so, it went on. She would see it and then next time she wouldn't. Unless something changed. There was a lady that used her to type up invoices and such like for her business. When she first met her she had an orange adventurous hue around her. Then there was none. One day she turned up and she was surrounded in red. Puzzled, it wasn't until the lady told her that she had been away on holiday and had met a man, a holiday romance. Love and passionate red!

Maggie kept her new found skill to herself!! She really was just like her Granny Hunter!!

Summer came. And Eve had her first birthday.

They had a little party at the Todd's for her. She really was the apple of everyone's eye, even David and Marc Todd made a huge fuss of her. It was hard to believe that she was one year old. More the fact that Maggie had managed to keep her alive. She had so little experience of babies and what to do with them, but so far it bad been so good. It helped that Carole Todd was only ever a telephone call away.

Maggie had her first night out in a very long time. It was just to Linda's house for her hen party, but it had been a good night and it had been lovely making an effort and getting dressed up. It was nice to feel like a normal teenager, though she did talk an awful lot about Eve to schoolfriends who she hadn't seen for ages. At the end of the night, when she went home it was to an empty house, Eve was spending the night with Carole Todd. After all the high jinx of the hen party, the house seemed very quiet. For the first time in quite some time, when she lay her head on her pillows, she stared at the spot on the ceiling which she did when she was a bit off and thought about her life.

Would she always be on her own? Well not on her own, she had Eve. But would she ever be having a hen party in preparation for marrying the man of her dreams. Her second sight wouldn't allow her the luxury of giving her hope of this. There was just the sound of silence. A wave of loneliness washed over her, thoughts of the lush kissing with Tony Sharp flooded her mind. He was in her past though still very much in her future with regards to Eve.

Beautiful, sunny, funny Eve. Her heart swelled with love and pride. The loneliness ebbed away and Maggie fell into a dreamless sleep. Something woke her, something going bump in the night?? She woke but there was nothing, but if she had woken up properly, she might have heard the distant sound of alarm bells. She might had listened to the noise in her head and been alert to what was ahead. Dean Burns. She hadn't met him yet. But there was trouble ahead, somewhere in the distance there was heartbreak waiting for her. If only she had woken up!

37) *The Knight of Pentacles*

Linda and Paul had a beautiful wedding day. The sun shone and as they stood at the altar shafts of it filtered through the stained-glass window and danced around the church. Linda looked stunning, she looked so grown up, mature. It was her 18th birthday and they had all drank champagne together while they got ready in Linda's bedroom. Well Maggie, Jude and Linda did. The other two bridesmaids were just little so had fizzy lemonade, which Maggie switched for herself when no one was looking. Champagne wasn't for her.

The girls were all pretty in peach, at first Maggie had felt a bit daft, she had a crown of peach flowers perched on her head and she was sure it was going to fall off as she followed Linda down the aisle, but it had survived well into the dancing at the disco later in the night.

And it was at that disco to celebrate the marriage of her best friend Linda that Maggie met Dean Burns. The second man who would grab her attention. The second man who set off her alarm bells, only this time Maggie knew what the ringing was about, swallowed it down and dampened the noise until she couldn't hear it. This time when the lush kissing moved on to the next part she was into it as much as Dean was. It was what 'doing it' was all about, and she couldn't get enough of him.

Dean Burns was a workmate of the groom Paul. He was 21, dark and handsome but Maggie wouldn't describe him as tall, he was maybe an inch or two taller than her in her kitten heels. He had arrived at the party with a bunch of lads, varying in ages so Maggie assumed that they were all Paul's workmates.

They were a rowdy bunch, as lads tended to be and she assumed that they had been somewhere for drinks before their arrival at the social club function room where the celebration was taking place. Maggie happened to be with Linda when they arrived and as Paul introduced his new wife to his friends, he introduced Maggie to them too. Straightaway Dean Burns marked Maggie's card, promising her a spin around the dance floor later. Maggie didn't mind, she had noticed Dean the minute he walked through the door, there was just something about him and because she had drank a couple of glasses of cider, when his eyes met her gaze, she gazed at him right back. Dutch courage.

So, after the 'thank you all for coming' speech and the buffet, Maggie found herself being taken by the hand and led onto the dance floor by Dean. And there they stayed. They danced in a big circle with everyone else, they danced with the bride and groom and with Jude and Stephen and at the end of the night they just danced with each other. Out of the corner of her eye she could see Dean's workmates all looking and pointing, but she didn't care. Dean's arms around her waist, her arms around his neck felt the most natural thing in the world.

When the lights went on and they followed everyone out of the building to wave goodbye to Linda and Paul as they went off as their first night as husband and wife, Maggie had no hesitation in letting Dean Burns walk her home. She heard the bells, Dean was obviously dangerous, but what was the worst that could happen. Hadn't everything that could have gone wrong already happened when she got involved with Tony Sharp.

Whatever feeling it was that Maggie had for Dean Burns it was new and she wasn't going to let the thought of being pregnant and abandoned not let her take a risk. She was at least going to let him walk her home, she would tell him about Eve, if anything was going to put him off her that would. And if he was going to run off, at least she wouldn't have walked home on her own.

The fifteen minute walk from the social club to Maggie's front door took them over an hour. It was a warm night and they meandered along the street getting to know each other. Dean was a chatterbox. He talked of his love of cars, how there had been no other job in the whole world for him. How once he could get his driving licence that had been it. He liked to race, most weekends he would be away at some meeting somewhere or other racing his car around and around a track. He had bought a cheap car and had spent all of his spare time doing it up specially to race in. So far, he had done ok he said, he was no Ayrton Senna but loved everything about racing his car. And he was all of his mates best friend, as most mechanics were.

Dean lived across town, still lived at home with his mam and dad and two younger sisters, he seemed happy to still be there. As far as Maggie could make out there had been girlfriends in the past, nothing serious but at the minute he was footloose and single. If she did get involved with Dean, she thought her biggest rival for his affection would be his car. She could deal with that.

Maggie told Dean about Eve. She didn't go into the nitty gritty, but when he asked her questions about Eve and who the father was and where he was now, she simply told him. There was no point in hiding it, people talked and if they did become an item them someone would break their neck to tell him. Better to just get it out there.

And still he walked at her side.

By the time that they arrived at Maggie's front door, it felt like they had always walked side by side. They seemed to be instep.

Maggie was unsure what she was supposed to do. Should she invite him in. Eve was staying at Carole Todd's for the night so there would be no harm asking him in, but she was 17 year old with a baby, the images of all of those faces that said 'slut' when she was pregnant with Eve raced through her head like a slideshow. The alarm bells were ringing, not as loudly as they had done in the past, but still they were still there clanging along.

When Dean leant in and kissed her it was job done. The lush Tony Sharp kisses faded into history forever, they paled in significance. This was kissing Maggie thought to herself.

She could no longer hear the alarm bells ringing, her head was all whooshy with want and need and without any hesitation, Maggie Hunter lead Dean Burns by the hand, into her house, into her bed and into her life. It was what 'doing it' was all about and she well and truly 'did it!'

38) The Two of Cups

soulmate. or soul mate (sōl'māt') n. One of two persons compatible with each other in disposition, point of view, or sensitivity.

Maggie Hunter and Dean Burns were perfect for each other. He was the Ying to her Yang. They just fit. On the Sunday morning after the wedding, when Maggie woke up in her bed and Dean was there with her, she knew that she wanted to wake up with him there every morning. And he clearly felt the same.

From then on in it was a whirlwind.

If anyone thought it was too soon and far too fast, they never said. Not even wise and wonderful Carole Todd who was Maggie's oracle and advisor. All she cared about was Maggie and Eve's happiness and Dean Burns seemed to tick both their boxes. So, Carole welcomed Dean into the dysfunctional family they had made and he slid into the spot as if it had always been his.

Dean was hard working, reliable and kind. Maggie Hunter could not believe her luck. The alarm bells that had first started ringing when she first met Dean Burns all but vanished, for a while anyway.

And how Eve took to Dean. She would smile and bat her eyelids at him. Shout for his attention if he ignored her and as soon as she could crawl would climb up his legs the minute he arrived at the house.

Dean virtually moved in straightaway. For the first few weeks he would just do weekends, but then a Sunday night was added on, he would just go straight to work from Maggie's. And then he would come for his tea on a Wednesday and just stay. Before long he was there every night of the week. Some nights he would arrive home from work later than others, there was always someone's car to fix or his own 'race car' that would need something done to it. But Maggie didn't mind, she was as busy as ever with her typing work, as long as he turned up by bedtime, she was happy. More so that she got to wake up in a morning with him.

Every weekend he took himself off to some race somewhere, at times he would be missing all weekend because they had to travel and it took ages with the race car on the back of a trailer, but his friend James had a van so they would sleep in that. Again, Maggie didn't mind, she still had Eve and would often take herself off to Carole Todd's for Sunday lunch and a catch up.

Maggie had her 18th birthday, she didn't want any fuss, she had caused enough already in her life, but they all went to Carole's who tried not to make any fuss and only did a buffet and got her a cake. More of a get together than a party. Linda and Paul had been invited and of course Jude and Stephen and Shaun who brought his girlfriend, which was a surprise for everyone because he hadn't even said he had one.

There had been no card off her mam and dad, not that Maggie thought there would be, but she had still hoped that her 18th might have been an opportunity to reach out with the olive branch. Shaun was still living at home, but he barely spoke about them and as ever, Maggie didn't ask.

She had so much to be grateful for and more so than ever with the arrival of Dean Burns into her life.

Maggie had seen sight of her mam and dad. The first time in almost two years. She had been in Dean's car and had instantly recognised her dad's car coming towards them down the road. They didn't see her, they would not of known about her travelling in her boyfriend's car, so as his car passed theirs Maggie got an opportunity to look at them without them noticing. They looked exactly the same. Maggie could feel the lump in her throat and the tears begin to prick behind her eyes. How could this have happened? How could her parents drive past her and not only not be able to acknowledge them, but know that even if they saw their daughter, they would ignore her.

And then they were gone, and Maggie put all thoughts of any reconciliation to the back of her mind. She had her own family of sorts now and she would concentrate on them.

Dean's family had turned out to be lovely. Eve was a good little ice breaker and any awkward moments about how Eve had come to be were soon forgotten as Eve Hunter stole the show. Dean said that all that his mam and dad ever wanted was for their children to be happy, he was the happiest he had ever been so in turn they were happy too. It made no odds that she already had a child, they just hoped that there would be more.

A wish that was granted sooner than they would have thought. Because just as Maggie took the little Christmas tree she had purchased the year earlier out of her loft, the nausea returned. Unfortunately for Dean, it had been brought on by the smell of oil and petrol, a smell that hung on him constantly. But this time it seemed to be the only thing that set her off. This time she knew what to do. This time she was in a completely different situation. She loved Dean with every fibre of her body, and she instinctively knew that he loved her completely the same back.

Christmas was both joyous and triumphant. Christmas Day with at Carole Todd's with all of the family, Boxing Day with Dean's family. Stephen had proposed to Jude on Christmas morning which made Christmas extra special, Stephen had ran it past Maggie, he was so needlessly insecure because there was no doubt that Jude wouldn't say yes.

So as the New Year rolled in, the three school friends lives were beginning to look very grown up. Maggie had Eve and now Dean and a new baby on the way, which was still under wraps. Linda and Paul were newly married and now there was to be another wedding to plan in the shape of Jude marrying Maggie's big brother Stephen. The future was looking bright.

With her pregnancy confirmed, which looked like it was going to be another June baby, Maggie and Dean spread their glad tidings. The sickness that had blighted the first couple of months passed and this time, Maggie bloomed.

She was under no illusion that having 2 under 2 was going to be easy. But Dean was so good with Eve and fussed around Maggie constantly that she knew no matter what they would cope. It was just the whole labour thing, the pain, the alarm bells ringing in her head. As excited as she was to see her second child, she knew what lay ahead and that filled her with dread, it was way too soon. The memory of Eve's birth was still etched very much in her memory, but if she lived to be 100 it would still be there. Giving birth was barbaric.

And if trundled on. Spring became early summer and with that Maggie was once again the size of a detached house. Her energy knew no bounds and she would walk Eve to the park and back each day, scrub the house to within an inch of its life and poor Dean had no peace, her appetite for him was insatiable. Whenever there was an opportunity to 'do it' she was having it.

For Eve's 2nd birthday they had a party at their house. It was touch and go because Maggie's due date was within days of the event, so the slightest twinge would set Maggie spinning, she just wanted Eve to have her special day. And she managed to hold on, everyone came and for the first time in her life since her life with her mam and dad, Maggie was content.

Shaun still had his girlfriend who was less new and more part of the fixtures and fittings now. She was called Jill and went to the same college as Shaun doing something sporty. All the Todd's were there, Jude and Stephen who were in the midst of trying to not only buy a house but organise a wedding for around Christmastime. They were a jolly bunch who stood around Eve and sang happy birthday to Eve as she attempted to blow out the two little candles on her cake.

After they had cleared away and people were beginning to leave, Maggie had an overwhelming urge for Carole Todd to take Eve home with her. It was just a feeling, nothing seemed to be happening, but still. As soon as she voiced her thoughts, Carole had a bag packed for Eve and was ushering everyone out of the door, with a promise from Maggie that if anything happened she would call, no matter what time it was.

Dean helped Maggie into a huge bubble bath, she found it so difficult to get in and out of the bath these day. Just like Eve had done the first time around, the baby loved to be in the warm water being coo 'ed at and splashed with water. Maggie hadn't been in the bath 5 minutes when the bump she was pouring water onto did an almighty move, she felt something pop and the water was filled with goo and stuff as Maggie's waters broke.

Dean got Maggie out of the bath, dried and into some clothes in no time. He rang the maternity ward to tell them they were coming, followed by a quick call to Carole and had them into the car and on their way within minutes.

The alarm bells were ringing at a siren like sound as they pulled up outside the hospital, the porter sat Maggie in a wheelchair and she was pushed through the corridors of the hospital and into the delivery suite. No time to wait she thought she heard the midwife say as she was examined, but as it had been last time, she could barely hear through the sounds in her head.

The pain was if anything worse than the first time. Maggie didn't know where she wanted to be. It was wave after wave all over again. Dean looked terrified. Later he told her it was like watching a horror movie, he could see what was happening but couldn't do anything to help. And unlike a movie, he couldn't just stand up and walk out like he would have at a cinema. The pain just kept on coming. It was just pain.

And then it was the urge to push. The overwhelming, uncontrollable urge to push her baby out of her body as if it was burning her body alive. She pushed and she pushed and the alarm bells in her head got shriller and shriller and whatever the midwife was trying to instruct her fell on deaf ears. She actually thought that this baby was going to split her whole body in two and at one point she even thought it was coming out of her bum!!

Every part of her body had a life of its own. And all she could do was push, she could see her actions were causing her midwife distress but she couldn't stop. At the moment that she felt her body literally tear itself in half, it was over. The alarm bells stopped ringing and the only thing she could hear was the crying of her new born baby and the quiet sobbing of her boyfriend.

Exhaustion overcame her and she fell asleep virtually at the minute the baby left her body. It must have only been for a matter of minutes, a pain tore through her body and she was wide awake. This time there were no alarm bells, there was a different midwife standing between her legs instructing what she needed to do. She heard every word. The placenta?? No one warned her that the placenta would feel like labour all over again, she couldn't remember this happening last time. What if they were wrong and it was another baby? But it wasn't and within minutes Maggie could feel something slither out of her body and it was all over.

39) The Ace of Wands

Maggie Hunter and Dean Burns had a son.

At almost 9lbs he missed being born on his big sister's birthday by minutes.

He was perfect, placid and by the time Maggie was discharged from hospital the day after his birth, he was named Ryan Dean Burns.

Eve thought he was a doll and kept trying to pick him up so Maggie found that she needed to have eyes in the back of her head. Dean was great with all of them and was almost pained when he needed to go to work each morning. He even gave up his weekend racing for the first few months so he could spend time with his family.

The Todd's were still a massive part of Maggie's life. Sunday lunch was almost a religion only now Dean came too. Jude and Stephen had put a deposit on a house and had set a date for their wedding. They were getting married on Christmas Eve of all days. They were getting married in a registry office and then had opted to have their do in Carole Todd's best room. It was going to be total chaos, the little ones would never sleep in time for Santa Claus coming. But the arrangements were made and if anyone could pull a wedding off, followed by a family Christmas it was Carole Todd.

More of interest to Maggie and Dean was the house that Jude and Stephen had placed a deposit on a new build house on an estate being built not far from where they lived now. There were good deals to be had with only a small deposit required for a limited time. It made Maggie and Dean think. Maggie's council house was only 2 and a half bedrooms really, not big enough for the kids growing up. It wasn't anything that made a difference at the minute, but in a few years, they would want more space. The kids could share the bigger bedroom, but Maggie knew as Eve got older, she would want a bedroom of her own, she could have thought of nothing worse than sharing a space with her brothers.

They went to see the show houses. They were amazing. All finished off to the highest standard and each came with its own drive and garage. Dean was sold. Maggie a bit more apprehensive, the three bedroom was more of 2 and a half bedrooms again, the 3rd bedroom could hardly be called a bedroom at all, more a storage cupboard. The 4 bedder was much more suitable. And with the extra bedroom came the extra big price tag. But it was stunning.

Unsure that they could even get a mortgage, Maggie and Dean made an appointment at the bank.   Maggie was taking typing in again, though in smaller amounts due to the kids, but it all helped, and Dean was on good money at garage, but his 'race car' took up any spare money he had so they didn't have a lot of savings. On paper not even the deposit.

But where there's a will there's a way and after speaking to the bank manager and seeing what their mortgage payments would be, which in truth was less that the rent that they paid on the council house now that Dean lived with her and they paid full rent. But still they needed the deposit. In Maggie's Post Office account was the money that Tony Sharp had given her, that would be more than enough. But still. There was nothing in her head telling Maggie not to do it. No second sight or alarm bells. Afterall it was going towards a nicer home for Eve!

So, they too paid their deposit on their new four bedroomed house on Prospect View and waited for their home to be built. Just as Jude and Stephen were. Neighbours! Everything was happening so fast.

40) The Ten of Pentacles

The run up to that Christmas was very exciting. Maggie Hunter had never been happier. The love of a good man made all of the difference. She hadn't been lonely on her own, but having Dean live with her made her complete. She looked forward to him coming home each night and the lovely feeling she had waking up to him each morning was as strong as ever. He literally was her soul mate, he completed her.

Both of the children were thriving. Eve was a competent walker and was doing her best to be a talker. Her fascination with her baby brother had worn off and they only time she had any interest in his was at bath time when they shared a bath and if she was tired and wanted her mammy or her daddy and they had Ryan. Then she would cause a commotion until the baby was put in his pram and she had taken his place on his knee.

Maggie continued with her typing when she could, more and more when Dean was home and he could keep an eye on the kids, it was proving to be more difficult to do with a toddling Eve and the baby when she was on her own. So, she would often be heard tip tapping away into the night. Every penny counted towards their new home and their new life.

As Christmas dawned Maggie found herself thinking about her mam and dad as she always did. They weren't attending Jude and Stephen's wedding, the only family her brother would have their would be Shaun, Tom and his good friend John and her. Jude on the other hand seemed to be having an abundance of relatives in attendance, most of them staying at Carole Todd's for Christmas too though Lord only knows where everyone would be sleeping. Shaun and Jill would be staying at

Maggie's, but Tom and John had insisted that they would just get a taxi home, they were going to spend Christmas Day with Auntie Joan and Uncle Ken, it would be the first time they had met John.

Would Dorothy and Leslie Hunter just be spending Christmas Day on their own? Shaun hadn't mentioned if he was going home!! How had her mam and dad managed to lose all of their children in the space of a few years?? Maggie felt a twinge of guilt, yes, she deserved to be treat badly, but they weren't going to Stephen's wedding and it seemed that Shaun just used their home as a base and spent an enormous amount of time with Jill these days. It was all just so sad.

Jude and Stephen had a very different type of wedding. There was no fancy wedding dress or bridesmaids, just a nice dress with a little posy and Stephen in a new suit that made him look so very handsome. They all cheered when the registrar pronounced them husband and wife and then quickly headed off to Carole Todd's where she had dressed it like a hotel wedding reception venue.

And what a great time they all had. It was a mixture of wedding and Christmas everyone drank lots and made merry. Carole's little ones were on the ceiling with all of the excitement and sugar and were up way beyond what should have been their bedtime on a Christmas Eve. A little bit tiddly and very happy, Maggie and Dean pushed the double buggy home through the streets to their little house, it would be their second Christmas together there and their last. The new house was scheduled to be completed in late Spring. Maggie had a lovely warm feeling, the sort you got when you were little and Christmas Eve was always the best night of the year.

Maggie Hunter had everything she could possibly want. She thanked her lucky stars.

Just as they almost reached their gate Maggie heard it. It wasn't the alarm bells ringing in her head, it was the roar of a car engine, she would know that sound anywhere. She didn't need to turn her head to see if she was right, she just carried on up her path and into the house.

There was a Christmas card on the mat, just like there had been two years earlier. It was addressed to Maggie and Eve and before she had chance to pick it up, Dean had it in his hand and took it into the living room while Maggie first took Eve out of the buggy and carried her upstairs and into her bed. She was pleased she'd had the foresight to get the kids ready for bed before they had left Carole Todd's knowing that the motion of the buggy going home would send Eve off into the land of nod.

Happy that Eve was settled for the night, she made her way back downstairs to get a bottle ready for Ryan, who was now sitting in Dean's arms on the settee. The roar of the engine and the Christmas card on the mat had unsettled Maggie. She was going to have to open it, by the size of it she knew that Tony Sharp had put some money in it. There had been nothing the previous year and although Maggie couldn't remember if she had even told Tony when Eve's birthday was, she was sure he would have had an idea. But there had been no cards for either occasion. So why this one?

Dean knew all about Tony Sharp. Everything!! Which was just as well when she rocked up with the deposit for the house. Dean thought Tony was a shit. But Maggie stuck up for him, needlessly she knew, because in her mind he was a shit too. But to be fair to Tony Sharp, he had known nothing about Eve until he had seen them on their way back from the park. Maggie knew way before Eve put in her appearance that there was never going to be a future for her with Tony. She had been flattered, but there had been nothing beyond the lush kissing. The rest had all been very mediocre, she knew that for certain now because 'doing it' with Dean was mind blowing. Now she got what it all meant.

But Maggie being Maggie, she sort of stuck up for Tony Sharp when Dean got on his high horse about him. Tony couldn't be expected to fix something that he didn't know was broken. Even if he did have a girlfriend when they were having their driving dates. Who knows what may have happened if she had told him she was pregnant? Maybe he would have wanted to stand by her, she may now have been known as Maggie Sharp. But she hadn't and she wasn't, and she knew without a shadow of a doubt that if she was Mrs Sharp she wouldn't have been half as happy as she was now, being Maggie Hunter and living with Dean Burns. Dean was the real deal.

Handing the bottle to Dean to feed Ryan, Maggie told him that she thought that the Christmas card was from Tony Sharp. Gesturing that it was on the side, Maggie reached over and opened it.

'To My Daughter at Christmas'

There was a picture of Rudolph on the front and opening it, there was a wad of cash.

Hi Maggie

I hope that both you and Eve are well.

I am sorry that I have not been in touch sooner. It has been quite a time, though no excuse.

If you need me for anything you can contact me via Quarry's End as I am no longer living at my parent's house.

I have enclosed some money for you and Eve, use it for whatever you need, it is for both of you.

Take care of yourself and of Eve, I think about her all of the time.

Tony xx

And that was that.

Maggie handed the card and note to Dean who was winding Ryan.

As he read Maggie took the money and counted it out. Another £2000. It was a mad amount of money. But it gave Maggie and Dean some rainy day money again. They hadn't used all of the money in the Post Office account but a fair chunk of it had gone and even though they were putting any spare cash they had back into it, it was a slow process. This money would definitely give them some peace of mind and even though Maggie could see Dean scowling, she wasn't going to look a gift horse in the mouth. Dean would just have to get over himself.

But he was fine, in fact he seemed pleased. They ended up sitting way into the night that Christmas Eve talking. They talked about Tony Sharp, his generosity when in reality he didn't need to do anything for them. About how much Tony was missing out on. He didn't need to be in a relationship with Maggie but he could see his daughter. But the opportunity of coming clean with his girlfriend or more than likely now his wife, had passed. To tell her about Maggie and Eve now would not just be cruel, but potentially a nail in the coffin of his current relationship.

They talked about their future. The new house, the kids. Dean asked Maggie about trying to reconcile with her mam and dad, but Maggie wouldn't. She couldn't! The very thought of rejection by Dorothy and Leslie Hunter was unthinkable. They would undoubtedly know where she was if they wanted to have a relationship with her, or even just to see their grandchildren. But they seemed to just be keeping themselves very much to themselves. There only seemed to be Shaun seeing them at all. And she had given up asking him about their wellbeing, he was always cagey and nervous about talking about them.

Another lovely Christmas, this year they reversed the order. Christmas Day at Dean's mam and dad's which was great, they loved having their grandchildren there, because in their eyes, Eve was their granddaughter and always would be. She was after all Ryan's sister. Then it had been Boxing Day at Carole Todd's and her family and extended family and everyone else who fancied a fun day. All in all, it was a great festive period and they looked forward to the New Year and all of the new things that it would be bringing.

41) The Eight of Wands

Their new house seemed to be getting built at a rapid pace. And then not. There was one snag after another and whereas Jude and Stephen moved into their new house in April, it was June before Maggie and Dean got the keys for theirs. Just in time for the kid's birthdays!!

They vowed they would never move again. Packing with two small children, Dean working full time, Maggie typing whenever she could and just generally day to day living was a nightmare. Maggie hadn't lived there that long, but boy had she accumulated some amount of stuff. But by moving day they were ready.

As tempting as it was to use some of the money in the Post Office to buy some new furniture, they were being sensible and taking their stuff with them, even if it wouldn't fit. They would make do and they did. The settee would remain in Maggie's home for a very long time, as long as she was there really.

Because although they were on the up, life had a funny way of knocking you back down. For Maggie Hunter it didn't happen straightaway. No she lived her most happy life in the new house with Dean and Eve and Ryan. She had good neighbours in the shape of Jude and Stephen and she had all the love and support she would ever need off Carole Todd and her lot. Life was good. But then one day she heard it. It was just faint and she had to take herself off into a bath of bubbles to really be able to hear it, but there was no doubt that it was there. The alarm bells were ringing. But for the life of her Maggie had no idea what they were ringing for. She had no foresight of what was about to come. Just that it was coming and it was going to hurt her. What though????

42) The Nine of Cups

Maggie Hunter celebrated her 19th birthday in her new house. They were supposed to be having a garden party, but the garden wasn't finished and although they had hopes of laying some wood down and putting deckchairs to sit on that, it rained for days before and the whole garden turned in to a quagmire.

So instead they had a kitchen party, well more of a house party. But it had been good to show off their new house to everyone and she liked playing hostess. Everyone who mattered to Maggie was there. Jude and Stephen, Jill and Shaun, Tom and John and of course Carole and Glen and the boys.

Eve was hyper as she always was when she was around David and Marc, Maggie could never tell if it was the additional sweets she was allowed to have or if it was just the joy of playing with the boys. God help them all when Ryan was big enough to join in too.

It was a happy day though, the house wasn't how they wanted it, it was all still very magnolia and lacked warmth, but the potential was there and the extra space gave it a light airy feel. The drink flowed, the food was devoured and everyone had a good time. As was always on momentous occasions, Maggie thought of her mam and dad. How different her life might have been if she had just gone to work at the hairdressers and not at Quarry's End. But Maggie could honestly say that given the opportunity to do it all again, she would still want to end up celebrating her 19th birthday with the people who she was actually with.

She could not possibly love anyone as much as she loved Dean. He was her everything, beside the kids.

They were just right together. They never argued although both of them could do a canny huff. There had never been anything that had pushed them beyond a slightly raised voice. Maggie thought that she sometimes got on Dean's nerves with her ability to dither around decisions, she doubted herself endlessly and Maggie hated Dean and his 'race car', although he had been doing it long before he met Maggie. And to be fair to him, he didn't go to as many meets these days, especially if it meant spending a night away.

Eve started at a nursery school in September, just mornings but it turned out to be quite the ordeal when she first started. The only children that she had ever really played with were David and Marc and that was all rough and tumble. So suddenly having delicate little girls around her was something Eve found hard. Whereas she seemed to be fearless and would launch herself off any bit of furniture, the other little girls in the group were a bit scared of her. Maggie was mortified to think that her little girl was a bully and made endless playdates for the little girls to come to their home so Eve could at least learn a little bit of etiquette and decorum.

Another Christmas and another New Year. Each year seemed to be better than the year before, if that was even possible. But they were with Eve having a little bit more awareness about what it was all about, it was all very exciting.

But the alarm bells were still there. Not loud, they were clanging somewhere in the distance, but Maggie could hear them. She didn't need to go and sit in a quiet corner to be able to hear them, they were just there. So, she watched over her family like a mighty lioness, nothing was being left to chance. There were no doors left open for toddlers to run into the street and be run over by a passing car. There were no pans of hot chip pan fat in reaching distance. There was no alien object left lying around for Ryan to put into his mouth and choke on. And she constantly rang Carole, Jude, Shaun, Linda and Tom checking that all was well.

There was nothing. But there was obviously something. But what.

Her mam and dad? Shaun assured her that Dorothy and Leslie Hunter were both fine and dandy. Well as fine and dandy as they could be, they didn't seem to be ailing or anything. Tony Sharp hadn't put in an appearance that Christmas, but then Maggie hadn't told him that she had moved, which did give her a moment of anxiety thinking of the windfall the family who had moved into her old house had received in the shape of the bulky Christmas card. But she had been around and collected any post that had been delivered and they didn't seem the type of family who wouldn't pass over the post. They had happily handed over all the junk mail that they had in her name and had taken a note of her new address if anyone came looking for her. He hadn't been, she knew he hadn't, the gift the previous Christmas was probably going to be his last, he had clearly seen her walking along the street pushing the double buggy with Dean. She wouldn't expect to get anything else now.

So, life went on, with Maggie on high alert. Her little typing business was going well and she seemed to be getting a good reputation for her proficiency and her timeliness.   The money helped. It wasn't cheap running a bigger house and although the mortgage was cheaper that the rent they had paid on the council house, the fuel costs were higher and then there was the food. It wasn't cheap feeding a family of four.

Spring sprung and they made a start on making the garden into a little haven for the kids. It was hard work, much harder than Maggie would have imagined. She could remember her dad spending hours and hours in the garden at home, but she had always thought it was out of choice and not necessity. But they persevered and they managed and by the summer, they had a lovely space for Eve to play in without any chance of her getting out and onto the road where she could be run over by a passing car! The noise just wouldn't let up.

And then one day she was making a mixed grill. The frying pan was singing away, and she dropped some sausages in. She had prodded them with a fork so they wouldn't burst. One for Eve, three for her and four for Dean. They had barely been in the frying pan a minute when it happened. Her life was about to change all over again.

43) The Three of Cups

Maggie Hunter stood shaking at the back door. It had been the only place she could go. She looked down at her feet, they were splashed with little bits of carrot. What the hell, she hadn't even had any carrot. But it wasn't the puzzle of how the carrot ended up on her feet, more the way it had landed there. Projectile vomit. The smell of the cooking sausages had totally disorientated her and the nausea was on her before she knew what was happening.

She had only just managed to turn off the pan and dive through the back door.

Fuck, fuck, fuck!! Maggie's head was spinning and there was the distant sound of alarm bells ringing, but they weren't loud, there was no imminent danger. They were just there, as they had been for months. What had made her throw up the magical carrots wasn't going to hurt her.

Leaning against the back kitchen door Maggie tried to think. She tried to think when the last time, as Dean liked to call it, the painters had been in. It hadn't been in the past month, that was for sure. They didn't take precautions, they used the rhythm method, Maggie was always as regular as clockwork and they were always careful, well as careful as two people could be when they were as physically entwined as Maggie and Dean were. But mistakes did happen. In the throes of their passion they sometimes had the odd mishap, they were obviously not careful enough.

So here she was again. Pregnant. Because there was no doubt in Maggie's mind what the sausages and carrots was all about. The sickness in the early months of both of her previous pregnancies was all the confirmation that she needed. At 20 year old she was going to be the mother of 3 children, all under 5! Lordy me!!

She was shocked, but not sad. It wasn't going to be easy, and her typing may have to go by the wayside for a little time when the baby arrived, it would be almost an impossible task with 3 little ones, but they would cope. New house, new baby. They should have been a bit more careful, but hey ho. Maggie was actually smiling as she made her way back into the kitchen and to the frying pan with the still raw sausages. Tea needed to be made, she would just have to put a peg on her nose, there was no time for her to be sick every five minutes, she had her man and her babies to take care of. Doing a little calculation in her head, baby number 3 would be here by turn of year. She couldn't wait to tell Dean, he would be over the moon.

And of course he was. Proud as a peacock. And he assured them that they would manage, he would give up the racing once the baby arrived, his 'race car' was worth a fair old packet so that would help. And he would pick up a bit over time if it was available. Carole Todd wasn't pleased, she knew herself how hard it was to have two little ones so close in age, three little ones was a near impossible task, but she would help, Maggie knew that without a shadow of a doubt that any time it got too much, help would be on hand in the shape of Carole Todd.

Time passed and Maggie's tummy grew. After the initial couple of weeks of nausea, she felt really well. She would push the double buggy out every day, weather permitting and this time she only seemed to have a bump and the rest of her body was relatively slim.

The alarm bells were still ringing, sometimes she thought they were getting louder, she would often hear them even when the kids were in full voice, but she couldn't be sure. She just found that high alert was what she did now, everything and everyone was double checked. But despite the ringing everyone remained safe and well. Maybe her second sight wasn't what the ringing was all about, maybe she had tinnitus or blood pressure or something. She even mentioned it to the doctor on one of her pregnancy appointments, he assured her that as far as he could see, she was fit and well.

So, Maggie remained careful and protective. It was difficult when Eve started proper nursery school in the September, she couldn't stay with her, Eve's teachers would think she was mad. So, she would drop Eve off at school and then be like a cat on a hot tin roof until it was time to collect Eve again.

Eve was much better behaved around the little girls who were in her class, her little play dates had paid off, though she did still launch herself off desks in the classroom, these occasions were few and far between and usually when she was showing off in front of the boys. So, her teachers said anyway. But she was equally as happy to go into nursery as she was to come out and with each week Eve's confidence grew.

And then there was another Christmas. Maggie's bump was huge, her due date was 2nd January so realistically if she made it through

Christmas, it would be a bonus. The thought of leaving the kids over Christmas filled Maggie with dread, it was her happiest time of the year.

It was Carole Todd's year, the reverse of the year before, it would be Dean's mam and dad's on Boxing Day. Maggie was always relieved when it was never suggested that she host Christmas, she had the room but nowhere near the confidence to feed an ensemble of people with different likes and dislikes.

She was lucky. She made it through Christmas Day and Boxing Day without her waters breaking and ruining everyone's fun. Christmas Day had been the usual riot, Carole seemed to have more and more there every year. As well as there being Jude and Stephen there, who had taken it upon themselves to go there Christmas Eve to celebrate their first wedding Anniversary and make the Announcement that Jude was having a baby. Which was the most amazing news for Maggie, it would be lovely to share baby talk with her best friend stroke sister in law and her actually knowing what she was talking about. It was sad for Linda and Paul though. Both Maggie and Jude knew how hard they had been trying for a baby, but it just wasn't happening, and Paul had consoled Linda with a puppy which he hoped would help ease the pain.

Then there was Shaun and Jill on Christmas Day too, somehow, they were as ingrained in Carole and Glen Todd's family as the rest of them were. As were Maggie's cousin Tom and his special friend John, who weren't there for lunch, but came for the rest of the festivities. It was another good day, filled with children and tears and laughter, copious amounts of alcohol, obviously not for Maggie or Jude in their delicate conditions, and enough food to feed the 5000.

But even above the din, Maggie continued to hear the alarm bells. Were they getting louder, she couldn't really tell, they were such a constant in her life that she almost didn't hear them. As her pregnancy advanced so did her fanatical protecting everyone. Even over Christmas she checked the fairy lights at Carole's and at Dean's mam and dad's to make sure they weren't fire hazards blah blah blah. But all was well and all was bright.

It was just Maggie.

Moneywise it had needed to be a much cheaper Christmas. They cut back on the kids gifts, realistically they both had everything they needed and were so small that even a few gifts would be enough for them. They had bought Eve lots of girly things like dolls and a pram and Ryan had got Tonka toys and a little train he could push himself along on. With him being on his feet he was all over the place now and his favourite thing to do was to sit in one of Eve's doll's pushchairs and wheel himself around the living room. By Boxing Day, it was all change and Eve was playing with the Tonka toys and Ryan was pushing Eve's new pram around into every piece of furniture in the living room. Typical.

Dean had been as good as his word and had picked up overtime when he could and he had someone interested in buying his 'race car' which Maggie would be glad to see the back of. She hated squashing past it in the garage getting to the tumble dryer. The car would be gone by the new year and that would fluff up their ever-depleting nest egg.

Once again there had been nothing from Tony Sharp. Where ever he was and what ever it was he was doing, he had stopped thinking about his daughter, his first born . Maggie was secretly relieved, the money would have been nice, but she couldn't be doing with Tony Sharp popping in and out of their lives like some rich Santa Claus. Dean was Eve's daddy, that's what she called him and that's what he was. All three kids were Deans.

So, the alarm bells ringing were nothing to do with Tony Sharp. As far as Maggie was aware he was now history. There had been no contact so just like she did with her mam and dad, Dorothy and Leslie Hunter, she placed him to the back of her mind and tried not to give any of them a second thought, they hadn't thought about her or her children, she was literally taking a leaf out of their own books.

44) The Tower

With Christmas over Maggie relaxed. The baby could put in an appearance any time it liked now. They had no plans for New Year, they would probably see it in in bed, Maggie's appetite for Dean was as strong as it had been when she neared the end of carrying Ryan. So, a little bit of nookie would be the perfect way to end the year and start the new one. Poor Dean, Maggie thought, she always seemed to wear him out as the baby's due date grew nearer, not that he complained, but being woken by his amorous other half a couple of times a night would test the patience of most men.

The alarm bells were most definitely getting louder. As alert to the danger of every day living as she had ever been, Maggie put it down to the imminent arrival of the baby. One morning the alarm bells were so loud that they woke her, and she fumbled around on the bedside table thinking it was the alarm clock going off. It hadn't been, it wasn't a work or school day and the alarm clock had never been set. It was all in her head.

There were only 4 days until her due date, so chances were that with this being her third baby, that day would be the day and that was what all of the fuss was about.

After waking Dean and having her wicked way with him before the kids woke up, she made her way downstairs and started on breakfast. Her hospital bag was packed and ready in hallway and the only thing to do was drop the kids off at Carole Todd's on the way to the hospital. Everything was arranged. And even better, Dean was getting rid of the bloody 'race car' that day. Some blokes had been to see it a couple of days earlier and had paid pound notes for it straight away. All Dean had to do was drop it off on the trailer and his race days were over. Maggie did feel a bit sorry for him, he loved that car, but he loved his family more and the car had brought a fare old bit of money. Money that would be put to good use when Maggie wasn't able to do any typing for a few months while the baby was so small.

Later Dean left with the trailer and Maggie spent the afternoon on the floor playing with the kids and their new toys. Toys they insisted on swapping, so Ryan was wandering around dragging a doll by its hair and Eve was again playing with the Tonka toys again.

The alarm bells continued to ring, and Maggie kept checking for signs of her waters breaking or the first tell tale pain letting her know that the new baby Burns was on its way. But there was nothing. She made the kids tea and still nothing happened. The alarm bells were getting louder. Maggie pushed on her tummy, the baby wriggled so all was well there.

It was getting late. It was dark outside and the kids were getting tired. They could have done with a bath, but she was enormous and had struggled for weeks bathing them and in the end had to leave them for Dean to sort out, she was terrified that one of them went under the water and she wouldn't be able to move fast enough. No, she wouldn't risk the danger of the bath.

So, they were in their jarmies, had their milk and biscuit and Eve helped Maggie get her little brother up the stairs and into his cot.

Monitor on, Maggie listened to their movement and knew that within a few minutes, both her children were in the land of nod.

But Maggie couldn't settle. She hadn't listened to where Dean was taking the 'race car' too, but she had assumed that it wasn't far away because he said that he wanted pie and chips for tea. But it was after 8 and there was still no sign. And the baby was definitely going to put in an appearance because the alarm bells were less bells and more siren, any second now there would be a gush and the water would flow. Then she would have to telephone Carole to come and get the kids and make her own way to the hospital.

On top of the sirens Maggie could feel herself starting to get Annoyed. She knew that one of his mates had gone to give him a hand unloading the 'race car', no doubt they had called into pub on the way back and Dean had forgot the time. And forgot the fact that his girlfriend was just about to give birth with his baby too by the looks of it.

Maggie must have dozed off because she woke with a start. This time it wasn't the alarm bells, though they were still at siren level. No something else had woken her. She checked, her waters hadn't broken and they was the mighty force of a kick in her tummy so all was well with baby. What had woken her. Then she heard it, there was someone knocking at the door.

Dean must have forgotten his keys again, he had a silly habit of doing that, especially when he chopped and changed cars test driving them for work. Easing out of the chair, she cursed under her breath at Dean, she hoped that he hadn't had one pint too many, she would be back to scenario one and Carole Todd having to come to them and them to travel to the hospital in a taxi.

Opening the door, she was taken aback to see two police officers standing there. There mouths were moving the noise in her head was so loud that she couldn't make out what they were saying. All she could do was beckon them in to the house and close the door behind them.

In her living room they looked like giants. They asked her if she needed to sit down, she did. She needed to be able to muster up all her resolve to hear what they were saying to her above the noise of the now screeching sirens. They must have thought she was stupid because she knew that she was cocking her head to one side, just like a dog would do when you were talking to it.

Yes, she was Dean Burns girlfriend. One task passed but why would they want to know that. Yes, he was driving a red Vauxhall Vectra. And then she heard everything that the police officer said as clear as day. There had been an accident. A drink driver had crashed into the car. The driver of the car had died instantly. The passenger died at the scene along with the drunk driver. It had been a fatal accident.

The screeching alarm bells stopped and there was nothing but darkness.

45) Death

'Happy Birthday to You, Happy Birthday to You, Happy Birthday Dear Dana, Happy Birthday to You!!'

Maggie sat and looked around the room. It was a room she knew well. Carole Todd's best room. It had been decorated and had a new set of curtains, but it still had the same safe feel it had when Maggie had stayed in it all those years earlier as a pregnant 16 year old. Of course, she had been in it many times since that time, but it was a place Maggie would always feel safe in.

It was New Years Eve and everyone that Maggie loved was there. Well nearly everyone. There was obviously no Dean. It had been 7 years just the day before since she had lost him. It had been 7 years since her own life had stopped still, for a long time anyway.

She remembered the day he died as if it was yesterday, right up to the point that those two policeman had filled up her living room with their form and told her that her soulmate, the love of her life had died in a car crash. After that there was nothing abate snippets of a life going on around her as she sat still and lived a living death.

Everything that she knew about that time had been told to her, by Carole or Jude or her brothers. There was no memory of anything, just a black hole. The little girl who they had just finished singing Happy Birthday to was Maggie and Dean's daughter. She had been born hours after her daddy had died. Maggie knew nothing of it. All she knew was that she had an 8 inch scar on her tummy thanks to the emergency cessarion section she had been given when it was deemed both Maggie and the baby were in danger of not making it through labour.

There were photographs of her youngest daughter. Lots of them. With her big brother and sister, with Dean's mam and dad, with her brothers and with Carole Todd and all of her family. There were none of Maggie and the baby. The little girl was a toddler before Maggie's face appeared on any of the snap shots. She was just too ill.

The baby had been discharged from hospital, Maggie was of no use to her. Maggie stayed. Moved from one part of the hospital to another where she stayed for weeks on end. At first, she was just left to sit with her thoughts, though if she had been sitting thinking, she couldn't think of a single thing she had thought about.

Unbeknown to Maggie, social services had been alerted to her situation, the death of her partner who was the father of her children, it was thought that they should be taken into care. If Maggie had been even the slightest bit corpus mentos then it would have been over her own dead body. But she wasn't and it left to her Stephen and Shaun who were technically the kids next of kin, to decide what would happen.

Once again it had been Carole Todd who was a heroine. In the first instance anyway. Eve, Ryan and the baby went to stay with her. There was no way on earth she was going to let Maggie's children go to strangers. It had taken all of them, Carole, Glen, her brothers, Dean's mam and dad and Maggie's friends to convince social services that living with the Todd's was the best place for them. They knew the Todd's and their home.

Social Services relented. They agreed that living with Carole Todd would be of benefit to them, but they would be monitored. For all of their sakes. There was no way of knowing that Maggie Hunter would ever recover from the ordeal, that her state of absolute comatose would ever lift. The children couldn't be expected to remain with Carole and Glen Todd and their own family for any length of time. But for the short term it was a solution.

The best room had once again been made into a make shift bedroom for the two older children and the cot that the new baby had never slept in at her mam and dad's house had been dismantled and made ready in Carole and Glen's bedroom.

Maggie Hunter had no recollection of anything that happened at that time. She knew that people came to see her. She could see their faces. Stephen and Shaun, Tom, her friends Jude and Linda and of course Carole. Maggie would see their faces and not hear a word they said. She heard nothing. There hadn't even been any alarm bells ringing. It was only the sound of silence. Maggie sat in her silence and couldn't utter a word. She had literally been struct dumb.

Pills kept her calm, but she even if there were no pills there would be no reaction. She didn't scream or shout and there was no cry of woe is me for the love that she had lost. There was nothing.

Every decision with regard to the kids was made by everyone else. Dean's mam and dad were having to deal with their own grief. They had lost their only son so to add the general well being of their grandchildren seemed to be more than they could have hoped to cope with. But it was Carole Todd again who made sure that every decision, every small step was relayed to Mr and Mrs Burns and even if they had no opinion of any of it, at least they knew.

Dean Burns funeral was attended by many, as only a funeral of a young person killed so tragically could be. Mr and Mrs Burns did well to hold themselves together, they clung on to Dean's sisters as if their life depended on it. All of Maggie Hunter's 'family' were there, the only visible absentee was Maggie. There was no way that she would have been able to cope with it all. Her sadness was so tangible adding a funeral into the mix would have been just too cruel. So, they made no mention of when and where they were laying Dean Burns to rest and let Maggie continue to heal in ignorant bliss.

And while Maggie Hunter remained in hospital, everyone else rallied around to care for her children the best they could.

They collected what they could for the kids from Maggie and Dean's home. Mr and Mrs Burns packed up Dean's belongings only leaving behind things that they thought that Maggie would gain some comfort from when she eventually returned home. The rest was taken to charity shops or back to their own home to be kept until they could bear to part with them. The remainder of the house was shut up while it waited for the return of the little family that used to live so happily there. It was an additional heart break for everyone involved.

But they did it and then everyone's attention turned to the care of the kids and the help in trying to coax Maggie into re-emerging back into the land of the living.

Weeks had turned into months. The doctors at the hospital hadn't seemed overly concerned with Maggie's slow progress. In their minds not only had she just lost her partner, but she had also had the trauma of having a baby. They assured the family that they wouldn't really have expected her to doing any better or worse than she was. It was just a waiting game.

The care for Eve, Ryan and the baby soon became the norm for all of them. There were rotas and the odd frantic telephone call when care was needed at the last minute, but they managed. Every week Carole and Glen would take the kids into hospital to see their mammy. The older ones would run and sit on her knee and Maggie would cuddle them in and stroke their hair, but she didn't speak to them and sometimes she could barely muster a smile. As kids did, they adapted to their situation and if they thought that their mammy was behaving weird, they didn't react to it. Just hugged her when they left and waved cheerily at the door. Carole didn't have the nerve to hand over the baby to her, she had no idea how Maggie would react to her.

All of the children thrived. Eve asked about mammy and daddy but was happy with the answer of mammy being in hospital poorly and daddy being a star in the sky. They were all so small.

Baby obviously couldn't stay baby forever. She needed a name. Mr and Mrs Burns were at a loss, no one could think of any names being mentioned for the baby by Maggie or Dean before her birth. Someone suggested DeAnna after her daddy, but it didn't sit with the chubby faced baby and Ryan already had Dean as a middle name. It was Shaun who said Dana!! The baby really did look like a Dana, and it did have most of the letters out of her daddy's name so Dana Marie Burns it was, the Marie was after Dean's mam. If Maggie didn't like it, then that would have to be an argument for another day.

46) The Nine of Wands

So, it was Mr and Mrs Burns who had once again to go to the registrars, this time for a more joyous event though none the less upsetting, they had only been there for Dean's death certificate weeks earlier, now they were registering the birth of their first granddaughter and informing them that the name of the father on the birth certificate would have to read deceased.

But Dana made everyone smile. She was the most pleasant of babies, it was if she knew that everyone had already been through enough and her job on the earth was to make everyone feel a bit better. She rarely cried, unless she was hungry or wet and as soon as she had mastered it, she smiled at anyone who looked at her. Even if Eve or Ryan were a bit rough with her, or Carole Todd's own boys gave her a fright, which they seemed to like to do knowing that after the initial start she would giggle, a yelp was suffice and then she would be smiling again.

The Todd's house had an ever evolving door. Maggie's brothers were there almost every day and when Jude started her maternity leave, she almost moved back in. Everyone took their turn with the kids and Maggie's cousin Tom and his good friend John became like maiden aunts to the kids and would always turn up with a bag full of treats for all the children in the house. If everything wasn't so tragic it could have been thought that they lived in one big happy commune.

There of course with the practicalities relating to money. Maggie and Dean had a mortgage on their house and although the Post Office book had been found, there was no way any of that money could be used without Maggie being present. There had been enough money in the bank account to pay for the mortgage and some necessities for a few months and Mr and Mrs Burns offered to help whenever or whatever was needed, but it was only a short term solution. They had to decide what to do with the house and a decision was probably going to have to be made without Maggie having anything to do with it.

They just all had to make the best of a bad job, hope that Maggie would recover and made as happy an environment for the kids as they possibly could.

Week by week and month by month they lived. Jude gave birth to a baby girl, they named her Emily and she was as pleasant as Dana was. Carole Todd's home was fit to bursting with children because Jude tended to spend her days helping out there while Stephen was at work, with 6 kids in total all under 10, every day was like a children's party.

All the while they took it in turns to go and see Maggie. There was improvement, the doctors were talking about letting her go home for a weekend to see how she got on. She spoke, but not a lot, she tended to be in her own little world, though was very compliant when they asked her to do anything, there were no kick offs or weeping and wailing, it was like her spirit had flown when Dean's had. She looked like Maggie, but to those who knew her well, they could sense there was a sadness about her. They were going to start weaning her off her medication slowly, see if some of the old Maggie emerged, after all she was so young, no one wanted her to live the rest of her life in some sort of half-life, they had to at least try.

The most shocking thing for everyone was that Maggie's mam and dad, Dorothy and Leslie Hunter never once showed their faces. Not to see Maggie, not to see their grandchildren, there had not even been a telephone call. They knew. Stephen and Shaun had gone to see them not long after the accident. But there had been nothing, not even a card of condolence, it was if Maggie Hunter had never even been their daughter. In Maggie's darkest hour there had been nothing.

Little by little the mediation was reduced, and Maggie began to wake. They knew she was coming back, she cried silent tears down her cheeks whenever any of them went to visit. She would ask how each of them were, how the kids were. And when Dana was a little over 4 months old, Maggie Hunter held her daughter for the very first time. Dana Burns gurgled with glee, it was if she knew that it was her mammy who was holding her, the little girl would help Maggie heal.

Maggie had a weekend at home. Another bed had been put in the 'best room' at Carole Todd's and Maggie spent two nights sleeping in the same room as her eldest children. To the kids their lives went on as normal, they played and they fought and they slept and all the while Maggie watched them with wonder and awe.

No one pushed Maggie to talk, she would talk when she was ready, but she had seemed to enjoy the hustle and bustle of the house, laughed with everyone and when she needed a moment of quiet, would make her way back to the best room and have her self a few minutes. There had been no talk of going to her own house, there had been no mention of any practicalities and there had been no mention of Dean. Everything was kept as calm as it could possibly be despite the chaos.

Maggie returned to hospital, there had been no dramas, she settled back to life on the ward and the decreasing of the drugs continued and Maggie became to come alive.

The weekend home visits became more and more frequent until just as the 6th month Anniversary of Dean's death approached, Maggie Hunter was discharged into Carole Todd' care. The best room once again became her home and there she stayed with her children until it would be deemed not just by Maggie's medical team, but also by Carole, that she was able to live alone and take care of her children.

47) *The Five of Cups*

Maggie Hunter ended up staying with Carole Todd for another 18 months.

There were no warning alarm bells anymore in her head, they had done their job, Maggie just looked in all of the wrong places for the dangers. She had hated the 'race car' with a venom and had been so happy that it had been sold and that she had thought was the end of it. There had been no meetings, no racing. But it had killed Dean in the end. If he hadn't sold it, then he wouldn't have been out on that fateful December night and ended up in a head on collision with a drunk driver. Three lives had been taken and three families lives destroyed.

All Maggie now had in her head was silence. Once she had completely been taken off her medication she would listen for some sort of noise, she had thought at the very least she may have heard Dean because she certainly sensed him. But there was nothing but silence.

Slowly, inch by inch and day by day Maggie allowed herself to live again. The hurt of not having Dean with her was sometimes all consuming, she missed him so much. But she had her children and they needed her. Eve, Ryan and Dana brought her joy every single day. The made her soul sing even on the saddest of days.

At first she hadn't been sure if Dana was a good name for her youngest daughter, but everyone had been right, it suited her. Dana Marie Burns was perfect and Maggie would often chastise herself for not being there for her daughter in the early days. But everyone had looked after her so well, they all loved her and she loved everyone in return. She had a look of her daddy sometimes, as did Ryan, but it was Eve who reminded Maggie the most of Dean. The daughter who wasn't his daughter had seemed to have picked up all Dean's little ways, she would say something in a way that Dean did or would do something that would remind Maggie of Dean, it was strange, but then she had been the child who had spent the longest amount of time with him.

Dean's mam and dad were very supportive. In the midst of their own grief, they cared for Maggie and all of the kids. They would take the kids to their house for the odd weekend just to give Carole and Maggie a break, in a house that was so often full of people, it was a welcome act of kindness by Mr and Mrs Burns.

Sunday lunch became the day of the week that everyone congregated together. Month by month it became more of a normal occasion. Life was going on the same as always but somewhat very very different.

Maggie still couldn't face going home. Carole would discuss it with her, but it was the one thing that Maggie couldn't do. In her heart of hearts she knew that she would never live there again, no matter how lovely it was. It was sitting there empty eating up what little savings she had left. There was to be some sort of payment off an insurance company for Dean's death, but even with that, it would be way out of Maggie's financial comfort zone, she didn't even have a job.

So, the little house was put on the market and Stephen and Shaun went every weekend until it was all packed up and put into a garage some friend of a friend was going to rent them. Maggie didn't feel sad about losing it, it was bricks and mortar. Her memories would be carried with her where ever she ended up laying her head.

With time came clarity. Maggie would never ever ever be able to repay Carole Todd, her family, Maggie's own family and friends and of course Dean's mam and dad for taking care of Eve, Ryan and Dana when she couldn't. It made her shudder at the thought of the kids ending up in some foster home, she would never have been able to forgive herself no matter how poorly she had been at the time.

One thing she did know was that she needed to get her life back in some sort of shape or form. She needed a job, and she needed a new home for her and her children. She needed to stop putting on to every one else not just for the kids care, but her own. They were heading towards another Christmas and then it would be Dana's 2nd birthday, in her head she was beginning to formulate a plan that come the New Year she would branch back out on her own. She had been signed off by the hospital. They were happy that she wasn't going to hurt herself, lest the kids and she had an emergency number to call in case everything got too much for her, but she would never call that. She had her family and that was all she needed.

The funny thing was, once she had decided what she was going to do, she started to sense Dean more and more. Sometimes at night she would wake up and she could feel the weight of him on top of her. It would only be there for a moment and then it would be gone. It was him though, Maggie just knew.

Then sometimes she would get the slightest whiff of engine oil, she would smell it and then as she went to take in a bigger smell of it, it would disappear, but it was him, she just knew it.

A song on the radio, a robin in the garden, something the kids randomly said. All these things were Dean. He was with her. He was telling her it was all going to be ok. But she wanted more. She wanted to talk to him. She wanted to talk to him just like her Granny Hunter used to talk to people. She would talk to him through those funny little cards her Granny Hunter used to teach her. She still had them. Somewhere!! She would ask Stephen and Shaun to look for her jewellery box because she had the funniest feeling that the package her Granny Hunter had left her had been placed unopened in the bottom of it. Before the garage was locked away with all her belongings in it she would ask them for the jewellery box. She wouldn't say why, they would think she was odder than she already was. But it was a way, for whatever reason, second sight maybe. Maggie Hunter knew that her future lay withing the brown paper package wrapped up with string that her Granny Hunter had left her.

48) The Ace of Pentacles

The house was completely emptied and a For Sale sign had been erected in the garden. Maggie Hunter had no urge to go and see it for one last time. Every time she thought of the house, she thought of the giant policemen filling her living room with their presence and the words that Dean had been involved in a fatal accident spewing out of their mouths.

The memories of the house before that, the happy times she had spent there with Dean and the kids was more abstract. She had memories, but they played through her mind as if she was watching someone else's home video. She could see the happiness and feel the love, but more like watching a film where the characters got under your skin because they were so good playing their part. It was all so surreal.

The jewellery box was eventually located and given to Maggie, who placed it beside her bed and waited until not only did she have time, but also the courage. The urge to open her Granny Hunter's gift was all consuming. There were no alarms of danger, just the feeling that once she opened the package, her life would never be the same again.

The opportunity didn't arise for a couple of weeks. Dean's mam and dad were taking the kids for the weekend, they were really nice people and knew that by reducing the household by the three youngest children would give everyone a chance to catch their breath.

It gave Maggie mixed feelings. She had only just began to feel like she was having a relationship with her kids once again. She was happy rolling around the floor with them and if they cried, she didn't shy away from it like she had when she had first been discharged from hospital. She loved lying in her little bed and listening to the sound of their breathing. Dana was in the best room in her cot too and she had turned into the biggest snorer of them all, for such a little body she was ferocious.

So, the nights they were away were always a little strange. But it gave Maggie some much needed opportunity to have some time to herself and keep on with the healing process, well that's what her counsellor had said anyway. Carole Todd would leave her to her own devices, with the reassurance that she was there if she was needed. What would Maggie Hunter ever have done without that woman!!

Sometimes she would sit in her room and read. Usually a thriller or a horror, she couldn't be doing with Mills and Boon and all the romance. More often than not she would sit and stare into space. Her head was quiet, so it was easy for her to drift off into a world of nothingness, there was no crying or feeling sorry for herself, it was just nothing.

But that weekend she knew that the urge to open the brown paper package wrapped up with string that her Granny Hunter would be the main focus of how her hours of solitude would be filled. And she had been right, she had placed it in the bottom of the jewellery box. How many years had it been sitting there waiting to be opened?

And then she did it. The string was off, and the paper pulled away from the contents nestled inside. There were the funny picture cards her Granny Hunter had played with her all of those years earlier. She could smell her Granny Hunter, the scent of her had remained on the cards, Maggie's heart gave a lurch.

There was a letter.

Maggie read the first few lines and had to stop. Her eyes prickled with tears and the writing became blurred as she tried to stop them falling onto the paper and ruining the words. Wiping her eyes and blowing her nose, she had another go!

My Dear Little Maggie

I hope that while you are reading this letter you a very old lady, but alas if the cards that I have now passed to you are right, I think that you maybe not too much older than you were the last time I saw you. A women, but a very young one.

For my dear I saw heartbreak. I think perhaps you have lost the love of your life, I think that perhaps he has passed to the other side. I hope against hope that I am wrong, I truly do for I feel that amidst the heartbreak you feel, that there are three little hearts beating. Did you have children?? I am assuming that you have.

And I think that the reason that you are now holding my cards and reading this letter, is that you need help.

My dear girl, the answers for me have always lay within the cards, I know for sure that you will find what you are looking for by using them. I cannot show you how to use them, I believe that you may have a gift greater than mine ever was. Hold the cards, look at the pictures and listen to what they tell you, for they will talk to you.

Be kind with them. Do not use them for spite. You can use them for money, I myself have had to turn to them to make myself a few extra bob or two.

Maggie they are your friend and your greatest gift, especially if you are as lost at this moment as I think you are. Let them guide you and I promise that you will find peace.

One day we will meet again. I think I have an arm around you even now, that I am never far away from you. I promise you that if I could have warned you about the tragedy you have had to go through, I would have done everything in my power to do it, though I have no idea how I would be doing it.

Keep the faith beautiful girl. One day you will be happy again.

Always remember I love you.

Granny Hunter

Maggie folded the letter and placed it back into the jewellery box. And then she let the tears fall, followed by great big gasping sobs. She didn't try to control herself, she rolled herself up into a ball and lay on her bed. And then she slept.

She had no idea how long she slept, but some startled her. Maggie listened and listened, there was nothing. Was it the alarm bell in her head sending out its warning? No there was nothing, it must have been a dream. The alarm bells remained silent. She lay on her bed and picked a point on the ceiling to stare at. For some reason she felt better. More at ease. Her Granny Hunter was with her, had always been with her. She said even before her death that she would warn her the best she could of the tragedy that she would face.

And then it hit her. To Maggie it was not as clear as day. The alarm bells ringing in her head had been her Granny Hunter. She had said she would do everything she could, and she had. She had given Maggie a second sight. When ever something was going to hurt her, there had her Granny Hunter been, ringing that bell as loudly as she could.

Maggie Hunter's body did that funny shudder thing it did when someone was walking over your grave. Her Granny Hunter again telling her she was right. If she had been right about all of the hurt, then she would be right about the funny picture cards or the tarot cards to give them their right name. Maggie's future was dependent on the pack of cards.

Her tummy did a funny little excited turn, again her Granny Hunter agreeing that she was right, the cards were where her future lay somehow. It was time for Maggie Hunter to get off the bed and start studying the tools to get her to where she needed to be.

She was ready. She was ready to embrace her 'oddness' and see if, how or even what the gift her Granny Hunter so adamantly foretold she had could do for her!

49) The Star

Carole Todd was the only person that Maggie showed her Granny Hunter's letter to. As the house settled itself down for the night, Maggie sought Carole out in the kitchen and passed her the letter to read. Carole cried. Maggie didn't ask why, in her heart of hearts she knew that if only Maggie had read that letter years earlier. Would it have made sense?? Would it have made a difference?? Maggie wasn't sure and she certainly didn't want Carole to feel bad for her. It had happened and there was no turning back time, Maggie understood that. But she had a feeling that Dean would still be very much part of her future. The cards would call him, and he would be there for her.

She told Carole she was going to start learning how to use them. But only if it was ok with Carole, people had funny ideas about tarot cards and the reputation that they would bring all sorts of ghouls and ghosts. And it was after all her home. But she was happy for Maggie to give it a go, said that she had lived with her 'oddness' long enough not to be freaked out by it and who knew, it could be a good money earner for her if she honed her skill well enough.

So that was what Maggie did. Well, she didn't really have to learn anything. Instinctively she knew what she needed to do. The first thing was that she would keep the little cards on her person so that they could pick up her energy. She had no idea how she knew to do this, she just knew that it was right. That she could not even begin to decipher what the cars meant until they had connect with her.

In the bottom of one of the suitcases that she had in the best room were a few items she had asked Dean's mam and dad if she could have. There wasn't much, his leather jacket, a sweatshirt that they had shared and the shirt that he had worn for Jude and Stephen's wedding. It was silk and he had looked so handsome when he wore it. He had thought that he looked stupid, he was so far out of his comfort zone. But Maggie had loved him in it. Taking it into the now empty kitchen, she cut into it and made herself a square, then sat quietly into the night and hemmed all of the edges. The tarot cards needed protection and Dean's shirt was the perfect thing to do just that. She wrapped the silk around the cards and used a ribbon belonging to Eve to keep it all together.

With the cards placed under her pillow, Maggie slept for the first time in a very long time with a feeling of optimism. No matter how much she was hurting or how much she was missing Dean, she had to make a life for Eve, Ryan and Dana. She had to take responsibility for herself, and her children and she had to give Carole Todd her best room back again.

And she found that once she got a feel for the old tarot cards, it came easy to her. Each picture told its own story, and when they were placed with other cards, she could read the meaning. She asked simple questions of them at first, using just one card, the more confident she got in her ability the more cards she used. Dean was most definitely with her, as was her Granny Hunter. She found she could have conversations with them just by shuffling the cards and deciphering the answers. The test would come when she started doing readings for other people. But she was a while away from that. She kept the cards close, practiced when she could and decided that first things first and she needed a job.

She had her typing skills, she could start taking in typing again, but she wanted something more. What she didn't want was to work with the same people day after day. She didn't want to have to bear her soul. So realistically an office job was out of the question. She needed something with a constant stream of ever changing people. Somewhere where she could go and smile sweetly and not really have to be engaged in anything beyond pleasantries.

And if she could do that then she may also do some typing at home, though with three young children she had no idea when she would be able to fit very much of it in no matter how quickly she typed. Something would materialise, she knew it would.

Then there was somewhere for her to live. The house she had shared with Dean was sold and the small amount of profit she had made on it was nestled in the bank, but she wouldn't be able to get another mortgage, it had been Dean's steady job that had given them the stability to be able to get the last one. On hindsight she maybe shouldn't have sold the house, time was healing her and although she could not imagine spending one night in the house without Dean, she maybe has just got over herself and given the children a home of their own in a house they knew well. But if was gone now and there was no use in crying over the milk that had been spilt.

So, she rang the council and once again got herself put onto the housing list. She had no idea how she would pay the rent, but surely there were some benefits she would be entitled to. Maggie filled in the form and waited for something to happen.

In the meantime, she started looking for a job. It was a lot harder than she had anticipated, there would be childcare issues and although Carole Todd had said she would have the kids anytime, three was a lot and she would have to put a lot of thought into what she would do before she considered applying for any job.

And all the while she kept the silk covered cards with her, got them out and asked them questions and knew that in the no time that she would be moving on to whatever the next phases of her life would be. Eve, Ryan and Dana were happy, growing every day, blossoming in the dysfunctional family they lived in the middle of. Despite everything Maggie Hunter eventually had hope. There were no more brain numbing tablets, she had clarity and she was beginning to have some faith in herself. That she could make a home and that she could bring up her children just like her and Dean had planned.

50) The Chariot

Maggie Hunter applied for a few jobs, a couple in shops, another working in a café and one working on a stall on a market. She had interviews, but none of them felt right. As much as she needed a job, she needed the right job, not just a make do one. So, she didn't interview well and wasn't surprised that she hadn't been successful in any of them. Along with her new found ability to read her tarot cards, the aua visibility was back. It had probably always been there, but the more she was learning to rely on her senses and read signs, the more vibrant the colours surrounding people became. All of the job interviews she had attended had been with people with shades of green, envy and jealousy, she didn't need anything dragging her down more than she could already do to herself. No green auras weren't the answer!!

The council offered her a home, Maggie rejected it. It was on a rough estate, and it was miles away from Carole Todd and Jude and Stephen, she didn't drive, and it would be two bus rides getting to Carole Todd's and back. And then there was school, the last thing she wanted to do was cause more upheaval than was necessary on Eve and Ryan. She still had two more offers to have. She would take the risk it.

Everyone continued to rally around to help. Sunday lunch at Carole Todd was still chaos and still Maggie's favourite day of the week. Sometimes the kids were there, sometimes they would be with Dean's mam and dad and would come home just as the dishes were being cleared away and in time for pudding. Dean's mam and dad would pull up a chair and tuck in to whatever dessert Carole had produced for the five thousand that week. They belonged with them all as much as everyone else.

It was Dean's dad that said that there was a new pub stroke restaurant opening in their little town. He had seen it being built everyone morning on his way to work. He said there was a sign outside saying that they were recruiting staff and there was a telephone number to ring. Work in a pub?? Maggie hadn't thought of that, she had no bar skills but her fear of being open to the scrutiny of being with the same people day in and day out and forever having to explain her situation and dealing with their pain of knowing that the young girl had so tragically been left alone with three young children would certainly be limited if she worked in such a busy environment with an ever evolving clientele. It was definitely an option.

So, she walked along to the area that Dean's dad said the new build was, noted the number and then detoured to the park that she used to take Eve to years earlier, it was time to show Dana the ducks! All the while she had a good feeling about the pub. The hours would probably suit her and somehow working at the Geordie Ridley felt right. She would call the number as soon as she got back and start the application process.

This time when she went for her interview she actually tried. The building was all new and shiny, the man who greeted her for her interviewed glowed with a pink hue. Tender, caring, emotional and sensitive. Maggie Hunter liked him at hello. His name was Jason, and he was another of what her Granny Hunter would call him a friend of Dorothy, or at least a friend of her cousin Tom Grey and his good friend John. Maggie knew instinctively that this was a man she could work with. He was the one and The Geordie Ridley the place.

Despite her lack of experience and the fact that she was a single mam and at that moment she was living in her friends best room, Jason Street obviously saw something in Maggie he liked. He explained about the pub, how he and his 'business partner' had each ran city centre pubs but had always had the dream of having their own place. When the original Geordie Ridley pub had come up for sale, they knew it was time for them to strike up on their own. But the pub had been empty for so long that it was rotten to the core and would need thousands and thousands spent on it to renovate it. The cheapest option would be to tear the old place down and rebuild. And that was exactly what they had done.

Jason was proud that they had managed to remove and keep many of the original features, that they had kept the name and the legend that belonged to Geordie Ridley and his ditty the Blaydon Races. Maggie immediately felt at ease. It had a familiar feel about the place. She loved it and hoped that Jason Street liked her enough to offer her a job there.

With a warm hug, he told her to call at 5pm the next day, when he had had the chance to speak to his business partner. Of course, she would call, she really wanted to go and work with the lovely man who stood in front of her. There was a serenity about him that Maggie could use.

Dean's dad called to ask how the interview had gone, but more than that, he had news of a house she could rent. It belonged to someone he worked with at his accountancy firm, it had been his mother's house and the house he had been brought up in. He himself had some swanky house somewhere so had no intention of moving there, but he didn't want to sell it either. He obviously knew all about Maggie Hunter, she was the mother of Mr Burn's grandchildren after all but was happy for her to go and view it before he thought of letting it to anyone else.

What a good day it was. If she firstly got the job and secondly the house, she would surely be back on the road to some type of normality.

Maggie met Dean's dad at the house the next morning. It was in between Carole Todd's house and the Geordie Ridley, so the location would be ideal. The house itself was an old terrace, from the outside it looked very well cared for, as did the rest of the houses in the street, it looked like a nice street. A nice place to live.

The lady of the house had gone into a care home, so although all of the personal belongings had been removed from the house, the furniture was still there. It was all a little bit dated, but not old fashioned old fashioned and some of it Maggie would be able to make good use of, especially the appliances as she hadn't been able to remove any of the integrated ones from her old home.

She liked the house. She sensed that it had once been a happy home and knew that it could be again. There more than enough room for a family of four, 3 bedrooms, living room, dining room and there was a little back yard that would be ideal for the kids once it had been tidied up.

The rent was reasonable, and he hadn't asked for a bond or anything. There was enough money in the post office account and the bank to be able to pay the rent for way over a year without even thinking about it. Maggie Hunter would be more than happy to live there and told Dean's dad to say yes.

Maggie was so excited.

Though the thought of having the 3 kids on her own was a little scary, she'd had so much help for so long she had only been on her own with them once or twice in the past 2 years, but they were her responsibility, and she was sure if it all got too much, and she shouted help would be on hand.

51) The Queen of Cups

And then at 5 o'clock she rang Jason Street. With the realisation that it had always been her Granny Hunter warning her of the things that would hurt her, there were never any noises in her head now. She had stopped asking the cards to help her, they had done enough for her to earn her trust in them and vice versa. If there was anything to be said from beyond the grave, it was there in the cards without it having to be asked. There had been nothing in any of the decks that she had read recently, she could only think that she was on the right path.

Jason asked if Maggie could go back in and meet his business partner Peter. That it would be easier to discuss things in person. It could only be a good omen. So, leaving the kids once again with Carole Todd, Maggie made her way back to the Geordie Ridley, past the street that had what was to be her home and through the door of the pub that had every chance to be part of her future.

Peter was just as nice as Jason, it was well seeing that they were not just business partners, but more than likely partners in life too. Peter's green hue complimented Jason's pink, they looked like a tree of cherry blossom together. Maggie immediately loved them both.

More so when they said that they would love her to come and work with them. They knew her circumstances, that she had children at home so were offering her flexi working hours, part time at first, at least until the pub opened properly in the next month or so. They appreciated that she had typing skills and they really needed someone to take on more of an admin role, stock, accounts etc, all things that they would work with her to perfect. Obviously, there would be bar work too and serving food to tables, and maybe some cleaning.

They said they would be happy if she could rota her hours in a week ahead, it was all just so perfect. Maggie could think of no better place to work and no better people to work with. Walking home she looked up to the sky and thanked Dean and her Granny Hunter for the great work they had done, a home and a job. It was just too good to be true.

Everyone was happy even of a little apprehensive. There was so much happening in a short time, the house the job; they didn't want Maggie taking on too much and reverting back to the place she was 18 months earlier. Maggie didn't think she would, she felt hopeful for the future. Every day one of the kids or all of them amazed her. Eve still reminded her of Dean, it was the most bizarre thing, she was happy when one day Dean's mam said it too, if Maggie was crackers, then Dean's mam was too. Whatever mannerisms she had picked up from Dean had stayed, the child who he wasn't the biological father of was more like him than the ones he was.

Looks wise Ryan looked like her brothers Stephen and Shaun, a little mash up of both of them and Dana looked like Maggie, she was literally a mini version of herself. After everything they had been through, they were well adapted and mainly well behaved even if every now and again the grappled as a group on the floor and screamed at each other.

The keys were dropped off for the house and the next few weeks were filled of cleaning and making good what was there and the furniture and belongings that had been in storage were brought in a van to the house. It was a bitter sweet time.

And then it was time. Carole Todd was getting her best room back. They both cried. As much as the buoyancy of moving with the kids and starting her new job the following week, the reason that Maggie had been staying with Carole Todd in the first place was still there. On the last night they talked way into the night, Maggie knew without a shadow of a doubt that Carole would always be there for her, she was the mother she hadn't had for such a long time. They had been through some of the darkest times together, but they had been through some of the most joyous. Carole had been at Maggie's side when Eve was born, they had been together when Jude had firstly fallen in love with Stephen, then married him and now they had their beautiful daughter with another on the way.

There were reasons to smile everywhere.

Carole Todd asked one thing of Maggie before she left. She asked if Maggie would read her cards.

Maggie had never done anything with her cards beyond communicate with those that had gone before. She had not attempted to read someone else's life. But Carole had asked and how could she refuse after everything that she and Glen had done for her. They had opened up their home for her, twice. They had made her and hers feel like they belonged, and they had loved them all unconditionally. A card reading was the least she could do.

The tarot cards were always with Maggie. If they weren't in a pocket, then they were stuffed in her bra close to her heart. At first, they had felt bulky, but she was used to the feel of them now, her amble bosom missed the feel of them when they were in her pocket. It just felt like the right place for them to be.

So, taking them out she shuffled them and asked Carole to do the same. She took the pack off Carole and divided the pack into three and placed them in front of Carole and indicated for her to choose a pile. She had no idea why she did this. It just seemed instinctive. Carole chose one and Maggie spread them out in front of her. She asked her to choose 3 cards and each one was placed in order of how they were chosen. Past, present and future.

And the rest came easy. They were Carole's life as it was in front of Maggie. There was the baby she had when she was young and then Glen and the boys and there was her enormous heart and her sense of giving. There was no drama to be foretold, everything looked like a happy family life, at least in the short term anyway. Maggie had no idea how far into the future that the cards could predict. There was a baby on the way, but then Jude was pregnant, but Maggie voiced the baby anyway. Only for Carole Todd to turn ashen. Not for one minute had thought that any baby that may be born would be Carole's. But she hadn't had a period for a few months, had out it down to change of life and sort of forgot about it. She didn't feel pregnant but thought that maybe a test would be the order of the day. Maggie doubted that she could be that clever and they both laughed it off.

The cards were stacked back away, and Maggie placed them under her pillow as she settled herself down for what would be her last night in the best room, ever she thought. It had been her haven, her safe room, but that had happened twice now, surely that would be it and this would be the last time.

After a night full of tosses and turns, moving day arrived and it was so busy there was no time for any tears. Dean's mam and dad came and took the kids away for the day, all of the kids David and Marc included so the adults could get everything to the new house and make it a home before the three youngest children arrived back at teatime.

By the time Maggie Hunter was placing her little pack of silk wrapped cards under her pillow that night, the new house was in order. Everyone had been there helping. Stephen and Shaun, Carole and Glen, Tom Grey and his good friend John came with bags full of little treats to help the family to settle in. Jude kept the coffee coming and Jill spent ages putting big transfers on each of the bedrooms that were to be the kids to make them a bit more child friendly. It had been a good day. More so when Maggie's record player had been located and the house was filled with music. Maggie had a good feel about the place.

Her sadness would never leave. She just had to think about Dean and a wave of loneliness would wash over her. They had been so close. He had been her soulmate, her best friend and her lover all rolled into one. She missed the intimacy. She doubted that she would ever find it again with anyone else, they had just fit. She could remember the days of the driving dates with Tony Sharp, the kissing had been lush, but the sex had been poor. If that was all that there would be if she wasn't 'doing it' with Dean, then she just wouldn't bother.

Jude and Linda told her she had to remain optimistic. That she was so young and there was so much time in front of her that she had to consider that sooner or later there would have to be someone that she would take to her bed. But Maggie doubted it. She doubted if there would be anyone that would ever make her feel the way that Dean had. She doubted that she was even capable of lusting after another man. But she could never say never. She hadn't even reached her mid-twenties, she couldn't write love off altogether. It would just be placed on a back burner until it came a knocking.

51) The Tower

And so, her life began again. As a single mother to three children, part time administrator/barmaid/waitress and Uncle Tom Cobbly and all at the Geordie Ridley.

The flexible rota system worked, most of the time. She arranged for the kid's to be looked after so she could work and even though every now and again, she would end up taking them in to work with her, Jason and Peter didn't mind.

They were the best of bosses. Their kind hearts and sunny outlook made the Geordie Ridley the success it was. They themselves became yet another extension of Maggie Hunter's family. Jude and Stephen had their baby boy, James's Christening at the pub and for the first time in forever, Carole Todd's best room wasn't used for Christmas Day. When the last of the punter's left on Christmas Day afternoon, Maggie's lot descended on the pub and the dysfunctional family that they had become grew even larger with all the added space.

Beside Carole Todd and all of her lot and all of her extended family, there was Shaun and Jill and Tom Grey and his good friend John. Obviously, Jason and Peter and both sets of their parents and there was one unexpected guest, well not so unexpected to Maggie and Carole Todd, because it seemed that Carole wasn't going through the change of life after all and Scarlett had arrived a few months after Maggie and the kids had moved out. Maggie certainly had a gift.

And how Maggie Hunter loved her job. It was varied and it worked out as she had hoped it would and there was so much footfall around her, outside of Jason and Peter, she didn't have to tell anyone her sorry tale of woe.

She continued to learn to read the tarot cards, they were always with her. With the arrival of Scarlett, she grew in confidence and would happily read for other people. She progressed from just 3 cards to bigger spreads, she liked to get the full picture.

The colourful auras were still there too, and the smells of people long gone. She still sensed Dean, but not as much. The more settled she became, the less aware of him she was.

The children grew, settled into their new home and by the time they were celebrating Dana's 7th Birthday in Carole Todd's best room all was well with Maggie Hunter and her children. But then life had a funny way of knocking you back on your bum when things were going too well. Nothing major, just a few things happened one on top of the other, well there was major, but they were from the past that intruded on the present. The first one was that Dorothy Hunter died.

Obviously, Maggie Hunter hadn't seen her mam and dad for over 10 years. She had been pregnant with Eve and now Eve wasn't far off secondary school, which was how much time had elapsed.

In all of that time they had never seen their grandchildren. Maggie knew they had seen Jude and Stephen's two, but Jude had said she had been once and wouldn't be going back. They had been made to feel so unwelcome. If Stephen had wanted his mam and dad to see the children, then he could take them himself.

So as far as Maggie was aware, of Dorothy and Leslie Hunter's five grandchildren, they had seen two of them once. What had that all been about. Jill and Shaun were married, but whether it was because there was already so many children in the family, to date they hadn't had any of their own and seemed happy to have it that way. They had lavish holidays for weeks on end and they had a social life second to none. There was time for them though, they hadn't quite reached their thirties.

To all intense and purposes, Dorothy Hunter hadn't been ailing. But one day she just dropped down dead. She was 58 years old. Maggie was at a loss as to what to do. Shaun and Stephen both went to see their dad, he hadn't said much beyond that he would let them know when the funeral was. He had always been a quiet man, even when his own children were little, it had seemed the time since Maggie left hadn't helped and if anything, he was even quieter.

Maggie would have to go to the funeral, how could she not. It was her mam. But she wouldn't go in a car with her brothers and her dad, or her Auntie Joan, uncle Ken and cousin Tom. No, she would just go and stand at the back of the crematorium and pay her respects for the woman who she used to call mam.

It was a strange time. She couldn't grieve like she would have been expected to be able to, there was too much time passed. All her grieving was done when her mam had laid into her, and she'd had to flee for her life. She still had the scar on her forehead as testament to that time passed. But she did feel sad, and she did feel a little bit sorry for her dad. Carole Todd thought she was mad for having any type of feeling for any of them, but then she had never been in that predicament.

So, on the day of the funeral, she made her way to the crematorium, waited outside until the family car and the coffin arrived and then quietly made her way inside and sat at the back for the service. Her dad seemed to have aged 20 years. He had a stoop he had never had before and instead of looking a sprightly 60 year old, he looked years older. Maggie Hunter gave a little shudder, she didn't think that this man who was her dad was long for this world.

She sat through the service. They talked of Dorothy Hunter's children, all three of them and her five grandchildren she was allegedly so fond of. Maggie could not believe what she was hearing. But she would never speak ill of the dead and if that was how her dad wanted to portray his wife then so be it.

Leslie Hunter must have seen Maggie as she filed passed him at the crematorium door, but he did not acknowledge her. There was nothing else for Maggie to do than to cuddle each of her brothers, her cousin Tom Grey, his good friend John, her aunt and uncle and then make her way home. She had paid her respects to the mother who had cared for her until she was 16 and now she was going home. That had been that.

There had been no warning from her Granny Hunter, there had been no alarm bells ringing in her head. Nothing in any of her readings. Nothing. Because there was nothing there to hurt her. It had upset her how much her dad had aged, the shock of losing his wife so suddenly would have taken its toll on most people. She had had some sort of aneurysm; it would have been all over very quickly. Sad, but any thought of reconciliation had gone, at least in this life anyway.

52) The Ace of Pentacles

Maggie Hunter had just about got over the shock of her mam when there was another blast from the past. Tony Sharp stood in front of her as large as life as she worked the bar one night at the Geordie Ridley. It was a Saturday night, and the bar was busy, so busy that Maggie had felt obliged to put the accounts books down and go and stand behind the bar with Jason, Peter and a couple of other bat staff and help out.

She often worked Saturday nights. Dean's mam and dad would take the kids for the weekend Friday to Sunday and on those occasions Maggie would put all her hours in for when they were away from the house. It was normal for her to work a Friday night, Saturday all day and night and even sometimes work on a Sunday morning, even if it was just helping with the clear up from the night before.

The Geordie Ridley had proved to be a very popular pub. Jason and Peter were perfect hosts and knew their trade well. The pub had become a vital hub for the local community, people went for a quiet drink, or for tea or party. They had live bands and no matter what time of the year it was they celebrated everything from Pancake Tuesday, the Grand National, St Patricks Day or New Years Eve. Any excuse and the pub was dressed and the atmosphere was party central.

Maggie loved working there. No two shifts were ever the same and Jason and Peter became her work family who often mingled with her real family and the rest of the dysfunctional family that she was also part of. But it was more than that, she was virtually a bar manager, she could turn her hands to the accounts, she could control the stock and the staff and every year when Jason and Peter took their Annual holiday, Maggie took charge.

They loved Maggie's oddness. Not long after she started working for them she told them what she thought each of their personalities were, Jason and his pick hue full of sensitivity, love and oozing sexuality, he might have been a gay man but he was certainly eye candy for the ladies and when he was working the bar, he would flirt with all the lady customers sometimes better than a straight man. This would of course wind Peter and his green aura up, he who was prone to a little bit of jealousy, he needed his life to be balanced, he needed to be soothed. But Maggie knew that Peter had no need to worry. Behind closed doors, when the punters had gone, Jason only had eyes for Peter, the floor show would be over for another day and Jason would revert back to just being Peter's bloke.

Maggie sussing them out so quickly had blown their minds. They made her read the other staff's aura, she could see them now so happily dissected the barmaids or kitchen staff or cleaner. They were even more in awe when she told them that she could read tarot and produced the little bundle of cards wrapped in Dean's silk shirt and Eve's ribbon.

A table was cleared and she found herself doing a horseshoe spread for first Peter and then Jason. And then anyone else who needed some sort of guidance. With each reading her confidence grew. The meanings seemed to jump out to her, she really was a natural. She was no longer scared.

The boys wanted to have a Clairvoyant Night in the pub. Maggie had initially laughed it off, but they kept going on and on. They said it would be a nice little money earner, for Maggie and for them. It would have to be a ticketed event, after all Maggie couldn't read loads and loads of them, but she thought she would be able to manage maybe 6.

In the end she agreed, but she didn't want people to know it was her. She didn't want it getting back to the kids and their friends and their teachers. She didn't want to embarrass them. They suggested a stage name, which sounded much more professional than it actually was. But it was a solution. Madam Mags, Clairvoyant Margaret, the list was endless. Then they were all sitting having a coffee one morning, well Jason and Peter were, Maggie still hadn't grown up enough to drink tea, before the opened the doors to the customers. On the wall was one of the relic's from the old Geordie Ridley pub, it was a ditty: -

> She's a Big Lass
>
> She's a Bonny Lass
>
> And she Likes her Beer
>
> And they Call her Cushie Butterfield
>
> And I Wish She Was Here!

The three of them had looked at the framed ditty at the same time. This was it, the name they had been waiting for. There was no need to be Madam this or Madam that. Maggie would have the stage name of Cushie Butterfield when she was doing her readings. They were all in agreement, she wasn't a big lass as such, but she was tall for a girl, the boys said that she was a bonny lass and she had become quite partial to the odd beer two, they would call her Cushie Butterfield, and they were all glad that she was there.

A poster went up and within a day the 6 spaces were taken. It was a bizarre feeling doing readings for money, it didn't seem to matter as much if she got things wrong if people were having readings free of charge because they couldn't really complain. Not that she had ever thought that she had ever got it wrong. It was a gift. First the aura when someone first sat down in front of her, that was a good indicator on to where that person was in their life, it was her chance to tune into them as they shuffled the cards. But still, she hoped that once she started charging a bob or two as her Granny Hunter had, her ability was still as honed as ever.

And what a success she was. Each person who had a reading went into the bar to regale who ever would listen how amazing Cushie Butterfield had been. Maggie had loved it. There was a little snug room that they had allowed Maggie to have for the readings and to be honest, the night flew over.

It was such a success that more and more people asked for more Tarot Reading Nights. Maggie couldn't expect to have the snug room for free, so agreed a price with Jason and then she worked it into the price of the reading. Another poster and another sold out night. It was proving to be lucrative for both Maggie and for the Geordie Ridley. Having money for readings wasn't dampening her skills, if anything the more frequent she used the cards the more insight she seemed to have. Sometimes she thought she could feel someone standing behind her looking over her shoulder, but it would only be Granny Hunter or Dean and that gave her more comfort than fear.

But even so, having Tony Sharp standing in front of her ordering drinks took the wind out of her sails. Where was Granny Hunter when she needed her, she hated all these surprises, at least when she had alarm bells ringing, she remained alert. But there he was, standing in her workplace and didn't look much different to the last time she had seen him which again was over ten years earlier.

Maggie Hunter might have got a fright, but there was no somersaulting tummy. He meant nothing to her now, if he ever had beyond the flattery. But he was Eve's dad and if he asked then she would have to tell. He didn't ask, he just ordered his drinks, said he hoped that she was ok and then left. Rude, Maggie thought then watched his head bob up and down towards the seating area at the far side of the bar.

Keeping an eye on the area, it wasn't until they had rang the bell for last orders and the last drinks had been served and the bar area cleared did Maggie Hunter get chance to see where Tony Sharp was sitting. He was with his wife, well at least Maggie assumed that was who it was, she looked about Tony Sharp's age and was very well groomed and dressed immaculately. She looked like money. In contrast Maggie was in jeans and a t shirt and looked every inch the hired help. Maggie would just stay out of their way and because the bar was quieter, she made her way around to the little room that was used as an office and started finishing off things for the night.

By the time she re-emerged from the office, put on her coat for home, the Geordie Ridley was empty and Tony Sharp had gone.

That was fine she thought as she let herself into the house. He knew where she worked now so if he wanted to chat that would be fine. There had been no money off him since they had lived in the old old house, he had never looked for her as far as she could see and if he had said anything to her dad, the messages would never get back to her.

But still, it did shake her to see him. He was out of her life by choice, as large a part as he had played, not he himself but the legacy he had left her with in the shape of Eve, it wasn't like with Dean, she hadn't really had a relationship with Tony Sharp, just driving dates and the lush kissing. Maggie and Dean were all consuming, the void that he left in her life was something that could never be filled, not in the same way.

In the quietness of the house Maggie Hunter did something that she didn't do very often. She let the tears low, gulped on huge sobs and let the wails out. She had no idea how long she sat in the middle of her living room, it was already late when she had got home but deciding that she wanted one of her big bubble baths, she glanced at the clock and was shocked to see that it was already almost 3am.

She slept because she had to. She had an early start cleaning in the Geordie Ridley in the morning and then she would be going to Carole Todd's for lunch where the kids would be getting dropped off in time for dessert. The warmth of thinking about the kids lulled her to sleep, where she dreamt of driving in cars and lush kissing, though she couldn't be sure that it had been Tony Sharp in her dream or someone else. Never the less, when the alarm clock went off, she was overwhelmed with loneliness with the empty space on the other side of her bed.

53) The King of Swords

Maggie never worked the same week twice. She always made sure she got her hours in throughout each month, but some weeks were more hectic than others and she was so dependent on others to help with babysitting that it was always like a military operation. But she was coping, they had to. Carole Todd helped, and Dean's mam and dad were amazing. Jude and Stephen would help with school runs seeing as Emily was in the same school and sometimes Auntie Tom and Auntie John would come and have sleepovers.

Money was always tight. The kids didn't stop growing and the older they got the more they seemed to need. Maggie had no idea how she would have managed to get Eve's school uniform for secondary school if it hadn't been for Dean's mam and dad insisting. To all intents and purposes, they treat Eve no different to the other two kids. Eve knew that Dean wasn't her real dad, but Eve loved everyone whether they were related, or not so loving Mr and Mrs Burns came easy to her and the readily loved her back in return.

She earned a good wage at the Geordie Ridley and then she had the little bit extra that she earned now and again when she was Cushie Butterifield, but she was always watching the pennies and when a big bill landed on her doorstep for the gas or the electricity, Maggie would tailspin and panic. The little nest egg she kept in the Post Office account had gone, just living a life had put paid to that.

There was no way she could do more hours at the Geordie Ridley, it wasn't fair on everyone else and to be honest the thought of getting her typewriting back out and banging away on that for hours on end didn't fill her with joy, it was a big commitment for not very much money. She had a skill at her fingertips but beyond the Geordie Ridley sessions and doing reading for friends and family, she had never thought about making a bit more of a business of it.

There was definitely a demand for it. Her little sessions at the Geordie Ridley were always filled in hours and there was always a waiting list in case someone cancelled, her Granny Hunter had said she earned a bob or two when she needed it, maybe that could be the answer. She could do private readings at home. Maybe in her dining room.

Eve was old enough to keep an eye on the other two, something she would relish if Maggie could slip her a bit pocket money for doing it, she had all of a sudden started to want little bits of make up and clothes. Maggie couldn't remember being that interested in fashion in her pre-teenage days, but kids were much older than their years those days.

It was something to think about anyway. And in reality, she hadn't worked on a Friday night in the Geordie Ridley since the night that Tony Sharp had been in 3 weeks earlier. She should have known that he would be back, she should have known that he had been back in the intervening Friday nights to see Maggie. This time he didn't have his wife on tow. This time he asked if he could speak to her and this time, when she handed him his drink, she made excuses to Jason about spotting an old friend and followed Tony to the corner of the room where it wasn't as crowded, and the music wasn't as loud.

Maggie felt ok about seeing him. She had no feelings for him, no more than that of what he was, an old friend. He just also happened to be Eve's dad. They exchanged pleasantries. Maggie really wasn't sure what he knew of her life in the years since they had last spoken. When had that been? It had been the Christmas Eve of the year that Eve had been born, so long ago and yet it just felt like yesterday.

All she could do was give him a quick recap of her life since him. He seemed to be visibly upset about Dean, said he could remember how happy they had looked when he had dropped off that Christmas card the last time, that was why he had decided not to intrude any more, she had seemed so happy. He hadn't known about the accident, he hadn't known about her youngest daughter being born or Maggie's breakdown or the kids having to live with Carole Todd with the support of the rest of the family, or the family home having to be sold. He looked bereft. He said he would have helped if he had known.

Tony Sharp did know that her mam had died. Leslie Hunter still worked at Quarry's End but hadn't uttered a word to Tony since Maggie had worked there. So, there had been no snippets of gossip for Tony to hear, he said for such a long time he sort of forgot all about Maggie and Eve. Until a few Friday nights ago when he had popped into the Geordie Ridley to meet up with some friends that had cancelled at the last minute.

He told her she looked well, she doubted that she did, but it was nice to be told none the less. Yes, that had been his wife he had been with. They had two boys, one a little older than Ryan the other a little younger. He was still working at Quarry's End, his dad had retired so it was his baby now. Apparently, Maggie wouldn't know anyone there now, Mrs

West had left not long after Maggie had to look after her elderly mam and Ann had gone to work at Newcastle Airport. But business was good it gave him a good lifestyle, just as it had done all of his life.

Jason came to the table and hovered as if waiting for an invitation, Maggie ignored the pleading eyes and asked him to bring a couple of drinks over. There was plenty of time to explaining to Jason who the good looking bloke she was sharing a table with was. It made her smile thinking of Jason and Peter whispering together thinking that ice maiden Maggie had pulled.

No, he had never told his wife about Maggie and Eve. It had gone way beyond it being a sensible conversation to have now, it would be all hurt and betrayal now, Maggie could understand him not wanting to tell her all those years ago, she couldn't even begin to think what effect his confession would have on his marriage now.

Tony asked about Eve. Maggie Hunter told him all about her, what she looked like, what her likes and dislikes were, what she excelled at in school and what she hated. Maggie wished she had kept some photos in her bag, but she hadn't. He just had to trust Maggie when she told him that she was going to be a heartbreaker.

Maggie actually felt sorry for Tony Sharp. He had everything he could ever have wanted. Good job, plenty of money, a lovely wife and sons, but Maggie could see his aura and she knew that there was a sadness there. She sensed that he would have had a relationship with his daughter if it was at all possible. Was it too late?? Maggie's instinct said it was, there would be too much hurt for Tony and his family and there would be too much confusion for Eve. She knew her real dad was out there somewhere, but to date she had never really asked, a dad was something she never really missed. Dean, she missed Dean and had very clear memories of him. But she also had lots of men in her life who individually took on a father like role, none more so than Dean's dad, Glen Todd and of course her brothers.

There was to be no happy ever after with Tony Sharp, there was nothing to say, no hope to give. Things were best left as they were.

Jason arrived with their drinks and Maggie steered the chat back to less choppy waters. She told him about working at the Geordie Ridley and she told him about Cushie Butterfield. He was amazed and a little taken aback with Maggie and her ability to read cards and people, he didn't think he had ever known that about her he thought. He made her laugh when he said he might book a reading for himself, she told him to save his money, she knew everything she needed to know about him and anything he wanted to know she could tell him there and then without the little pack of cards or him parting with his money.

It actually turned into a nice hour or so. If Jason and Peter were narked at her for abandoning her post they never said, just came and put another couple of drinks on the table when the ones in front of them were almost empty.

They didn't talk about anything of any importance. Maggie did ask about her dad, was he coping did Tony think. But he was as green as she was about the health and wellbeing of her father. He talked of his plans for Quarry's End and told her if she ever needed a typing job she only had to ask, but they both knew that she would never do that. He offered her money. He said he knew she must be finding it tough on her own, Eve would no doubt be demanding now she was growing up. But as skint as Maggie was, she had pride. The nest egg he had given her had served her and her family well enough, she wouldn't take more off him. She had already decided that Cushie Butterfield would be working out of her dining room, but that was something she was doing on her own. If she needed money she would earn it, she wouldn't take a handout off Tony Sharp no matter how rich he was.

And then it was last orders, and it was time to say goodbye to Tony Sharp again. How many departures had they had now?? Two?? Three?? He was a nice bloke, he just wasn't her nice bloke and he probably never was. She had been young and flattered and a little bit in awe of the older boy who just happened to be the owner of the company's son and who drove a swanky noisy car. But he was also Eve's dad and looking at him he could see Eve in him, something she had never seen, especially since Dean had died and all so ever saw was Dean and his traits. But with her hand on her heart, she could see a startling resemblance between Tony and Eve and she once again kicked herself for not having a photograph of her in her handbag.

With a cuddle and a kiss on the cheek he was gone. Maggie had the strangest feeling that this would maybe be the last time she would ever see him. But it was only a fleeting thought and then it was gone, just like he was.

The door had barely closed on him, and Jason and Peter were over to see who her 'date' had been, the nosey buggers. She wished she had a camera with her because the look on their faces when she told them it was Eve's dad was priceless.

That would teach them for trying to teach their Granny to suck eggs and think that they could predict who the handsome man she had whiled away an hour or two with was. With a kiss on both their cheeks she started picking up dirty glasses, it was the least she could do, it was going to be another late finish. But she had a smile on her face, and she felt all was well in her world once again… but was it???

304

54) The Magician

Life carried on.

Cushie Butterfield became a massive part of Maggie Hunter's life. By inviting people into her little dining room for readings, her life became a little bit more manageable. Two or three times a month she would invite clients to her home, and she would read their aura, spread out the cards and see what life had in store for them. Good and bad. She had researched Clairvoyants, see what was said about them and found that they mainly had bad press.

It seemed to be a business that was open to abuse, to charlatans who would take money off mainly vulnerable people, because if your honest, happy people don't tend to look for answers in the lap of the Gods, no people sought out answers from a higher level because they had concerns. Cushie Butterfield knew she was the real deal though, she had already gained quite a reputation from her evenings at the Geordie Ridley. All she needed to do was be honest. Already in the past when she had readings and there was nothing there, she would give the client their money back. She would rather do that then blow smoke up their tail. She would know the moment the client entered the room, the aura would be dim or none existent and the spread of the cards would just be confusing. It didn't happen often, but it did happen.

Cushie Butterfield even honed a way that allowed her to foretell a client bad news, a bit like the alarm bells that she herself had once had. A gentle push to be guarded without scaring the bejesus out of the client.

Just like she had done years earlier, she placed little postcards in the local shops and waited for the telephone to ring. Which it did and much to the kids Annoyance, it happened very often. The bookings were made, and the people came.

They came in ones and twos and sometimes a group would book her for the full night, again much to the kids Annoyance when there would be 6 or 7 people sitting in their living room and they were banished to their bedrooms.

Maggie Hunter had some sort of peace. As she worked as Cushie Butterfield she would often get her Granny Hunter or Dean mischievously pop into the reading. It gave her some kind of comfort. Maggie knew that even without the alarm bell warning in her head, if there was something she needed to know, then it would be there.

There was a couple of pieces of narrative keep coming through to her. The first was movement, in almost every reading she did, there was the movement motion. What was that about?? Was she going to have to move house again, she thought not. There had been no noise from her landlord about wanting her to leave, she paid her rent in a timely manor and wasn't really any bother.

But the cards seemed to be insistent, and it wasn't until Eve had a complete meltdown one night because Cushie Butterfield was having a group booking in for readings on the same night that Eve was having friends sleepover, did the penny drop. Maggie Hunter needed to learn to drive. She needed to be able to go to clients homes herself when there was a few of them wanting readings together. She needed to give the kids their home back.

She could afford a small car, she could afford some driving lessons and if she could rope someone in to learn her to drive or a least learn her the basics.

And that was the second piece of narrative in the cards. Reconciliation. With the thought of learning to drive there had only been one person who had popped into her head. Not her brothers, that would have been like World War 3, neither of them were the most patient of drivers, she had seen first hand how Annoyed they got the minute they got behind a steering wheel. No, the only person she would ever have considered helping her to learn to drive was her dad.

Once the thought of her dad was in her head, it was all consuming. What was the worst that could happen, he closed the door in her face. They had done that years ago, she could take the rejection. She just needed to try. Her heart hurt when she thought of him living in the family home all on his own. Tony Sharp had said he had seemed to age since her mam had died. She had seen his stoop herself at the funeral. Surely it didn't have to be this way though, that he simply slipped away all on his own. Maggie knew about grief, about the all consuming sadness, she still felt sad all of these years later. But Dean's death no longer defined who she was, her mam's death didn't have to be all that Leslie Hunter was about.

She was just going to have to brave it out. At least try.

Knowing that he wouldn't be at work on a Saturday morning, she took the opportunity the next weekend that Eve, Ryan and Dana were staying with Dean's mam and dad. It had been almost 15 years since she had last set foot in her family home, she wasn't even sure if she would set foot in it again. She only knew that the urge to see him was a little bit all consuming.

55) Judgement

The front garden was as well kept as ever, obviously her dad was still taking care of it, but the house itself looked shabby and a little bit uncared for. She knocked on the door once and there was no answer. She knocked again and stood waiting. It took a long time for her to hear the latch on the door being pulled back, so long that she thought that she had been wrong, and her dad wasn't in.

But the door opened, and her dad stared at her with an utter look of shock on his face. 'Dad??????...'

Maggie Hunter smiled at him, she needed to show him that she meant him no harm. Her heart went out to him, he looked so fragile.

Leslie Hunter pulled the door open and beckoned her inside. The house was as shabby inside as it was out. It wasn't messy, everything seemed to still be in its place. The coat stand, the telephone table, it was all there just as it had been when she had last lived there. They went into the kitchen, it hadn't changed one bit. But her dad had.

The stoop was still there, maybe it was all the years working at Quarry's End that had put a curve into his back or was it that he was a broken man. Maggie thought the latter.

He offered her tea, no she would just have juice, she made him smile when she told him that she still wasn't grown up enough for hot drinks.

Passing her an orange juice that he had made from a bottle he found in the 'pop' cupboard which looked like it had been sitting there the last time Maggie had been in the kitchen, he busied himself making a cup of coffee and then sat down Maggie in front of his only daughter.

It was awkward.

The father and daughter hadn't spoken for so long. They had never been big talkers in the first place, there were all those strained journey's to and back from Quarry's End, they had talked but never about anything important, she had just been 16 for God's Sake. Now she was a grown woman, and he was an elderly man. But it needed to be done.

Maggie needed to bring this broken man out of the shadows and into the midst of her dysfunctional family. He needed to meet his grandchildren, he needed to have a reason to live.

Taking a deep breath, Maggie opened her mouth and what ever it was she had been wanting to say for over a decade came out. Warts and all. She could hear herself talking, she sounded like her mam, she wasn't talking to him, she was talking at him. Stopping she apologised, she just had so much to say. He smiled at her and in that moment, she knew that within the shell of a human being that he was now, there was her dad.

In parts he talked. He tried to apologise. Maggie would have none of it, that as all long gone. She remembered something that her Granny

Hunter used to say, her son would no doubt have heard it in his lifetime too, but it seemed a fitting thing to say!

'Dad, if God hadn't wanted us to keep looking back, he would have put eyes on the back of our head and not the front. We need to keep looking forward!'

'Your Granny used to say that! Granny used to say that! You are very like her Maggie.'

More than he could ever have imagined. So, Maggie told him about Cushie Butterfield and the little business she ran and how that was the very reason that she was there that day. Of course, he would love to teach her to drive! He would even help her look for a car.

In the end she was there until tea time. She ended up having to put on her make up in his little bathroom, which again seemed to have been stuck in a time warp. She was tempted to look in her old bedroom, but that would be for another day. She had to get to work.

Maggie Hunter had no recollection of ever cuddling her dad. But before she left to go to her shift at the Geordie Ridley, she held on to him as hard as she could. It was the best feeling. It was made better when he cuddled her back.

They had agreed that going forward everything would be done in baby steps, she didn't want to overwhelm him, he had been living quite a solitary life for a long time, even when her mam had been alive. But he had agreed to go and look for a car with her, Thursday night when he finished work.

And so Leslie Hunter reconnected with his family. He had still seen the boys, Stephen not so much, Shaun called every week. But it had all been strained since Maggie had left. The talk never came easy, and Leslie couldn't blame his boys for getting fidgety after 10 minutes and wanting to get away.

To say everyone was shocked by Maggie's olive branch to her dad was an understatement. Stephen and Shaun thought that she was mad, he didn't deserve it, they didn't get it. But Carole Todd did. She understood that her dad was a sad and lonely old man, he would never have come to Maggie, his pride wouldn't have let him. But he had a great big family there that would embrace him into their lives just like they had everyone else that had followed Maggie into their own lives. It was something that Maggie wanted, had she not been through enough?? Carole said to anyone who raised an eyebrow at her intentions. None of them would forget, but surely, they could forgive, especially if it was going to make Maggie happy.

So, the dysfunctional family waited on the side line until the time was right.

Maggie bought a little Ford Fiesta and Leslie Hunter turned up when ever they had any free time and taught his daughter how to drive. In all that time there had only been the two of them. It was their time. A time to talk and a time to heal. Maggie Hunter could probably have passed her driving test months before she actually did, she passed first time with flying colours.

They had talked a lot. Well Maggie had, her dad tended to agree or disagree and grab the wheel when she became animated and distracted. Leslie Hunter would have a very good idea about each and every one of Maggie's dysfunctional family before he had even met them. His grandchildren were all dissected personality wise, Dean was talked about a lot and of course Carole Todd and her brood. Even her cousin Tom Grey was spoken about, his good friend John and her new best friends Jason and Peter. The world was changing and they should be embracing it. That was one subject her dad gave no opinion of, but he was old school.

And they talked about Tony Sharp. She was so sorry that she had caused so much hurt. Her head had been turned and she had been very flattered. If she could turn the clock back she would and do everything differently, but it was done, and she was sorry. It had been the last driving lesson before her driving test and it was a subject that hadn't been broached, but it was the elephant in the room and it needed to be talked about, because once the lessons were over, it was going to be showtime and Leslie Hunter would be eased into family life.

But he was a quiet man and even though Maggie Hunter did the whole talk at him thing, he did not respond. Tears trickled down his face, Maggie saw them and expertly pulled the car to a safe spot at the side of the road, dug into her handbag and passed her dad a tissue. She had said what she had wanted no needed so say and now that was that. She had no need for her dad to say anything back in return, him and her mam had obviously been living in some type of purgatory all of these years. It was over now. It was time for Leslie Hunter to meet Eve, Ryan and Dana. It was time for the family to put their arms around Leslie Hunter and welcome him. He was family.

So little by little he became a part of the family that he had shunned for so long. It was all done in a drip drip fashion, nothing to scary. He got to know Maggie's children first, they asked no questions about where he had been all these years, just accepted that he was their Granddad, Maggie's dad and let the life they lived flow around him.

With each visit, Leslie Hunter grew in confidence. Somehow his stoop didn't seem quite as curved, and he chatted to all of the kids with ease. Shaun and Jill would sometimes call knowing that he would be there and when one day Jill suggested that they had a little family picnic, it turned into a real family occasion when Jude, Stephen and their two turned up too. It was another hurdle out of the way.

With her new freedom in the shape of her Ford Fiesta, there was less need for people to come to the house for their Cushie Butterfield readings, it was surprising how many people liked to see her in groups of 6 or 8 and they were happier still that she would travel to their homes.

So, art least once a week, Maggie Hunter would take herself off for a nights work and sometimes, which at first, she had to coax him to do, Leslie Hunter would be there to look after the kids.

56) The Six of Swords

Carole Todd had been a little harder to convince. By the time it got to Christmas, Leslie Hunter had still not been to her house. She made excuses and he made excuses and it never happened. But it was Christmas and this year they were all going to the Geordie Ridley, and everyone would be there. Which included Carole Todd and her exceptional extended family, Maggie and all her lot as well as cousin Tom Grey, his good friend John, Jason and Peter, Dean's mam and dad and of course Maggie Hunter's dad.

They could all just like it or lump it.

Maggie was far too busy on the run up to Christmas to worry about any of that. Cushie Butterfield was as busy as ever, she seemed to be getting a really good reputation and to her, it wasn't really work. She loved the half hour or so she spent with each of her clients, a little snippet into their lives. Some were looking for something that they would never find, others had lost people and just wanted to connect to know that everything would be ok. The younger ones tended to want to know about love and babies, the older ones whether their husbands still loved them or were cheating on them, there would be the odd one that wanted to know about a job and then the older ones just didn't want to be lonely.

Cushie Butterfield always gave her best. Even if their future looked bleak she would encourage them to try a different path and then come see her again in a year or so. It had happened, a small tweak to their lives and the next time she saw them there would be a brighter aura and the cards would look better.

She still sensed her Granny Hunter in the cards, she still sent the odd message to her personally, on reflection, Maggie thought that it had been her Granny Hunter's doing that she had reconciled with her dad. The signs had been there, subtle hints. Dean was far less apparent. If she wanted to sense him, she would pull on his leather jacket or wear his sweatshirt. She still hated the bed being empty next to her, but the days when she would wake thinking she could feel the weight of him lying on her were long gone. She could now think of him without it hurting so much. Time did heal.

When Linda asked Maggie to read her cards, she had no hesitation. She had done it many times for her in the past. But Maggie had a sneaky feeling that she might be wanting her to spot the pitter patter of tiny feet in her reading. Maggie was all braced for it, but despite asking Linda to choose a few more cards there was nothing. Linda knew there was no baby, she was wanting Maggie to see something else.

Movement and travel were everywhere. Maggie looked at her oldest friend! She was emigrating! Linda said she could think of no other way to tell her, they had got their final papers a few weeks ago and would be heading off to Australia in February.

Maggie was blown away. She had always thought Linda and Paul as being home birds, but one of Paul's workmates had gone to Australia a year or so earlier and they were living a dream life. Linda and Paul had to give it a go! Maggie re-read her cards with her new found knowledge and there was nothing to say it was going to be the wrong move. As gutted as Maggie was to be losing her best friend, it was only the other side of the world, they would see each other again. And another two people were added to the Christmas Day guest list.

Maggie Hunter worked as much as she could. The kids had asked for so much for Christmas and none of it was cheap. So, she worked at the Geordie Ridley through the day when the kids were at school, did the odd Cushie Butterfield party and if she could get any additional babysitting, she would pick up a shift at the pub.

She was working the bar at the Geordie Ridley the Friday night before Christmas. She hadn't intended being in the bar, she had wages to sort out and end of year bonuses to be paid to the staff, but one of the barmaids had rang in sick and the place was fit to burst. There was a live band on and they were belting out Christmas tunes, it seemed that every business had left their place of work and made their way to the pub. The place was packed to the rafters, but the mood was jovial as only works Christmas drinks could be.

The kids were with Dean's mam and dad. She had plAnnd on working as much of the weekend as she could, there weren't many shopping days before Christmas and Eve had her heart set on some shoes she had seen in the city centre, thank God she drove now or else it would have been an all day job going for them, as it was she would be able to go get them Monday morning, she'd had a pair kept back for her.

With a constant shopping list running through her head, Maggie wasn't really concentrating on who was in the bar or who she was serving. She did it all with a smile on her face and a Santa hat on her head. Thanked each one that tipped her and then moved on to the next customer. But she could feel eyes on her. She scoured the faces of the people at the bar waiting to be served. Beside a couple of regulars that came in all of the time, she didn't recognise anyone.

But the feeling didn't go away and when she took a second to think about it, her heart did a little flutter, not in a sinister scary way, like an excited way. That something lovely was about to happen. She was obviously over worked and over tired, her radar was playing up. But she was smiling, it was hard not to when there was so much jolliness in the Geordie Ridley that Friday night. If there was something momentous about to happen to her, then bring it on!! It's Christmas!!!

57) The Nine of Cups

A Christmas that went surprisingly well. There was no awkwardness on Christmas Day as Maggie thought there may be. Watching her dad, he seemed happy to be in amongst it and even though he got everyone muddled up he had actually played a blinder, he came to the Geordie Ridley dressed as Santa Claus with a gift for each of the children, even little Scarlett hadn't been left out. It was lush because none of the kids knew him well enough to recognise the man under the beard or the familiar sound of his voice. By the time everyone had been given their gifts and he left with a big Ho Ho Ho there was only Eve who grinned at her mam and gave her granddad a huge cuddle when he made his way back into the pub. Partners in crime Maggie thought to herself. But a lovely gesture and if she wasn't mistaken, a new tradition.

The whole of Christmas was lovely. Bitter sweet because of Linda and Paul leaving so shortly in the New Year, but it was the right thing for them to do. No baby had materialised, and she knew without a doubt that both Linda and Paul were worn out by people asking when they were going to be having a baby of their own. Maggie had the strangest feeling that there would be a baby, somehow when they got settled there would be the pitter patter of tiny feet, they had both longed for, what Maggie couldn't be sure of if the baby would be one they had made!! Time would tell.

Maggie continued to work in the Geordie Ridley through the rest of the festive period. Her dad was as good as gold and didn't mind driving over and sitting with the kids until she finished her shift, he seemed to be relishing in the fact that he was needed. Again, Maggie thought that his stoop wasn't quite as stooped these days. And he looked so smart, all of the clothes they had bought him for Christmas were being well worn.

He had turned out to be a better man than Maggie could have hoped for. He had pulled Carole and Glen to a side on Christmas Day and thanked them for everything they had done for his daughter and grandchildren, he didn't explain or apologise, he just thanked them. It was enough. The awkwardness was gone and the dysfunctional family they were grew. And Leslie Hunter seemed to mosey along with everyone else, even Tom Grey and his good friend John or Jason and Peter didn't seem to phase him. He may not have agreed with the relationships much less understood them, but he accepted happiness and they were happy.

Back in the Geordie Ridley the eyes were always on her. Each session was busy with there being so many people off for the Christmas period. But the feeling that she was being watched didn't go away. Nor did the fluttering heart. She was so curious that she had even done herself a reading, something she didn't normally like to do, if there was anything she needed to know then she would usually be able to pick it up in other peoples reading. But she hadn't done any readings since before Christmas and the curiosity was getting the better of her.

So, she did a simple three card spread: -

        Past   -   Three of Pentacles

        Present -   Wheel of Fortune

        Future   -   Knight of Cups

Interesting Maggie thought to herself. Basically, it meant that she had been using her skills to make a better life, which she had. A move of house?? Hopefully not. But there was a turn for the better coming, some luck and there was a man, well a young man, who was well travelled and fair of face. He would be her love and her lover and her best friend!!

There was definitely something amiss. The eyes, the fluttering heart and now the cards. A man?? It was something that she had never really thought about. It had been such a long time since she had been intimate with someone, she didn't give herself time to think about it. She just assumed that was probably going to be it for her. She had loved and she had lost. But if she was being honest, she did miss 'doing it', well good doing it like it had been with Dean. Maybe he had been a one off though, Tony Sharp had certainly been a disappointment. The thought of getting her clothes off to have disappointment would certainly finish her off for the rest of her life.

Getting her clothes off?? Now there was something too! Her body was still only layered with a little fat, she was never off her feet running after the kids or around the Geordie Ridley, she had never kept fit and had always just ate what she wanted but maybe if she was going to get naked anytime soon, she may have to take a long hard look at herself. Bubble bath after work was on the cards!

She continued to keep a beady eye out for her fair of face young lover. There were so many faces in the Geordie Ridley each shift that they tended just to morph into one. But there was someone, the eyes were boring into her very being now and her heart was more of an albatross taking flight than a flutter. Maggie actually felt a little bit excited. But with another shift over, she made her way home, had a warm milk with her dad and then waved him off. He really was like a new man.

As she waited for her bubble bath to run, she took a good long look at herself. She had a scar running across her middle from where they had done an emergency caesarean section on her when Dana was born. And there were stretch marks, little silvery ones now, not like the purple that had been there where she was enormously pregnant. Her boobs were a nice shape and so far hadn't attempted to go South, but how long would they remain like that, she wasn't getting any younger. But all in all, if she had to get naked, she thought she may well cope!

Lying in the bath, she laughed. What the hell was she even thinking about. There was no one, she hadn't been asked out by anyone since Dean, she certainly didn't encourage any of the punters in the Geordie Ridley, she was friendly but never flirty. And if they were regulars, they knew that she had an alter ego in the shape of Cushie Butterfield and to those mere mortals, that was witchcraft!

So, she had never been out of a proper date for years and years and years and there was no one on the horizon who was trying to get into her knickers, so having worries about her body was a needless task. With that thought in her head, she submerged herself under the bubbles with the thought of there being an unopened tin of Quality Street in the living room with her name on it.

By the time they had celebrated Dana's birthday and seen in the New Year, the feeling of being watched had gone. Whatever it was had vanished and even though she didn't really mean to, she felt a little bit disappointed. A chance missed.

The New Year saw the departure of Linda and Paul to Australia, it was sad but happy. Maggie hoped that she would see two of her oldest friends again. She hoped that she would be able to see how they were through her readings. At least that gave her some sort of comfort.

Then life went on as usual. She worked at the Geordie Ridley, she did her little Cushie Butterfield group readings and she cared for the kids and everyone else she had in her life. It was a very sedate period.

It may well have been the calm before the storm.

58) The Page of Cups

Because the storm did arrive.

Working in the Geordie Ridley one night the feeling was back. There was someone watching her, she felt it again. Her heart was fluttering all over the shop. This time she wasn't working the bar. She had been in the office doing some book work and had only left to go and get herself a drink.

She had no sooner got the door of the bar when she felt it. Whoever he was he was here. He hadn't been here since Christmas so wasn't a regular. Sitting at a stool at the bar she asked Peter for a coke and instead of taking it back to the little office, she remained on the stool and sipped the coke through a straw, all the while discreetly scAnning the room for the 'watcher!' This time she wasn't going to let him slip through her hands, she wanted to know what all this was about.

So, she sat and she sat and she sat a bit longer. Peter brought her another drink. Even though she was officially working, she did so much more than was asked of her that it was never a problem if she had herself an extended break. It didn't happen often, but sometimes Carole and Glen Todd would pop in for a drink, or one of her brothers and of late, her dad! He had been an unexpected surprise one night when Jason came to tell her there was someone in the bar looking for her. She had lost count of the number of times he had been there since then. He only ever had two pints and then took himself off. But even if she didn't have time to sit and chat with him, he seemed happy sitting at the bar and talking to whoever happened to be sitting next to him. He was full of surprises.

Maggie Hunter was almost through her second glass of coke, when all of a sudden, her face started to flush up, her ears were burning, her heart was hammering in her chest and there was something pulling at her back. It wasn't a physical pull on her back, it was something else. She knew whatever or whoever it was that was causing all of this was behind her. For the first time in a very long time, Maggie was scared. Something like this had never happened to her before.

Tony Sharp had flirted with her, but there had been no body changing experience about it. Dean had danced his way into her heart, quickly, but still it wasn't quite love at first sight but more of love at first night. Still her body hadn't burned up and her heart hadn't felt like it was going to burst out of her chest. But then, back in the day, she hadn't been in tune with her second sight, it was something that she suppressed. Nowadays she embraced it, loved it, it had helped her live in oh so many ways.

She was going to have to turn around. If she didn't, she feared that she would instantaneously combust sitting on the stool at the bar and no one wanted to see that. So, taking a deep breath she span herself around in her seat to see what the fates had thrown at her……..

The bar had become a bit more crowded in the half hour she had sat on the bar stool. There was no one standing behind her, no gift. Just lots of people milling around and a few playing pool in the corner.

Maggie Hunter literally scratched her head. What had that been all about??? The burning up, the thumping heart, the ears and the pulling on her back?? She was at a loss. The back tugging had gone but the rest was still there. Was she missing something here?

Chewing on her lip, she smiled at a couple of people she knew. She felt like she was in some sort of surreal episode, it was like life was going on around her and she was having some sort of weird out of body experience. She was struck dumb, stock still.

And then there he was. It was like the parting of the sea. There had been lots of people between Maggie and the pool table, but the people dispersed and there was a group having a game of pool. There was a bloke bent over the table about to take a shot when he glanced up. Eyes locked and that was that. It was him, he was here. Fair of face and young, well younger than Maggie! She had no idea what he looked like, she could only see his eyes.

He dropped his head, took his shot and then started moving around the table finishing off his game. Maggie felt stupid. She must have looked like a proper idiot because she had the feeling that as she stared at this man, her mouth had opened wide enough to catch flies.

Jumping off the stool she almost ran out of the bar and back into the safety of the little office. She was an idiot. How could her second sight have done all of that out there. She must have looked like a desperate women, eyeing up a man she had never seen before, worse eyeing up a lad she had never seen before. The feeling was still there, but that was probably a mixture of addenelin and humiliation. She would stay in her little office until the bar was empty and the building closed for the night. Thank God she wasn't back into the Geordie Ridley until the middle of next week. She only hoped no one had seen her bizarre behaviour out there.

By the time Peter popped his head in to tell her they were just about tidied up for the night and they were ready to lock up, Maggie was feeling more like herself. The only remanent of her earlier humiliation was that her left ear was still burning away. Granny Hunter popped into her head 'left for love, right for spite.' The little rhyme had always made Maggie laugh when her Granny Hunter said it. She was told that if it was her right ear burning then she had to lick her fingers and then place them on the burning ear. Whoever it was that was being mean about her would wet themselves. Maggie thought that was a great trick to do and had done it herself many times over the years, but she had no idea if it worked, but it always made her feel better.

Maggie said her goodnights to Jason and Peter, if they thought she was behaving extra odd that night, they never said and she left the building.

59) The Knight of Cups

She had barely stepped outside when everything that had happened earlier was back. The thought of being watched, the thundering heart and the burning face. He was here. And there he was, leaning against a wall, staring at her just as she was staring at him.

This time they moved towards each other. Both stopped and stared and then continued to stare as if both of them had been struck mute. It seemed Maggie managed to pull herself together first. 'Hi, I don't know if this is just me, but I feel like we need to talk!!' The boy nodded and unsure of what else to do, Maggie beckoned to him that they would walk and he fell into step beside her as she made her way back to her house.

Maggie talked. Well, more interviewed him. His name was William, Will never Billy. He lived on the other side of the town, the opposite way to the direction they were walking. He was a soldier, based at Carrick so had chance to get back home on leave quite a bit. Hence the absence between Christmas and now. Yes, he had spent quite a bit of time in the Geordie Ridley over Christmas and New Year. Yes, he had seen her. Yes, he had watched her. And no, he had no idea why, he just knew that he needed to meet her. He said it had literally blown his mind.

All the while they walked she had no fear of him. When they got to Maggie's house, she had no hesitation in letting him in. She thought that they both needed a drink and she was sure she had a bottle of something or other in the fridge from Christmas. Eve was staying at a friend's, Ryan and Dana were at Dean's mam and dads. They had the house to themselves.

It was white wine, not a favourite of Maggie's or of Will's by the face he pulled when he took his first drink, but it would do for now and she knew that if she had a look around the cupboards there may be something a bit more drinkable, but that would be later. For now she needed to talk and look at Will. It was the strangest of feelings.

Will was young, way younger than Maggie which made her feel quite uneasy. But as they talked it became very clear that Will was an old soul, wise way beyond his years. Maggie gave him an extremely shortened version of her life. Eve, Dean, Ryan, Dana, Carole, Leslie Hunter and Cushie Butterfield. Will took it all in. He said that his life was boring in comparison, joined up at 17 when he wasn't sure what he wanted to do, loved the Army and had a long term girlfriend called Joanne.

The bottle of white was gone, as Will went for a wee, Maggie found a pack of beers stashed in the kitchen cupboard, she had forgot all about them, had bought them for her dad to have one or two when he looked after the kids. The pack had been untouched. So, grabbing them and some crisps she made her way back to the living room, just as Will returned. There eyes met and they were each as confused as each other. The surreal feeling returned, Maggie felt like she wasn't actually there, or it could have just been the white wine.

Drinking beer and eating crisps, Will asked her about Cushie Butterfield. What could she tell him?? So, she told him the truth best she could, about always being a bit odd growing up, about her Granny Hunter and the cards, how that at her worst moments there were always alarm bells ringing that would sometimes turn into siren, about the letter, the cards and the auras. Will asked Maggie about his own aura.

Maggie had seen it straightaway. It was of the type that she only saw now and again, usually people just had one hue, they were green or red, just one solid colour. Sometimes people may have a blend of two. Will's aura was like a rainbow. It was blue which made him calm, smart and trustworthy, then it was yellow for warm and energy and then pink for love and sexuality and orange for attraction and happiness. If she looked hard enough there was probably other colours. But for now she told him what she saw. She hoped and prayed that he wouldn't ask her for his cards to be read, she had the feeling that they would be a mess with the state they were both in.

They were very comfortable with each other. They had barely known each other a couple of hours but felt like they had been sitting talking like this their whole lives. Will said that it had really freaked him out the first time he had seen her. She had been serving behind the bar and he had been gutted when one of the blokes served him and he had no idea why. He said he felt like he was stalking her. That he had watched her all of that first night, working the bar, smiling at customers wearing her Santa hat. He said that the urge to talk to her had taken the wind right out of his sails. He had a girlfriend and said up until that point had never looked at another female, but Maggie was something else.

He said every opportunity he had he would find his way back to the Geordie Ridley, if she wasn't there he said it felt like his heart had broken. It had scared him. He had no idea what it was all about, so he did nothing, watched her from afar and then went back to is regiment. But she was always on his mind, more than his girlfriend was and tonight had been the first time he had been on leave since Christmas. When they had locked eyes across the bar earlier, he knew that what ever it was he was he knew that it had affected Maggie the same way and decided that it would be best to approach her away from prying eyes.

Maggie told him she knew he was coming, that she had read her own cards and there was someone young and fair of face in her future. It was all a bit mad. The beers were helping, they took the edge off. That and the bottle of wine they had shared. Taking the cap off another couple of beers, she passed Will's to him and their hands touched. It was like a bolt of lightening shooting up her arm, looking at Will, it had been the same for him. They both chose to ignore it, carried on drinking their beers and chatting about whatever came into their heads.

She had no idea where any of this was going. The urge to reach over and touch him was unbearable, but he was so young. And what would he want to do with her, single mother of 3, it would be no more than a one night stand. But it had been so long since she had been kissed or touched or 'done it' and he was so handsome. Once couldn't hurt could it???

'Fuck it!' she thought. Maggie put down her beer, crawled across the floor to where he was sitting and she had no sooner got in front of him when he was kissing her as hard as she had wanted to kiss him. She was done for! Never in her wildest dreams could she have imagined that she would be able to feel the things that Dean had made her feel. Will made her feel even better. Undressed he had the most beautiful body Maggie had ever seen. She couldn't get enough of him. All the frustration and loneliness she had felt over the years ebbed away as Will whose surname she still didn't know worshipped her body as if it was that of a goddess, scars and stretchmarks and all.

It was the most amazing night of her life. They just had it. It was if everything in the world aligned, and this was their moment.

But then the next morning was their moment too.

And the next night. And the following morning.

And then he was gone and she had her kids back and life went back to normal. Well not normal, it would never be normal again.

Will. Will James. At the tender age of 20 he had completely rocked Maggie Hunter's world in a way no other had, not even Dean who she loved completely. Will James was on another level. Another level who had a girlfriend, was a soldier and was over 10 years younger than her.

Was he Mr Right?? Probably. He was Mr Right now. He would be on leave again in six weeks. Six weeks all of a sudden felt like a very long time!

60) The Ace of Cups

The six weeks passed though. Maggie decided that she wasn't going to say anything to anyone about Will, she kept mum about her night of passion, though people kept asking if she was okay? There was something different about her. But she had no idea if Will would even be coming back to her. He was young and already had a girlfriend, she might have been to him exactly what it had been; a one night stand!

That was something though. Maggie Hunter had never been or had a one before. It made her smile. That and the fact that even though there was distance between them and she no way of contact him, Will James thought about her – a lot. Her left ear would glow hot, and she knew that it was him. It gave her a little warm feeling and made her stomach flip. Silly she was a grown woman and he was just short of being a boy. But boy what a man he was. Not just 'doing it' but his whole being. How he talked to her, how he looked at her, how he touched her and how he made her feel.

She would be patient, let the God of Fates sort this one out for her. But she asked them all the time to cut her a break and bring him back to her! Please!! The desire to read her own cards was strong, but she stopped herself so many times and instead looked for little messages in the other readings she did. There weren't any!! It was like they were taking the micky out of her.

So, she got on with her life. Worked as Cushie Butterfield more and more, she really was gaining a good reputation as a good reader. There were less groups of giggling girls who had booked her for a hen party and more people who just needed some guidance.

Cushie Butterfield was a marriage guidance counsellor, mental health nurse and confident all rolled into one. People opened up to her and she found that sessions were getting longer and longer. She upped her prices and reduced her party size. It just felt a better thing to do, made her more exclusive and the client got more of her. It worked, if anything she was doing more bookings, it took a little bit less time and brought in more money.

Because of all the extra responsibility she had at the Geordie Ridley, her salary was more that of a bookkeeper these days and less of a barmaid come cleaner. The pub was thriving, it was one of those places that ticked all the boxes, quiet drink, party night, meal for two. It catered for everything and the hosts were second to none. All the hard work that Jason and Peter had put into it was paying off, so much so that they thought about opening another pub in another town.

Her Post Office account was actually starting to grow again, this time it was her earnings and not some windfall from a long past boyfriend. Very soon she would have enough deposit to buy her house, it had always been an unspoken agreement, if Maggie was ever in a position to buy it, then it was hers. Maggie did want it. Even though she knew that one day the kids would leave and the house was huge, there would be grandchildren that would come and fill the bedrooms, she would always need the space. Buying the house was definitely on her 'to do' list.

And then Will James was back. He had told her before he left the date of his next weekend at home. Maggie wrangled so she would be at work and the kid's would be staying at Dean's mam and dad, well Eve and Ryan were at friends, they were getting too old and too cool to spend full weekends with their grandma and granddad, but Maggie knew where they were and was happy for them to be there.

When Jason opened the office door and said someone was asking about her in the bar, Maggie knew it was Will. She had taken her time getting ready for work that night. Jason now raised an eyebrow at her, a silent 'I knew you were up to something' but she didn't care. She asked if it would be ok if he came into her office, Jason flounced off to get him and Maggie quickly ran a brush through her hair and had a spray of perfume!

Will James was standing in front of her. Jason closed the door and it was business as usual. It was just as well there were no camera in the little room that Maggie used as an office. Half an hour later Will was making his way back to the bar, Maggie went back to her rotas and all was well with the world.

He was waiting for her as she left the pub, she knew he would be. Will James was already so familiar to her. It was like she had known him forever, his laugh, his smell and there was something about his hands. She wanted to hold them, for them to touch her, she just wanted them. Together they fit. There were no awkward silences, if they were quiet they were happy just being near each other.

By the time he went back to Catterick, Maggie Hunter knew with no uncertain terms, that Will James was the man that she wanted to spend whatever days she had left on earth with. She could hear her soul singing. Tony Sharp had taken her breath away, Dean Burns had held her fragile heart and made it better, only to tragically break it again. But Will James completed her heart, it was like those necklaces that people gave to each other, half a heart each. Only with Maggie, her heart had never been whole, not until Will.

Thank God he felt the same.

It wasn't going to be easy for them. Him being younger would always be an issue. And then there was the kids, how would they feel about their mam's soldier toy boy boyfriend?? It was something that they would deal with when they had to. And then of course there was Will's girlfriend. She lived near his Army base in Catterick and he had met her in a local pub not long after he had gone for his training there. All Will would say was that she was canny, or that she was sweet or that she would be ok if he ended it with her. Maggie wouldn't let it spoil what they had, Will was a decent sort, he wouldn't be a two timer for long, Maggie could sense that.

Will's leave came around every 6 to 8 weeks, they carried on as they were. They kept things under wraps for almost a year, almost no one knew that they were an item.

They weren't being sly or anything, they were just being sure. Their feelings for each other had been pre-empted before they even met. The force of them meeting so intense! They had to know if it was real.

But when she was with him he made her feel like she didn't want to sleep. She lusted after him, almost as much as he did her. But it was more. Will James made her want to be a better person. A better mother, a better daughter, a better sister and sister in law and a better friend. He made her feel good. About herself, her family, her friends about the whole bloody universe. Maggie and Will were the real deal.

People noticed the difference in her. Eagle eyed Carole Todd was straight on her case. But Maggie kept her cards close to her chest and said that things were just better now. Which was the truth of it. Cushie Butterfield was keeping the wolf way way from the door, she had managed to buy the house, which gave her a massive sense of achievement. It was something for the future, for the kids if anything happened to her, because she knew better than most how life could change on a sixpence.

They only people who had any idea about what was putting a spring in Maggie Hunter's step was Jason and Peter. They saw Maggie and Will together at the Geordie Ridley. They would see the handsome soldier come in and scour the bar for Maggie, they would see them lock eyes and they would know when the lock turned on the room she called her office, they knew not to knock.

It took about a year of meeting up whenever Will had leave before they decided that it was time to come out and tell everyone. They could take it, Maggie having a younger bloke, Will having an older woman; with kids!! Will had called things off with Joanne months earlier, there was no need for them to be in the shadows. They were solid.

Then just as they were about to go public, Will was informed that he was going on tour, he would be gone for 6 months before he would get chance of leave. To Maggie 6 months seemed like a lifetime. But it came with the job, he had told her from the beginning that it would happen, but still!

She was so tempted to read her own cards. It was something that she hadn't done since before she met him. But she didn't want to know, if there was anything she needed to know, it would be in the readings she did for others. Like when Ryan was being bullied at school and although he had gone quiet at home, he had never said anything. Or when Eve had got herself a boyfriend and he was a little waster. And there was a marriage, a marriage that the cards were very excited about, but made no sense and it certainly wasn't Maggie's, but it was someone close. There was always something said when there was something to be said.

Maggie would just have to make do with snatched telephone calls, burning left ear and the fluttering of her heart. It was enough. Everyone else would fill in the missing bits that Will would leave behind.

For the last leave before Will's departure or what ever it was they did, she took the weekend off work. They had never really been anywhere together, so she took the opportunity to book them into a little plush hotel on the coast. The kids were all going to be away themselves for the weekend, Dana to Dean's mam and dads, Ryan was at a football coaching weekend and Eve was going to stay at her granddad's with a friend to look after the house as he was away for the week. Maggie wasn't sure if Eve's friend was a boy or a girl, and her dad hadn't mentioned going away for a week, when had he ever done that. But she asked no questions because she didn't want any lies and sighed about the years that had been wasted between Eve and Leslie Hunter, they really were as thick as thieves.

So, without a care in the world Maggie and Will spent an entire weekend just being with each other. They ate in the hotel's restaurant and spent and enormous amount of time in the huge four poster bed. They walked on the beach and they talked. It was if they were cramming in enough memories to see them through the following months. Check out was early on the Sunday morning, but neither wanted to go home quite then.

They booked a boat trip to see the seals. The morning was bright and the sea looked calm, it would be a perfect way for them to end their weekend. The boat looked like it had seen better days, Maggie and Will exchanged wary looks as they shuffled up the queue. But they had paid for the tickets and the rest of the people in the queue seemed really excited. Surely the boat was sea worthy!

But as they left the harbour the boat was swaying from side to side as well as up and down. Everyone was hanging over the edge. Maggie wished she still got the alarm bells ringing in her head, she really would have liked a heads up. She wasn't normally a sickly person, unless she was pregnant of course, but the full English breakfast she had eaten early was really starting to scramble in her tummy.

Will was laughing at her but took her by the hand and led her to some bench seats in the middle of the boat.

They had just sat down when it happened.

Maggie forgot all about the motion on the ocean and the tumbling in her tummy. There on a bench directly opposite the one she was sitting on was her dad. Leslie Hunter was on a sightseeing boat with a woman!!!

She sat open mouthed as her dad put an arm around the woman as if keeping her warm. It was such an intimate gesture. Maggie had no idea that her dad had a lady in his life!! He saw her and even though Maggie thought that he would be embarrassed, he once again shocked her by smiling the biggest smile, jumping up off the bench and ushering his totally shocked companion over the space between them.

It was another very surreal experience. Maggie and Leslie Hunter on a sightseeing boat on the North Sea both with people neither of them knew anything about. It was Leslie Hunter who seemed to be the most composed. He introduced his good friend Eileen to Maggie and then looked at Will as if to say,' help me out here mate, if I know you, I can't remember your name' Will obliged and Maggie in return introduced Will to her dad.

Maggie couldn't help but think that she had met Eileen before. Maybe she had done a reading for her. But she was usually pretty good at remembering her clients, it was a good trick to have. No, she had seen Eileen somewhere else. Making their way back to the side, all thoughts of the boat crashing or Maggie throwing up forgotten, she asked Eileen where she had met her dad.

Eve!!! Eileen was one of Eve's friend's grandmas. That's how Maggie knew her, now that she knew it was from school, she could remember her picking up a little girl when Maggie was there for Eve. Between the two friends they had managed to set their grandparents up on a sort of date, Eileen and Leslie had taken to each other immediately and had been spending a great amount of time together. What was Eve like!!

And all the while, she could hear Will and her dad chatting away. She could hear Will saying he was going on tour, that he would be away for 6 months. She could make out what her dad was saying in return, but when Will said he would love to do that when he got his next leave.... All would be well.

An hour later they disembarked. The seals had been little dots, barely to be seen. But it had been a trip she would never forget. She could see her dad in front of her. Eileen was linking his arm and they were striding away from the boat towards where the cars were parked. She couldn't be sure, he was some distance away from her, but Leslie Hunter was walking tall, there wasn't a stoop in sight!

Her heart swelled. She had always been fond of her dad but growing up she could never have said that she was especially close to him. In that moment, watching him walk away a happy man, she felt nothing but love for him. She would only look forward. She couldn't erase the past, but she could certainly put it behind her. She loved Leslie Hunter. It was a long time in coming but it was here.

And how how much did she love Will James. There wasn't enough minutes in the day to say it. Walking back to her car Maggie Hunter was walking tall. Taller than her dad had. Lovely unexpectedly well balanced kids, a family she loved and friends she loved. And she loved those that had gone before her, Dean and especially her Granny Hunter, because without her she wouldn't be the woman she was today. She was twice any normal woman – she was also Cushie Butterfield!

61) The World

And that was her life!! To date anyway.

Maggie Hunter soon to be Maggie James.

After twenty odd years together, Will was leaving the Army and coming to live on civvy street. He was due home in a couple of months, his last tour would be over, and he would be coming home to marry Maggie in full uniform before hanging it up for the last time.

Her dress was hanging upstairs. It might have been her one and only wedding, but she was far too long in the tooth for white. It was the palest of khaki, to compliment Will. She hadn't been sure, but Eve and Dana had loved it. The colour and the style were her. She was bigger than she was when she had first met Will, contentment and happiness did that to you, but the dress complimented all of her assets and though it was way out of her comfort zone, she was excited to wear it.

Despite the age difference, Maggie and Will were perfect for each other. The big gaps of separation hadn't hurt their relationship if anything it made it stronger. Leave time was their time and he would no sooner be through the door than he would be back out again and they would be jetting off somewhere for some much-needed alone time. It was a good life.

The whole wedding thing had been unexpected. It was something that they had never really felt the need to do. But practical Will had always been concerned that if anything happened to him, there may not be a pension for Maggie, that had been his excuse anyway. But when he had asked her, officially asked her anyway, it had been perfect and any women nevertheless a cynical Maggie Hunter could have refused him. Maggie James had a nice ring to it!!!

She had sat a long time travelling back down her memory lane. She could see chinks of light through her curtains. She would make herself another cup of coffee (yes she was now grown up enough to drink it and actually kicked herself for never having drank it earlier) and then start making good for her guests, it was her turn for Boxing Day that year and the quietness of the house now would be a distant memory amid the chaos that would arrive with the family and friends.

It had quite a Cast – her life!

Maggie opened the curtains and the grey morning light flooded into the living room. The Blessing of a new day.

Coffee in hand, she would give herself one last rummage in the past. So, who were the Cast of Characters ……..

Dorothy Hunter	Maggie's mam – deceased
Leslie Hunter	Maggie's dad – currently living in sin with his girlfriend Eileen. Very much part of the family and has been Santa Claus every

	single year since he was reconciled with everyone.
Stephen & Jude Hunter	Maggie's eldest brother who married her best friend. Still happily married with 2 daughters. Jude and Maggie were still best friends.
Shaun & Jill Hunter	Maggie's younger 'twin' brother married to Jill.
Hannah Hunter	Maggie's paternal grandmother. Probably the greatest influence on Maggie's life. Hannah Hunter had second sight and had passed the gift down to Maggie. As a child Maggie was taught about Tarot cards off her Granny Hunter and on her death left her a gift that Maggie chose to ignore for many years. Her Granny Hunter was a constant in her life up until Maggie learned to use the skill of second sight herself. But her Granny remained in contact through the many readings Maggie made.
Linda & Paul	Maggie's other best friend who married her childhood sweetheart and emigrated to Australia. They will be home for the

	wedding. And thank God for Zoom these days!
Tom Grey & John	Maggie's cousin. Has lived with his good friend John forever. Has a small art gallery at Tynemouth where he makes a grand living selling his work. Still one of Maggie's greatest friends. And they both 'Aunties' to all of the kids.
Tony Sharp	Maggie's first boyfriend and father of Eve. Developed lung cancer and died shortly before his 40th birthday. On hearing of his illness Eve and her dad were reconciled, though Maggie had been right in her prediction, and she never saw him again. A substantial amount of money was left in his will for his only daughter Eve.
Carole Todd	The woman who saved Maggie's life, over and over again. Jude's mam and the person that Maggie went to when she found out she was pregnant. It was Carole and her husband Glen that took Maggie in and helped her heal. Carole Todd is Eve Hunter's God mother. In Maggie's eyes will always be her Guardian Angel and her house is still the go to house for Sunday Lunch.

Eve Hunter	Maggie and Tony Sharp's daughter. Lives with Joe and is mother to Brogan and Jessica. Eve is a geriatric nurse and remains close to her mam and her brother and sister.
Dean Burns	Maggie's first real love and father of Ryan and Dana Burns. Died tragically before his daughter's birth. Dean's death caused Maggie to have a nervous breakdown, Carole and Glen Todd took in all of Maggie's children while she recovered in hospital and then Maggie also lived with them while she recuperated after her discharge.
Ryan Burns	Maggie and Dean's only son. Married to Kirsty and father of Reggie. Ryan is Assistant Manager for Jason & Peter helping them run the chain of pubs. Of all of Maggie's children, Ryan is the only one that has any sort of second sight. He can see auras but is yet to pick up a deck of Tarot cards.
Dana Burns	Maggie and Dean's daughter. Dana was born the day after her father's death. In the midst of all the tragedy, Dana was a little ray of sunshine. Her sunny disposition remains with her still and its rare she is

seen without a smile on her face. Dana is the ultimate rolling stone, has been engaged a couple of times, moves out of her mam's house and then back in and flits from job to job. Is currently working the ski season in France but is joining a cruise ship after the wedding for the start of another adventure.

Jason & Peter — Landlords of the pub Maggie works in. Instantly bonded with Maggie and recognised not just her talent as a bookkeeper, but also her physic ability. Now run a successful chain of pubs throughout the North East but always spend Christmas Day with Maggie, her family and her friends.

Will James — Maggie's husband to be. The ultimate love of her life and her twin soul – no more words!!!

And last but not least. The leading lady:-

Cushie Butterfield. Maggie Hunter's alter ego who not only put food on the table but shaped Maggie's life. The people who she has met because of her. She had given hope when there was little and offered peace when there was only torment.

For over 25 years Maggie had lived with Cushie every day of her life, she is as real to Maggie as Carole or Jude is.

Maggie Hunter sat holding her tepid cup of coffee smiling. Her heart was fluttering, just like it always did since she had met Will, well before she met him. It was always such a comfort. There had been none of the warning alarm bells ringing in her head, there hadn't been for years. If only though.

The flutters got faster, and her face flushed up, just like it had when she was about to meet Will James. How confusing those days had been. The heart flutters and the heated face and the hot left ear. But her face was really heating up and flutters were less of a flutter and more of a pounding heart. Will?? Had something happened to Will?? He was in the Middle East surely not, he was about to retire!! WILL!!!!! The pain ran through her heart before she even knew what was happening. And then there was darkness!!

Maggie Hunter died on Boxing Day. The last thought and image were of Will James. It may have been sudden but for sure Maggie Hunter died a happy woman. And Cushie Butterfield died alongside her! Neither to be forgotten!!

'She's a big lass, she's a bonny lass and she likes her beer and they call her Cushie Butterfield, and I wish she was here!!!'

A Note From the Author

I hope that you enjoyed reading Cushie Butterfield as much as I liked writing about her.

In my eyes she is a Legend.

And if you did like it; please spread the word; it is so difficult getting books out to the masses when you do it all yourself.

But I have a head full of stories so check out the ones already written and keep an eye out for news ones.

Love Gill xxx

Printed in Great Britain
by Amazon